The Date

LOUISE JENSEN

Sphere
An imprint of
Little, Brown Book Group
Carmelite House
50 Victoria Embankment
London EC4Y 0DZ

An Hachette UK Company

sphere

www.hachette.co.uk
www.littlebrown.co.uk

SPHERE

First published in 2018 by Bookouture, an imprint of StoryFire Ltd.
This paperback edition published in 2019 by Sphere

13 5 7 9 10 8 6 4 2

Copyright © Louise Jensen 2018

A CIP catalogue record for this book
is available from the British Library.

ISBN 978-0-7515-7420-3

Printed and bound in Great Britain by
Clays Ltd, Elcograf S.p.A.

Papers used by Sphere are from well-managed forests
and other responsible sources.

MIX
Paper from
responsible sources
FSC® C104740
www.fsc.org

'It doesn't matter how old we get, how big we grow, we all need a mum, don't we?'

This book is for mine. With love.

The Owl and the Pussy-cat went to sea
In a beautiful pea-green boat,
They took some honey, and plenty of money,
Wrapped up in a five-pound note.
The Owl looked up to the stars above,
And sang to a small guitar,
'O lovely Pussy! O Pussy, my love,
What a beautiful Pussy you are,
You are,
You are!
What a beautiful Pussy you are!'
Pussy said to the Owl, 'You elegant fowl!
How charmingly sweet you sing!
O let us be married! too long we have tarried:
But what shall we do for a ring?'
They sailed away, for a year and a day,
To the land where the Bong-Tree grows
And there in a wood a Piggy-wig stood
With a ring at the end of his nose,
His nose,
His nose,
With a ring at the end of his nose.
'Dear Pig, are you willing to sell for one shilling
Your ring?' Said the Piggy, 'I will.'
So they took it away, and were married next day
By the Turkey who lives on the hill.
They dined on mince, and slices of quince,
Which they ate with a runcible spoon;
And hand in hand, on the edge of the sand,
They danced by the light of the moon,
The moon,
The moon,
They danced by the light of the moon.

EDWARD LEAR

SUNDAY

CHAPTER ONE

Something isn't right.

I know that as soon as I wake from a thick, muddy sleep. I know that even before I am aware of the throbbing at my temples. It's not the stab of disappointment I get every morning when I realise I'm not in bed with Matt, that I'm no longer living, or welcome, in my own home. It's something else. My head is pounding, thoughts cloudy, and the whole room feels as though it's spinning.

Something is wrong.

There's a sour smell in the room. A smell I can't quite identify and, at first, I wonder if there's someone in bed with me. I've a horrible sense of being watched, and not in the loving way Matt used to, when I'd open my eyes and see him propped on one elbow, gazing at me as though I was the only girl in the world. This feels creepy. Goosebumps spring up on my arms. I should never have let Chrissy and Jules persuade me to go on a date. I'm not ready, and besides, I'm still clutching onto a kernel of hope that my marriage isn't over. It was only last year Matt and I decided to try for a baby. My imagined future wrapped itself around me like a blanket, cosy and warm. That was before he ripped my dreams away with one sharp yank, leaving me hollow and icy, icy cold.

My friends had rallied round, as good ones do, and a few weeks ago we sat drinking wine as they persuaded me to create a profile on a dating app.

'I'm married!' I protested.

'Separated,' Chrissy said, and she made it sound so final, although neither Matt nor I had mentioned divorce. 'It would be good for you. You never go out. You don't have to take it seriously.' She flashed a grin. 'It's just a bit of fun. The odd dinner or drink. You don't have to do anything you don't want to.'

'Like set up a profile?' I pulled a face as Jules read aloud from the home page of *Inside, Out*. 'We don't post photos until we've got to know the person. "We're all beautiful on the inside".' She mimed sticking two fingers down her throat, but then she's off men too, separated like me. Chrissy is divorced. God knows why I take relationship advice from them. We are all a disaster.

'God, that's even worse,' I said. 'What if they've two heads or something?'

'When was the last time you saw someone with two heads?' Chrissy laughed. 'Besides, I thought you weren't interested.'

'I'm not,' I said, and I hadn't been, but I couldn't help scrolling through the app. 'What's ISO love – answers JBY?' It was like reading a menu in a foreign country.

'In search of love. Just be yourself.' Chrissy ripped open a bag of Doritos as she read over my shoulder. 'Everyone uses acronyms. Avoid LIPB.'

'What's that?'

'Living in parents' basement. He'd probably keep you chained in the cellar!' Chrissy popped off the lid from the jar of salsa.

'We might never see you again. Can I have your Michael Kors tote?' Jules asked. 'It's wasted on you anyway.' That much was true. I had feigned excitement during my first Christmas with Matt as I tugged open the bow, pulled at metallic wrapping paper as stiff as my smile, revealing the handbag that probably cost as much as my monthly food bill. I kissed him hard, indulging in the pretence, all the while wondering whether I should share with him why I was so uncomfortable receiving gifts. Of all the secrets I could reveal about myself, it was far from the worst.

'I can't go on a date,' I protested. But what I really meant was, I won't.

'What's the worst that could happen?' Chrissy asked, and before I could offer a list she spoke again. 'You might meet someone BABWAHC.'

'What's that mean?' I loaded a tortilla with chunks of tomato and peppers.

'Buffed and bronze with a huge…'

'You're making these up!' Laughing, I topped up our glasses and we spent the next couple of hours glued to our phones, sharing that Andy, 32, liked to meet a variety of new and interesting people: 'can't keep it in his pants', Chrissy said; and Lewis, 35, didn't want to define himself by his job: 'unemployed', Jules declared.

Later, I had hesitated a fraction of a second too long over a profile of a guy who loved home-cooked roasts, dogs and fishing. 'Boring,' said Chrissy, but I thought he sounded normal. Safe, I suppose. I was finding the thought of meeting a stranger utterly terrifying.

'He seems…' I hesitated '…kind.' And that was all it had taken for Jules to snatch the phone and send the reply she'd known I never would, giving concrete shape to my nascent singleton status at the age of twenty-eight.

Now I really wish she hadn't. The duvet compacts as I clutch it tightly, hands balled into fists, keeping as motionless as I can. As quiet as I can, pretending I am still asleep, listening for the sound of movement. Of breathing. But all I can hear is the birdsong outside my window and it sounds so loud. How much did I drink last night? I've never had a headache like this before. I was supposed to be driving; I had thought that if I stuck to lemonade I would be calm and in control. Fleetingly, I wonder where I left my car. Is it still outside Prism? It's all a bit of a blur. I'd chosen Prism, thinking a town-centre bar was about as public as you could get, although it's not quite my scene. I much prefer a country pub, but I hadn't wanted to allude to romance. I swallow hard. My throat is raw, and when I press my neck lightly with my fingers it feels bruised.

Despite the softness of the ancient mattress that sags beneath my weight, my shoulder is sore, and I gently touch it, feeling the skin torn and sticky beneath my fingertips. My lashes are clumped together with last night's mascara and I have to prise my eyelids open. The sun is pushing through the crack in the curtains, and the spare bedroom I have been lodging in at Chrissy's house since Matt and I separated is full of a soft amber glow.

Pain slices through my skull as I sit up. I raise my hand gingerly to the side of my head. A lump. Did I fall over last night? It's likely. I've always been clumsy, and I never did master the art of walking in heels. Prodding the wound as gently as I can, nausea crashes over me in sickening waves and I have the sensation of falling. Quickly lowering my hands to steady myself, I see it.

The blood.

Holding my palms in front of my face, I study them as though I've never seen them before, slowly turning them over. They are coated red, dried blood encrusted around my fingernails. It must have come from the cut on my head. No wonder I feel so ill. My gaze travels towards my wrists and I am alarmed to notice a smattering of small, circular angry bruises. I trail the fingertips of my left hand over my right forearm. There are four bruises, for four fingers? They are bigger than my fingertips, and as I turn my arm over I find a larger thumbprint and I know I have been restrained. Fear sweeps through me as my eyes dart around the room, reassuring myself I am alone. Why is there a blank space where my memories should be?

I yank back the covers, swinging my legs out of bed as though I can escape. But I've moved too fast. It feels as though the mattress is rocking. I close my eyes and wait for the queasiness – almost masked by the jackhammer in my head – to pass, and when it does, I slowly scan the room, searching my scant possessions for anything out of the ordinary. My clothes are scattered. Bra dangling from the wardrobe door handle as though it has been tossed there, tights balled up under the chair which is heaped with laundry I've yet to put away. The room is a mess, but that's not unusual. There's no sign of anyone else and, as I look at the pillow next to me, there is no tell-tale indent indicating someone has slept here. I run my hand over the sheet next to me. It's cool.

I fumble around on my bedside table, where – no matter how drunk I am – I always toss my mobile, and there's the usual array of loose change and tissues, *Marie Claire* magazine, *The Ladybird Book of Dating* Chrissy bought me – which should have made me laugh but some pages made me cry – but no phone. Where's my bag? I can't see it on the chair. Gingerly I stand but, even with my tortoise movements, the room tilts and sways under my feet and I stumble forward, landing heavily on my knees. Tears spring to my eyes as I rest back on my ankles, rubbing my kneecaps. The skin is pink and grazed.

Stretching out my hands I gather the clothes I wore last night. My thick winter coat is filthy and damp – at least that accounts for the smell. The bottle green strapless dress is torn along the seam. My cream scarf splattered with mud; the matching gloves appear to be missing, along with my black shoes with the pointy heels and silver bows. As I unravel my tights I see they are laddered and torn, and I am crying now. Heaving sobs I can't contain.

What has happened to me? Why can't I remember anything? The question circles my mind but, even as I ask myself, I think the worst. Have I been raped? By the man I met online? But I really don't feel as though I've had sex, consensual or otherwise, and I'd know, wouldn't I?

Wouldn't I?

The question slams into me. Bile rises, stinging the back of my throat, a deluge of saliva streaming into my mouth. I only just make it to the bathroom before I splatter the toilet bowl with vomit. Every tiny movement hurts my head, my stomach muscles cramping until at last I think the worst is over. Sitting back on my heels I unravel a handful of toilet roll and wipe my mouth.

I am shaking all over. Trembling so violently my teeth clatter together. Bare feet freezing against the bathroom tiles; legs boneless as I heft myself upright. I feel weighted with a sense of dread and I stand stock still, for a moment, trying to recall last night, but beyond the flashing coloured lights and the boom of the bass there's nothing. My head lolls, too heavy for my neck, and I'm so woozy I need to lie down again, but there's a horrible taste in my mouth and the urge to clean my teeth drives me towards the sink. As I reach for my toothbrush I pause, momentarily wondering if I am about to spoil evidence. Evidence of what? The question is cold and sharp, and I shove it away, but the caustic voice inside my head won't shut up. I'm barely holding it together. As though I can wash away my morbid thoughts I twist on the tap and hold my quivering hands underneath the cool water, watching it flow clear, at first, then turning crimson as the caked blood begins to soften, spinning like a tornado before it gurgles down the plughole. There is something else under my fingernails. Dirt? Blood? Instinctively I grab the nailbrush and scrub at my nails until they are pink, but I still feel dirty. Clean. I long to feel clean. As I shake the excess water from my hands my gaze is drawn upwards to the mirror.

The sight of my reflection triggers an overwhelming onslaught of fear and confusion, my breath sticking in my throat, until I force it out as one long scream. I tell myself I must be asleep. This has to be a nightmare. It *has* to be.

But it isn't.

Chapter Two

This can't be real.

Swallowing the acid that has risen once more, I close my eyes and take three deep, calming breaths before I dare look in the mirror again.

Nothing has changed.

The face reflected back at me is not mine.

It's impossible.

My curtain of long, blonde hair swishes as I turn my head from left to right. It's me. But it isn't. The features are not mine.

I must be asleep. Rationally I know this can't be happening, but I can't recall experiencing a dream so vivid. I can hear the thrum of a car passing by outside the window. Feel the cold drops of water trickling from my fingers. Smell the raspberry liquid soap I've just washed my hands with. But I can't be awake, I just can't.

I long to be back in my cosy bed, to fall into sleep, dark and warm, but I can't seem to move. Can't tear my eyes away from the image in the mirror watching tears pour down cheeks that are not mine. Slowly I unclench my fingers and raise a trembling hand towards my reflection, watch as the mirror-me does the same. My bones turn to dust and I sink to the floor.

What's going on? Drawing my knees up to my chest I lower my head, rocking backwards and forwards, as though

I can shake away what I have just seen. I can't. I don't know how much time passes. Minutes? Hours? I become aware of the cold, hard ceramic floor tiles beneath me, the way my entire body is aching. *Think*. There must be an explanation. There has to be. It's almost with relief I come to the conclusion I must have been drugged last night. Something slipped into my drink. Of course! That's why I'm hallucinating. Why I can't remember anything. The floor seems to lurch as I stand, and I walk tight-rope slow, arms splayed for balance. My voluminous lilac dressing gown is hanging from the back of the door and I slip it on, tying the belt around my waist. It doesn't bring the snuggly comfort it usually does.

Chrissy may be able to fill in the dark spaces in my mind. I pick my way unsteadily down the hallway to her bedroom. Her door is closed and, too impatient to wait for answers, I push it open without knocking.

Her room is empty. The box of chocolates she brought home weeks ago still sits on her bedside cabinet. Her Marc Jacobs perfume, the neck of the bottle a daisy, tossed on the bed. Chrissy's dressing table is covered with more make-up than the Boots Nº7 counter, and I have flashes of us getting ready last night, The Human League blaring out 'Don't You Want Me', as Chrissy coaxed me out of my usual jeans.

'I love this one.' She'd held my green dress up under her chin, smoothing the fabric with one hand. 'If you don't want to wear it tonight, can I borrow it again?'

'If you won't let me wear jeans, I've not much else to choose from. Most of my dresses are still at the house.'

I met Chrissy only six months ago, at the gym, but she'd been so easy to talk to that we quickly progressed from sharing an after-work-out cake to sharing confidences. Matt

had become increasingly hostile at my futile attempts to fix
things between us and, weary with our incessant arguing,
I had, reluctantly, moved in with Chrissy, to give us both
some space. I hadn't brought much with me, hoping time
would heal our rift, but it has driven us further apart.

I'd shimmied into the dress and pinned a smile to my
face, as I slicked glossy pink over my lips and tried not to
think of Matt, while Chrissy coated my nails with look-at-
me magenta.

Her bed is crumpled and covered with the vast array of
clothes she tried on and quickly discarded last night. It might
have been my date but she was coming to keep an eye on me.
To keep me safe. Except she didn't, did she? And by the looks
of things, she hasn't been home.

Where is she? I'm seriously worried. As much as I want
to pretend nothing happened last night it isn't working.
Already I am falling and breaking apart.

Nausea rises again and panic punches me in the guts. I
think once more of the blood on my hands when I woke,
the cut on my head. Thoughts attack me as the room shifts
and tilts. The world lets go of me and I fall onto Chrissy's
bed, curling into a ball as though I can ward off memories
that gather and retreat. Voices shouting. Misshapen shadows.
The fingers of last night reaching out, dragging me back to
a place I don't want to go. Despite my stillness, I'm kicking
and screaming. Fear, when it returns, is startlingly real. I
hug myself tighter.

A knocking on the front door cuts through the hazy
and indistinct images. Unease shifts in my gut. Branwell
barks and I remember I haven't let him out of the kitchen.
He must wonder what's going on. Usually the first thing I

do when I wake is let him into our small garden, watching him through the window as the kettle boils, circling the perimeter, sniffing at the borders as though something may have changed overnight.

This time the doorbell.

Slowly I stand. My inability to recall the details of last night has shrouded me with shame. I feel dirty. Sullied. Not wanting to face anyone who might look at me and instantly know what has happened in a way that I don't. But what if it's Chrissy? She often forgets her keys and can't be bothered to walk around the back of the house to reach the key safe. I have to see who it is.

*

Reluctantly, slowly, I inch downstairs, each step magnifying the stabbing in my head. In the hallway, the blind to the small window is closed, but through the safety glass of the front door, I can see a shadowy figure that is far too tall to be Chrissy. Is it him? My date from last night? Ethan? I can't quite remember his name. No, it was Ewan, I'm sure. I try to recall his face, but all I see is a blurry mass looming towards me.

Sweat pricks my skin. I'm so scared. I wrap my arms around myself, wincing, as I brush against my bruises. There's no way I'm opening the door. The knocking comes again, furious now. I stand statue still. Scarcely breathing. *Go away. Go away. Go away.* A throat clears, deep and loud. It's definitely a man. And then silence and light as the shadow disappears and, for a second, I think he has gone. Time is long and slow, until there's a jangling. The sound of a key scraping the lock. I'm frozen with fear as I remember my missing handbag, my keys, my purse with my ID. Has he come to hurt me again? To silence me?

The handle begins to twist. Every nerve ending in my body urges me to move, but I can't wrench my eyes away from the door. It begins to swing open. A tan shoe steps onto the doormat that says 'Welcome'. A denim-clad leg. And then he's in my house. This stranger. Unbidden, a scream is torn from my throat, sharp and loud, and the sound kick-starts my feet.

The aching in my body, the pulsing in my head fades to nothing as adrenaline speeds through my system. My bare feet slap against the laminate floor, arms pumping by my sides. I fall into the kitchen, slamming the door behind me. Branwell springs forward, delighted to see me. Standing on his hind legs, his front paws on my knees, his rough tongue laps at my hand as though he hasn't seen me for a year. Matt and I always joked if there was ever an intruder, Branwell would lick them to death. Now it's not funny. Too late I realise I should have run into the bathroom, where I could have locked myself in, or into the lounge, where there's a landline. Anywhere but this tiny room.

There's nowhere to hide.

Footsteps approach, loud and purposeful. My eyes dart wildly between the knife block on the counter and the back door, weighing up which I can reach faster. The door handle squeaks as it begins to twist. Instinctively I dart forward and yank a knife from the block, the stainless steel blade glinting in the weak winter sun that's threading under the roller blind.

The knobs of the oven press into the small of my back as I cower against it; the smell of my fear radiating from my pores. The man enters the kitchen, and I raise the knife, but my hand is shaking so violently it clatters to the floor. A cry escapes my lips as I drop to my knees. It's slipped under the breakfast bar and, at first, I'm not sure I can reach it, but I stretch and wrap my fingers tightly around the handle. Bizarrely, despite all that's going on, I notice a blackened chip under the oven and I wonder when I last cleaned the floor.

'Ali?' says a voice.

'Ben!' At the sound of my brother, I spring to my feet, thwacking my head on the breakfast bar. Pain pixelates my vision.

'Ben.' My voice is small now. Weak. 'There's a man…' I hold the knife loosely at my side. My vision clears. I can't see my brother at all. Only this stranger who now stands over me, reaching for me.

No.

His hand grasps mine. Crying now, I try to pull away, but his grip is tight. 'Ali?'

Utterly perplexed I stare at him. It's my brother's voice. Ben's voice. And he's wearing Ben's silver-framed glasses. But it's *not* his face.

'It's me, Ali-cat.'

No one else calls me this but him, yet I am not reassured. His face.

'There's no one else here, I promise. No one at all.' He speaks in the soft tone of when he was small and used to curl onto my lap, both of us unable to believe the tragedy that had befallen our family, begging me to read 'The Owl and the Pussy-Cat' again and again. Some semblance of normality.

Like the poem, this doesn't make sense. Branwell is pawing at the stranger, wagging his tail; the soft growl that usually vibrates in his throat when he meets someone new is absent. Could this really be Ben? The kitchen bobs up and down as though I am on that boat with honey and plenty of money, wrapped up in a five-pound note. Nonsense. It's all nonsense.

The Ben I do not recognise speaks again, but this time his words sound as though they are coming from oceans away. Blackness hurtles towards me and I welcome it with open arms.

Chapter Three

I have a sense of seasickness. An ocean of misery and confusion ebbing and flowing as I float on a cold, steel trolley. The faded blue curtains pulled around this tiny cubicle do little to cancel out the chatter of nurses, the slamming of doors, but the noise is nothing compared to the acerbic voice inside my head cackling *going mad-going mad-going mad* and I don't only listen, I believe it to be true. I have sent Ben to grab some lunch. We've already been here for hours and there is no sign of me being discharged. Besides, if I'm being honest, I can't bear to look at him.

My eyes are gritty with sorrow. I cried all the way to the hospital, huddled in Ben's passenger seat, pressing my body against the door as I clung to the handle, trying to create space between me and the man who sounded like my brother, who acted like my brother, and yet somehow, with the exception of his glasses, didn't look like him at all. On previous journeys we'd sing along to the Brit pop he was obsessed with, 'Don't Look Back in Anger', and the lyrics seemed to impart a message just for us. We'd chat about our days, laughing together, occasionally falling into a painful silence when I knew we were both thinking about our childhood. Often, we drew comfort in the space between the words; the lack of conversation sometimes saying more than we ever could. It was difficult to talk about what happened, still; perhaps it always would be. But it made us closer than most siblings I know.

But, this morning, as we sped towards Accident and Emergency, the atmosphere was tight with tension. To placate my sobs, Ben placed his hand on my arm, and I slapped it away, as though it was burning hot, unable to stand being touched by this face I did not know, and I could feel the hurt radiating from him, my baby brother who I have always strived to protect.

There was a roaring in my ears, waves rushing inside a shell, as I stared out of the window, trying to focus on the ordinary. Candy-coloured buckets and spades piled up outside the newsagents. Circling seagulls screeching as they swooped for food. The brown sign for the 'fun' pier; although the rickety wooden boards with sea snapping beneath clattering feet, the meagre array of slot machines with flashing lights and tumbling two pence pieces, the one solitary kiosk serving minute scoops of ice cream in often stale cones, was anything but fun. Still, better to look anywhere but at Ben's face. Each time I thought of it, thought of my own reflection, pressure formed in my chest, my heart in a vice.

'You must remember *something*, Ali?'

I heard the scepticism that poured from his lips as we waited at the junction. In the far distance are the cliffs where we had played as children in the crumbling ruined cottage we pretended was ours. Those memories seemed sharper to me than the indistinct fog from last night. But I couldn't tell him what I didn't know. The engine hummed, my cheek vibrating as it pressed against the window. I sensed rather than saw Ben's gaze boring into me but I didn't turn around.

'I've already told you, I *can't*.'

Ben had fired question after question at me in my kitchen after I'd come round, and I could sense his fury bubbling just below the surface. Had someone hurt me? He demanded answers over and over. Who was it? Should we call the police?

'No!' We'd exchanged a look. I had not been able to read the expression on his unfamiliar face. Ben was young when the police turned up, though he must still remember the way things were never the same afterwards. The way our world had fractured. Even now, my stomach still clenches like a fist whenever I see a police uniform.

'I think I just fell at the bar.' I'd been sketchy and vague as I'd shown him the lump on my head. My hair clumped together with dried blood. Tried to explain I couldn't recognise his face, that I didn't recognise mine. I hadn't told him my suspicions that I had been drugged and attacked. Shame washed over me whenever I thought about it. The scenarios my mind conjured became darker, more twisted with every passing second. How could I tell my brother my fears? Too often in the past, I'd had people gazing at me with sympathy in their eyes. Or disgust. I couldn't bear it from him too.

In the car, the questions kept coming and my agitation built. I glared at the red traffic light holding us up and there'd been a sudden spark. A memory from a few days before. Chrissy glugging red wine into my glass despite me shaking my head; pressing it into my reluctant hand until I submitted, curling my fingers around the stem.

'I'm having second thoughts about this date,' I said to her. 'I'm still married. I still want to be married.'

'*You* do,' she said, pointedly, before pausing as though filtering her words. 'Come on, Ali. It's just a bit of fun. You've dealt with a lot. And not just with Matt.' She looked at me with such sorrow that, not for the first time, I wished I hadn't told her what I'd been through; but my birthday is always such a difficult time for me, and her presenting me with a cake had been my undoing. The wine loosened my tongue. At the time, I'd felt such relief at finally telling someone; it was only afterwards I wondered if I could trust her to keep my secret.

'It'll do you good to let your hair down.' She patted my hand. 'What could possibly go wrong?' She dazzled me with her smile, her freckle-spotted nose crinkling. I'd taken a too-large sip of Shiraz, hoping it would quash the butterflies thronging in my stomach.

'Everything,' I sighed. And I hadn't known what I'd been more afraid of: that I wouldn't find my date attractive, or that I would. But she'd been right. Matt and I are over, and one of us will eventually meet someone new. Move on. Perhaps it would be easier if it were me first.

The fears I had then seem paper thin now. Inconsequential. Never had I envisaged this.

I tugged my sleeves down, covering the bruises that were already tinged purple.

The wheels of the car turned faster and faster, propelling us forward, and my heart galloped along keeping pace. By the time we turned into the car park I had convinced myself I was having a heart attack. Soaked in sweat, I clawed at the neck of my jumper, tugging it away from my throat, lungs burning, trying to suck in air. Ben circled the car park trying to find a space as I heaved in short, sharp, painful breaths. *I can't breathe.* Something jolted deep inside me when I realised I had felt this way before and, as though remembering, my hands circled my throat.

'Fuck it!' Ben screeched to a halt in a disabled bay and flung open his door, racing to help me out. My weight sagged against him as he supported me, and as the automatic doors of the Accident and Emergency department swooshed open, the sickly smell of disinfectant hit the back of my throat.

'Help,' Ben called, and heads of waiting patients swivelled like owls but nobody moved. Ben half-carried, half-dragged me to the desk, and the nurse rose from her seat.

'Bring her straight through to triage,' she said. She took my pulse and checked my blood pressure as I gasped and wheezed.

She rustled open a paper bag. 'Breathe nice and slow.' The fingers squeezing my rib cage loosened their grip. 'A panic attack. Have you had one before?'

I shook my head, instantly regretted it as stars exploded behind my eyes.

'What's your name, love?'

'It's Alison Taylor.' Ben had answered for me as he pushed his glasses up onto the bridge of his nose in the nervous way of his.

'Back in a sec.'

A welcome breeze had wafted in as the door to the room opened and shut. Minutes later it opened again.

'Let's fill out some details.' A different nurse stood in front of me, clipboard in hand.

'My name is Alison Taylor.'

'I know that bit. You just told me.'

Not her too. I stared at her in horror. *She doesn't look anything like the nurse that looked after me when I came in.* And the fingers squeezed and squeezed my ribs again as the bag was held to my mouth once more.

Please. I don't want to.

Fingers around my throat, vision tunnelling. I can't breathe.
A voice cold and angry.

Bitch.

Chapter Four

The sharpness of my hip bone digging into the too-thin mattress recedes as I close my eyes. It feels like I've been here for a lifetime and it's hard to believe it's still Sunday. I'm utterly exhausted and as I hear the curtains swish open it feels arduous to even turn my head.

'Mrs Taylor,' the doctor says, and I wonder if he was the one I saw before. 'Is your brother here?'

'He's gone to grab a coffee.'

'Is there anything you'd like to share while we're alone?'

'No.' I pick at the edge of the fraying sheet with my fingers. 'I fell. That's all.'

'Yes, you said. And the bruises on your arm came from your brother lifting you up?' There's a weariness to his voice as though he's heard all this before, and he probably has. The 'I walked into a door' or 'I slipped in the bath'. Excuses as flimsy as 'the swelling to my neck was caused by me singing too loudly', as though I'd been having the best night out ever.

Please. Stop. I don't want to.

'Don't you want to talk to the police?' Ben had asked when I'd begged him to lie to the doctor for me. To fill in the spaces in my fabricated story. 'Find out what happened to you?'

'I just want to go home.'

'You can't be on your own if you're concussed.'

Ben had texted Chrissy, to check she was okay, without telling her that I'm in hospital; I don't want to worry her. She'd replied she was staying with a guy. I had thought she was seeing someone; she'd been out more than usual lately. She'd said she was sorry she couldn't find me at the end of last night, and she'd assumed I'd gone home with Ewan.

'Whatever happened is over now. I just want to forget it.'

Ben understands. We had trusted the police before and they had lied to us. Promised to keep us safe. Safe was the last thing we were. I don't want to put myself through anything like that again. I don't want to put Ben through anything like that again. The trial tore our family apart. And, if I'm honest, I don't want to risk the police questioning my friends and Matt finding out I was on a date.

But there is a nagging part of me that thinks if Ewan has done something to me, he'll likely do something to someone else and I really should report him, but I wasn't asked for my address when I signed up for the dating app, so Ewan wouldn't have been either. I don't think the police would even be able to trace him.

'Your brother told you that you fell,' says the doctor. 'But you still don't remember. Don't you think it's possible?…'

'I fell,' I say again with finality.

The doctor sighs and I can feel disapproval rolling off him in waves. When he continues, his tone is sharper now. 'If you say so. I thought you might like to know your urine tests are clear. There's no sign of any drugs, but that doesn't necessarily mean you didn't ingest something. Generally, Rohypnol can be detected for seventy-two hours and GHB for twelve hours, though these times can fluctuate; and, of course, now we could be a good twelve hours from anything that might have been administered without your knowledge. You know. In case that was the cause of you *falling over*.'

'And the other tests? The faces… Your face. You said I'd met you before? I don't remember.' My words are thick, coated with tears.

'That brings me to your CT scan. There has been some bleeding to the brain.'

'Oh God.' I clutch the sheet tightly to me.

'I've shown the scan to the surgeons, and we're not going to operate. There is some abnormality to the temporal lobe, specifically the right fusiform gyrus.' He pauses as though that should tell me all I need to know. It doesn't.

'So?' My voice is too high. Too loud.

'It's too early to tell and not my place to diagnose, Mrs Taylor; the right fusiform gyrus coordinates the neural system that controls the ability to recognise faces. It is possible the head injury you have sustained has triggered a loss of facial recognition. This could well be a side effect of a bang on the head but we'll know more once you've had an MRI.'

Once more, that crushing feeling. I'm being suffocated by medical terminology I don't understand.

'Try not to worry,' he says, pressing his fingers against my wrist to take my pulse.

'But I'll be okay? It will only be temporary?'

The doctor writes something illegible on his clipboard but doesn't meet my eye. 'Try not to worry,' he says again.

I've been admitted for observation and rest and partly as a curiosity, I think, for the group of junior doctors who crowded around my bed this afternoon, staring at me as though I'm part of a freak show – 'you actually can't recognise yourself?'; 'you honestly wouldn't know me if I came back in five minutes?' – while shame at my ineptness painted pink spots on my cheeks. Despite the pounding in my head and my bruised and aching body, I'm longing to go home. Already I am thinking about tomorrow. Wondering who will fill in for me at the care home. I love my job. The residents, Mrs Thorn and her endless supply of After Eight mints; Mr Linton and his knock-knock jokes. Who will call the numbers for the Monday lunchtime bingo if I am not there?

Ben bundles the clothes I came in wearing into a bag – the smell of hospitals has permeated the fabric – and leaves to fetch my pyjamas and toothbrush. I turn to face the wall, curling up into a lonely ball.

I must have dozed because the next thing I am aware of is the sound of my tray on wheels squeaking over to my bed, a dinner plate clattering.

'Grub's up, Ali,' says a voice, with a soft Welsh lilt.

It's one I've heard before. There's a split second where hope skips in my stomach and I wonder if perhaps it's all over. The nightmare of this never-ending day. I turn my aching body. The nurse is smiling at me as she says: 'Jacket spud, cheese and beans with a nice salad – that'll sort you out. You feeling any better?' Miserably, I shake my head. I don't recognise her face, just her accent.

'You'll be OK. Your brother will be back soon, and it'll be nice to have your own night things on. Better than that gown with your arse crack showing.' She sloshes water into a glass.

The food on my plate is cold and unappetising. A small potato with pale skin, obviously microwaved, not dark and crispy the way I like them. Congealed melted cheese, a small heap of drying baked beans and a few wilted leaves imitating a salad. Food I recognise but I begin to doubt that what I see is what is really there.

When Ben and I were young, Mum used to fill Nan's silver tea tray with small items and we'd try to memorise each one. Kim's Game, she called it. She'd cover up the tray with a red gingham tea towel, and me and Ben would frown with concentration, counting with our fingers, a pencil sharpener, a safety pin, a satsuma. I'd remember everything, my memory had always been good, but Ben always remembered what he wanted to be there rather than what he saw, a chocolate bar, a pound coin, a football card. I'd often pretend to get things wrong, to let Ben win, but I always, always knew what was under that tea towel.

Now, I test myself again, covering my face with my hands, counting slowly to ten. Relief swamps me when I uncover my eyes. It's still a baked potato, cheese and beans and that must be a good sign, I think. It's only faces that seem to change each time I look away, and if there's just one thing wrong it must be easier to fix, mustn't it? I hold on to that thought as though it's a precious prize, curling my fingers tightly around it as I once held on to the ten pence piece I won for coming second, because believing my facial recognition will return is better than the alternative. If Ewan attacked me and comes back, I won't be able to identify him.

I'll never feel safe again.

WEDNESDAY

Chapter Five

WEDNESDAY

Ben is sitting to my left. He was supposed to be in Edinburgh today. He became acting assistant manager for a small but expanding chain of hotels. Although head office is located here, he often has to travel around the UK.

'I don't want to get you into trouble for missing your meeting,' I'd protested.

'You think I'd leave you now?' He looked hurt. 'You'd be on your own.'

The doctor had restricted visiting to family only. It's too distressing for me seeing faces I should know but don't. We're only a family of three. I knew stepping foot in a hospital would be too much for Aunt Iris, so I told her not to visit; yet, irrationally, feel disappointed she hasn't come, and I try not to equate it with the way she let us down before. We were *children*. Still, my heart breaks for all we've been through. Ben has been my only visitor and I'm worried about the pressure on him, feeling he has to be by my side, day and night. He's exhausted and tense. Stale menthol smoke clings to him, and I know he is smoking again. He always turns to cigarettes in times of stress. Although he was so young, I wonder if the smell of the ward is bringing it all back for him too. Jules, my best and oldest friend, and her cousin, James, who she lives with, have sent a card, along with a huge red and white bouquet that takes up so much space on my bedside cabinet there isn't enough room for my water jug. There are cards from Mr Henderson, my old neighbour, and Matt too. I'd spent ages analysing his message, the 'love' written in his looping script, wondering if he meant it.

My nerves are fluttering. Today I should get some answers and I'm glad Ben is here.

In my peripheral vision, I see his hands are clenched into fists as they rest upon his knees which jiggle up and down to a beat only he can hear. Directly in front of me, in an executive chair that swivels as he talks, is Dr Saunders, the clinical neurologist upon whom I pin all my hopes. I don't look directly at either of them. Instead I keep my eyes fixed on the shaft of sunlight streaking across the mottled lino.

'Ali can't remember anything about that night, can you?' Ben says.

'No.' Although there's something awfully disconcerting about not being able to remember the details, in a way it's a relief. But the not knowing doesn't stop the cord of panic tightening around my neck whenever I wonder what happened to me, as I frequently do. As soon as Dr Saunders has fixed me and I'm back at home, back at work, it will be easier, I'm sure.

'Your sister took quite a knock to the head when she fell,' Dr Saunders says. They both speak as though I am not here.

'But her memory will come back?' Ben asks.

'Possibly, although it's not guaranteed; and if it does, it might be incomplete. The cerebral shock Ali suffered could have been fatal. You really are quite lucky.' His chair moves again. Left to right. I fight the impulse to grab hold of the arms and keep it still. I feel sick, angry, scared. Anything but lucky. My teeth clench together and again there is the shooting pain in my head.

'We've already discussed your CT scan and MRI results. It certainly appears that the unusual shape of the lesion you sustained from a blow to the head has caused an abnormality to the temporal lobe, which is involved with face process-ing. It's this that's causing the loss of recognition. I want to carry out some more tests, if you're feeling up to it, Ali? A cognitive assessment session. Nothing too taxing.'

The last thing I feel like are more tests, but the sooner he can diagnose me the quicker he can cure me and so I nod my head, the room shifting as the ever-present nausea wells up.

'Are you sure? You look so pale.' Ben threads his fingers through mine and gives a gentle squeeze.

I flash him a grateful smile that dies on my lips as my eyes fall on his unrecognisable face, flickering between his mouth, his nose, his eyes. I pull my hand away and wipe my palm on my dressing gown.

*

The anger flares from nowhere, pulling me to my feet.

'It's too hard.' I pace across the room, putting my palms against the window, resting my forehead forward. My breath fogs the glass and I wipe it with the balled-up tissue that's permanently clasped in my fist. 'I don't understand what's happening to me.' For the past hour I've been asked to memorise faces I've never seen before and identify them again. I can't. Dr Saunders's ballpoint pen scratches against my notes.

'Sit back down and we'll try some famous faces now.'

Even as I'm shaking my head, I'm sitting back down. What choice do I have? He shows me the first picture.

From the hairstyle and facial hair I can tell it's a man but I've never seen him before.

'Come on, Ali.' The agitation in Ben's voice smarts.

'I'm not doing this on purpose.'

'But you *know* this one,' he insists. 'You wanted to marry him once.'

'Channing Tatum?'

'Well done,' Dr Saunders says and there's the scratch-scratch-scratch of the pen again. We all know I wouldn't have guessed right if it weren't for Ben's clue, but I allow myself to feel one small victory all the same.

'We'll try something different now,' Dr Saunders says, and I feel he's giving up on me.

As hard as I try it isn't any easier to spot similarities or differences between faces during the next test, even when their pictures are next to each other. Judging age, gender or emotional expressions is slightly easier and I don't feel quite so useless. Already I am learning to pick up clues, long hair, beards, jewellery.

'That's all the facial recognition tests.' Dr Saunders clicks the end of his ballpoint as he speaks. I hope I can rest before treatment starts, tiredness burns behind my eyes.

'What's wrong with her?' Ben asks.

'Just a couple more things and then I'll tell you what I think. I'm going to evaluate your IQ, Ali.'

'You think I'm stupid?' I *feel* stupid. I can't believe I didn't recognise Channing Tatum. Dr Saunders doesn't answer.

It feels as though I've been in this tiny, airless room for days. Dr Saunders has excused himself to make a phone call. I sip at warm water from a styrofoam cup. Ben checks his phone again. I feel lost without mine but arranging a replacement has been the last thing on my mind.

'I've had the locks changed, by the way,' Ben says. 'I had a scout around your bedroom, but I couldn't find the bag you said you took out with you, the grab?'

'The clutch.'

'Right. I thought it best to change the locks. Not that I think anyone would try to get in the house,' he adds to reassure me, but his voice is terse and I know he's worried too.

'But when Chrissy comes back she won't be able—'

'I've texted to let her know there's a new key for her next door with Jules. I couldn't remember the code to your key safe. Matt rang again to ask how you are. He says if there's anything else he can do…'

'I wish you hadn't taken Branwell there.'

'I can hardly bring him here, can I? Besides he's half Matt's dog. Matt is still legally your husband.'

The word husband has lost its spikiness. I've too much time to think here and Matt has been much on my mind. Although everything seemed so broken between us before, I can't help wondering if it's too late to put things right. The shock of being faced with my own mortality has left me feeling disempowered and vulnerable and longing for a sense of permanence. Life suddenly seems impossibly precious. Impossibly short. 'Does Matt know I went on a date, Ben?'

'He hasn't mentioned it.'

The door swings open and we fall into silence as Dr Saunders slips behind his desk. Suddenly I'm nervous.

'Ali, I've combined the results of all your tests including the MRI and the CT scan and, aside from the memory loss we've already discussed, I'm quite confident in saying you have prosopagnosia, although I've never come across a case in clinic before.' I detect a faint hint of excitement in his voice and irrationally I hate him, as though it's all his fault.

'And what does that mean?' Ben asks.

'Ali's mind can no longer identify features. She'll be unable to recognise faces, even those of close family and friends.'

'And is it common? This proso…' I falter. How can I have a condition I can't pronounce?

'Pros-o-pag-nosia.' He breaks it up. 'It comes from the Greek *prospon* meaning face and *agnoisa* for not knowing. It's also known as Face Blindness.'

The word 'blindness' terrifies me, and my eyes flash around the room drinking in the spindly spider plant on the windowsill with its brown and trailing leaves, the square black clock on the wall, as though reassuring myself I can still see.

'There are two types, the first of which is developmental prosopagnosia. You're generally born with this type, and it's far more common than you think. Roughly two per cent of the UK, or 1.2 million people, suffer from varying degrees of facial blindness. Many of them don't know they have it, often thinking they have a bad memory for faces or people look more alike than they actually do; if they have similar hairstyles for instance. It's often inherited although we haven't yet found a specific gene for developmental prosopagnosia. It's interesting that—'

'So I was born with this but it's only surfacing now? Our parents didn't have this, did they, Ben?' He's too young to properly remember Dad but we'd have known if this ran in our family, surely.

'No. You have acquired prosopagnosia, Ali. This occurs after a stroke or head injury. It's much less common than developmental. We already know from your scan there's some abnormality to the right fusion gyrus. This would be consistent with your head injury. Damage to this area can cause two subtypes: apperceptive prosopagnosia and associative—'

'How long will it take before I'm back to normal?' I cut in. It's all I care about right now.

There's an awkward pause. The creak of the chair spinning left to right. The click of the ballpoint pen.

'It's likely to be permanent, I'm afraid.' His voice sounds as though he is shouting from a large hole.

I can't process what I'm hearing. I take another sip of my drink. The styrofoam crumples beneath my fingers and water trickles onto my lap, but I can't cross the room to pluck tissues from the box of Kleenex on the windowsill. Dr Saunders's words have pinned me to my seat.

'So, Ali won't recognise anyone? That's crazy!' Ben says. 'I can't imagine.'

'It's difficult for those without the condition to understand,' Dr Saunders says. 'Face recognition is such an automatic process that many people can't imagine facial blindness is even possible. I've been involved in studies where patients have come in with their families and we've asked their families to change clothes and stand silently in a room with a small crowd of people and asked the patients to then identify their loved ones. It's heartbreaking to see the patient's distress when they can't. Children don't recognise their parents, wives don't recognise their husbands. Men, in particular, are so hard to identify, being often very similar when you take away their features, short hair, casual clothes. You'll come across a lack of empathy and understanding, and the best way to deal with this is education. Be honest with people. Don't be ashamed.'

But ashamed is exactly how I feel.

'There must be something you can do?' There's a pleading in Ben's voice I haven't heard for years. He used the same tone once to beg me to read just one more of the silly poems he loved.

They sailed away, for a year and a day, to the land where the Bong-tree grows.

This must be a nightmare, it has to be, because the alternative, that this is real, is more than I can bear.

'Certainly there are things we can do,' Dr Saunders starts, and I am pulled back into the room, but the swelling of hope his words brought deflates quickly when he adds: 'There are lots of compensatory techniques that can help you day-to-day.' His words blur into each other. Permanent. This is permanent. Already I feel I cannot cope. As Dr Saunders answers Ben's questions about the condition, he taps on his keyboard and the printer whirrs to life. 'I've spoken to Stonehill University – you know it?'

I nod. It's about an hour away, in the city.

'They work very closely with the National Hospital for Neurology and Neuroscience in London. You'll be in safe hands. There's a specialist, Dr Wilcox, based there running a research programme. I've just spoken to him, and he's eager to meet you. There's a trial for transcranial magnetic stimulation which may get some function back. It's not my area of expertise,' he adds quickly, cutting off my questions. 'He's writing to you directly with an appointment, it shouldn't take too long. In the meantime he's sent through a handout with some more information and coping strategies. I'll discharge you now. I bet you'll be glad to go—'

'Wait! I'll never recognise anyone again? You can't just send me home.'

Dr Saunders must notice the utter misery on my face, the tears filling my eyes, because his voice is sympathetic as he speaks again.

'You'll probably recognise one in a thousand people. Not much admittedly, but perhaps better than nothing. That's usual and, if it happens, try not to get your hopes up. It doesn't mean you're recovering. It's a lot to take in, I know. Physically there's nothing else we can do for you here and emotionally…' He clears his throat. 'Look, I appreciate it's tough but we really need the beds. You know how stretched the NHS is. Sorry. I'll see you again though. Make an appointment with my secretary on the way out. Do you work?'

'Yes. I'm a care assistant. Oh God. How am I going to tell the residents apart? I won't… I can't…'

'For now you need to rest and recover. I'll sign you off for two weeks and give you some painkillers to take for your head, and we'll reassess how you're coping with… with everything after that. Okay?' He hands me my papers. I cling to them as though they are a buoy as he opens his office door and I am cast out onto the choppy waters once more.

On the ward I dress in clothes Ben has brought in, a pink summer skirt and a clashing red and orange floral top. He's remembered bra and pants but forgotten tights and shoes, and I shiver as I shuffle out into the winter-cold car park in my slippers.

*

It's only four o'clock but already dusk is sucking the daylight away. As we drive I lean forward in my seat as though I can make us go faster, longing to shower away the stench of illness that clings to my skin, to sleep in my own soft bed that smells of summer meadow fabric softener. To be back among my own things, if not my own home, safe and familiar. My mind drifts to Matt. I am incredulous I won't be able to recognise the face of the man I married although I can still picture him clearly. Long black lashes framing hazel eyes. The mouth that used to lift into a smile when he saw me but later became a thin, straight line whenever I walked into the room.

Ben cuts the engine and reaches for the door handle.

'Do you mind if I go in alone?' As soon as I've eaten and showered I want to go to bed.

He hesitates. 'If that's what you want.' He pushes my new door key into my hand.

'Is it okay if I whizz up to Edinburgh tomorrow? The site up there is haemorrhaging money. I need to find out why.'

'Of course,' I say. 'I've James and Jules next door if I need anything, and I'm sure Chrissy will be back any day.'

There's a beat.

'Honestly, Ben. The painkillers have wiped me out. I'll probably spend all day sleeping.'

'You will call me if you need anything or if you remember anything?' Ben asks.

I nod, and he leans to kiss me on the cheek, as is our way, but hesitates as I lean away from him. He squeezes my arm instead. The edges of our relationship have become sharp and jagged. There's a distance between us that wasn't there before. I know I'm unfair to treat him differently, when I'm the one who has changed, but I can't help it.

My body is leaden, almost sinking into the path as I stumble towards the front door. At the bottom of the driveway, the shadow of my bright yellow Fiat 500. It's disconcerting to think I might have driven it the state I was in. What if someone had got hurt? It doesn't bear thinking about.

There's a bouquet of pink roses on my doorstep. As I pick them up, leaves scatter like dust.

Inside I kick the door shut with my foot. 'Chrissy?' But although the scent of vanilla from our plug-in air freshener is strong, the air is thick, as if no one has been here for days and I know she isn't home. The house feels empty but I'm too exhausted to collect Branwell today. I scoop the post from the mat and toss it on the work surface, dump the flowers in the sink. The mail is mostly junk; there are get well cards from work signed by the staff and, touchingly, one from the residents, their handwriting as shaky as their balance. Turning my attention to the flowers, I pull open the drawer and rummage around for the scissors to snip the stems. Among the batteries, the crumpled receipts and freezer bags are my keys. Odd. If they're not in my handbag they are always hanging on a hook by the front door. If it weren't for the flowers I might never have found them. Ben needn't have changed the locks after all. I lift the roses from the sink. Inexplicably I feel chilled. Almost reluctant to open the small envelope sellotaped to the bouquet, my name handwritten on the front. These haven't been delivered by a florist. I pull out the stiff white card, yellow roses decorating the corners. Four words. Just four words scrawled in thick, black pen.

Enjoy the date, bitch?

Chapter Six

Oh Ali, I wish I could see your face as you open that card. I bet you thought your nightmare was over? It's only just beginning. We're going to have some fun. And by that I mean I'm going to have fun. You? You're going to scream.

Chapter Seven

Someone must have seen who left the flowers. I rush next door to ask Jules, grateful again that Chrissy had rented the house next door to James and now we are all neighbours. It's been the one good thing, the only good thing, to come out of my separation, being able to get together with my friends and share a bottle of wine without worrying about driving or taxis.

The doorbell peals. A chilling wind bites at my nose, my ears. Snow is forecast later, clouds covering the stars invisible. Wrapping my arms around my middle I bounce up and down on the balls of my feet, desperate to keep warm.

The door swings open. It's a man. I tell myself there's nothing to be frightened of, it's only James, but still I keep my eyes fixed firmly on the floor, unable to look him in the eye, wanting to picture his face the way I used to and not see the image my brain will tell me is in front of me. His boots are scuffed at the toe, and I hold the tiny scratches in my gaze as I blurt out: 'Someone left a bunch of flowers on my step. Did you see who?'

'Ali!' he exclaims, as though I am the one who looks different. 'Jules is out but come on in.' James is an accountant, although he told me once over a glass of wine he hates his job, he's saving to buy a boat. Get away from it all, I suppose.

'No, thanks,' I say, feeling a desperate sadness as I realise just how uncomfortable I am around people right now – before this James felt almost like another brother. We share the same taste in music and he's offered me tickets to gigs a couple of times, chilled-out folk who would bore Matt senseless.

'The flowers?' I prompt.

'Sorry. I haven't seen anyone. Wasn't there a card?'

Tears flood my eyes.

'Are you okay?'

I shake my head.

'Of course you're not.'

There's little else to say except, 'Can I have the door key Ben left with you?' I'm going to put it in the key safe.

He darts inside his house and seconds later presses the cold metal into my hand. 'I'm sorry,' James says. 'About what happened to you. Do you remember anything yet?'

'No.' Cheeks stinging, I turn and walk away. He calls my name, his voice cracking with emotion, and I hesitate but all I hear is the wind battering the trees and I know he is not going to speak again and, even if he did, there's nothing he could say to make me feel any better.

Ewan has my address. I check the front door is locked behind me three times. *He has my address.* My blood is hot, rushing through my veins at lightning speed. I'd been careful not to give out any personal information. We'd met in a public place. Has he tracked me down or did he come home with me that night? What does he want?

Enjoy the date, bitch?

My eyes scan the message again and again, as though I can morph those four words into something else. Something nice. 'Get well soon, Ali' or 'I love you. Ali'. I can't remember the last time I'd heard that one. I turn the card over in my hands. There's no logo on the back and it could have come from anywhere. *He was here*. My logical mind tells me to call the police, but my cynical mind questions what they can actually do. This anonymous bunch of flowers could have come from a dozen supermarkets, and they're hardly likely to rush over and offer me twenty-four-hour protection for a bouquet, are they? They didn't protect us before and the threats then were real and relentless and utterly terrifying. Briefly, I consider calling Ben but I know he'd insist on coming straight over and he needs a good night's sleep before his long drive tomorrow. If something else happens, I'll tell someone. I will.

The scent of the roses is cloying. I snatch them from the sink and step out of the back door, shivering, as I head for the bin. The darkness is absolute. Our garden leads onto wasteland, one of the reasons Chrissy rented the house – bikini summers, making breakfast in bra and pants. I'd loved our private, sheltered space, but now I'm seeing potential hiding places everywhere. A rustling. It could be the wind. It could be something else. Someone else. Dumping the flowers in the almost overflowing bin – it was Chrissy's turn to put them out last week, but she forgot – I scurry back inside. My heart pounding, my hands trembling as I slam the door, turning the key. Checking it's locked, again and again.

After I've showered, I trust in my favourite red-check fleecy pyjamas to relax me, but they don't. Although I'm sleep-deprived and painkiller-hazy I still feel edgy. A quick supper and then I'll fall into bed. In the kitchen I ignore the lingering scent of roses and switch on the radio. A blast of the 80s music Chrissy loves fills the kitchen – A-ha's 'Take on Me'. Twiddling the knobs I adjust the volume and retune it to Classic FM. Vivaldi's *Four Seasons* drifts from the speaker. Rummaging through the cupboards, I pull out a tin.

Heinz tomato soup spins in the microwave. Branwell's wicker basket sits lonely by the back door, red blanket crumpled and sprinkled with sand from our last beach walk. His favourite monkey chew toy spreadeagled on the floor. The house seems so empty, silent, without his claws clip-clopping against the kitchen tiles, his low growl as foxes sneak into our garden. It's beetle-black outside. The spotlights in the kitchen have turned the glass to a mirror. A shudder runs through me as I stare outside into the depths of the wasteland behind our fence, wondering again who delivered the flowers. Cold kisses the back of my neck.

Tugging the cord, the blind drops until it brushes the taps on the sink. The sunflower fabric has never been long enough to cover the glass, but it didn't seem important before. Chrissy liked the print, 'a little bit of sunshine no matter how dull the weather', she had said but now, with the two-inch gap at the bottom, a gap deep enough for a pair of eyes, I feel horribly exposed. For the umpteenth time I rattle the handle of the back door, before doing the same with the front door and again meticulously check each window is latched.

The ping from the microwave shatters the silence. The bowl is scalding. Quickly, I lift it with my fingertips onto a tray, and then twist open the loaf of bread, checking the crusts for mould, before taking my supper and hurrying into the lounge, where the curtains are tightly closed.

Despite my sense of disquiet, it's good to be home, I think, as I sink onto the sofa. The pastel pink wallpaper patterned with dove grey birds automatically soothes me. Chrissy and I are polar opposites. This is such a contrast to my minimalist home but, tonight, I'm grateful for the shelves crammed with the weird angels without faces, ornaments Chrissy loves, wings spread, protecting an invisible flock. The candles. The books. For once it feels homely rather than oppressive.

Another yawn escapes me. I hadn't slept much in the hospital. The rattle of trolleys, the hum of the night lights, the low murmur of nurses was constant, but that wasn't what kept me awake. As soon as I stepped through the doors, into A & E, and inhaled that hospital smell, it all came rushing back. Hospitals may help, may heal, but even now I equate them with loss, and the nurses' uniforms, much the same as police uniforms, send my heart spiralling like blackened smoke. Despite the years that have passed, I have never got over what happened. Not really.

Slurping soup, I aim the remote at the TV, intent on finding something mindless to distract me. I'm behind with the soaps, so I open iPlayer and as the *Eastenders* theme begins I feel my shoulders start to relax. We had a ritual, Mum and I, we'd always be in our pyjamas, snuggled on the sofa, and whatever the weather we'd each have a mug of hot chocolate, an open packet of custard creams between us. We'd dip our biscuits into the malty liquid. There was a knack to getting the timing right. Too long and the biscuits would turn to mush at the bottom of the mug.

Ben would always be in bed. Whatever had happened in the day, whatever abuse had been hurled at us, whatever we'd had to deal with, it was our one constant. Our special time. I miss that. I miss her.

Trying to remember what happened in the last episode, Phil Mitchell's growly voice lances me and the bread I have dipped orange and soft sits hard and solid in the pit of my stomach. I don't recognise him. Suddenly the enormity of the impact prosopagnosia will have on my life crashes into me. Soup sloshes onto my lap as my body shakes with the force of the howl that rips through me, my tears splattering into the bowl.

As Dr Saunders had explained the condition, I hadn't fully taken it in, but now, as I kneel in front of the TV as though I am praying, tracing the faces of the characters on screen with my fingertips, it seems horribly, horribly real. These people in Albert Square feel like family to me almost, the family I lost, and I might never recognise them again. I might never recognise *anyone* again. It was impossible to imagine how life would be with my friends, my family, looking like strangers. I'd never once thought about TV. Movies. Theatre. I jab the screen to darkness with such force the DVDs housed on the shelf below tumble to the floor.

Although we stream most of the things we watch, I always buy my favourites on disc. The box set of *Friends*. The *Step Up* movies. *Bridesmaids*, our go-to bad day movie, which Chrissy and I have watched far too many times, sliding a box of Maltesers between us, topping up our gin with fizzing tonic, stomach muscles sore with laughter.

There will be no re-watching my favourite films. No watching new ones. The actors' faces will become unrecognisable to me the second they leave the screen, morphing into someone else as they return. I feel I haven't just lost them, the characters in the programmes I love, I've lost a piece of myself too and, inexplicably, I feel like I'm losing Mum all over again. My life will never be the same and I fold in on myself, my forehead resting on my knees, and I sob and sob as though my heart is breaking. As though my heart is breaking again.

A crashing sound from the back garden.

Fear beats its wings. A scraping now. Something rooting around, and I tell myself it's a fox. If Branwell were here his hackles would be raised, a low growl in his throat, but he is not here, and I am utterly alone and utterly terrified. Out of the kitchen window, there is nothing to see but blackness. I know if I were to fling open the back door it would scare away the fox – if it is an animal that is skulking around in the dark.

If.

Rummaging through the junk drawer I find the Maglite buried under tea towels and takeaway menus and, quickly, I stride upstairs. Opening my bedroom window wide I peer out into the garden, arcing the torchlight over the lawn, illuminating the roses scattered over it. I tell myself the wind must have caught the lid, blown the bouquet to the ground, but even I can see from here the heads of the flowers have been torn violently from their stems.

A fox foraging for his dinner. That's all.

I shine the torch on the bin. It is upright. The lid firmly closed.

Chapter Eight

I can't settle. The thought of the shredded roses conquers sleep. The hours slide by as I lie on my back, the mattress curving up around my body, sagging and sighing as I roll onto my side. The hour is late. Cars thrum past infrequently now, and the pub at the end of the road must be closed. In the distance, a dog barks. Every sound is amplified, slicing through the silence. My fingers scrunch the top of my duvet. As a child I was scared of monsters and I used to draw the covers over my head. The fingertip-bruises on my arms, the still-throbbing lump on my head remind me that monsters are real. They walk among us, looking like us, talking like us. Unidentifiable. While I was in hospital I was desperate to be at home, but now I am here I am longing for the sanctity of the ward, where the constant background noises reminded me I was not alone. The pain in my temples pulses. I wish a frazzled nurse would tip painkillers into my hand, handing me a warm plastic cup of water. Stupidly, I've left the co-codamol I was prescribed on the coffee table, in the lounge. I sit up. An engine outside roars and revs, there's an angry slam of a door. A squeak. Our gate? Chrissy returning early from her break? The front door hasn't creaked open but then I remember the new lock and I can almost imagine Chrissy chewing her lip in frustration, poking her key again and again, wondering if she's drunk too much. If she's got the right house. The right door.

Jamming my feet into my slippers and shrugging on my dressing gown, I traipse downstairs to the dark, narrow, hallway. Chinks of moonlight push through the gaps in the blind covering the small window to the left of the front door.

I'm holding my breath though I don't know why, afraid to flick on the lights, wishing now that I'd asked Ben to stay the night, but James and Jules are only next door. I'm okay. I am.

There's a shuffling outside. A muttering.

'Chrissy?' My voice is barely audible.

The door handle rattles up and down. I step forward. My fingers grip the key but, instead of twisting it, I sidestep and hoist open the blind so I can look out of the window. A face presses against the glass. I stumble backwards in shock. The face stares back at me. It isn't Chrissy, this much I know. Automatically I think it's a man. It's too dark to see clearly but there is no long hair poking out of his beanie, the type workmen wear. It can only be seconds that we stand, eyes locked together, but it feels like an eternity.

He raises his gloved hand and slams it against the glass. Slowly, methodically, over and over. Thud-thud-thud – until the thumping on the window merges with the thudding inside my head. I clasp my hands over my ears and screw my eyes closed, praying this is a medication-induced nightmare, but when I open them again the face is still there.

His hands still banging the glass.

It's like something out of the horror films Matt used to love. He'd wrap his arm tightly around my shoulders, plant kisses on the top of my head as I pressed my face against his chest every time there was a scary bit. Stuffing toffee popcorn into my mouth, my crunching dulling the sounds of the screaming coming from the screen. But this isn't fantasy, this man outside my window, fogging the glass with his breath. This is razor-sharp real, and utterly, utterly terrifying. If it were a movie I'd be yelling at the actress to move, to run, to do *something*. My legs feel like paper as I back down the hallway, slow steps, unable to tear my gaze away from the window as though it might shatter if my eyes are not on it. It must be him. Ewan.

He can't get in I tell myself but that doesn't calm my frantic heart. It doesn't dry the sweat that is running in rivulets between my breasts. Suddenly, I'm desperate to call the police. Fumbling behind me I twist the door handle to the lounge, and I stumble backwards, righting myself as I switch on the light. The landline we have for the broadband is on the bookcase and I swipe it from its cradle, the shaking fingers of my other hand clicking on the table lamp. I banish the dark but fear has still swallowed me whole. The tomato soup I had for supper rising in my throat as my thumb stabs the call button. Holding the handset to my ear, I wait for the reassuring whirr, picturing every bad movie I have ever seen. Is it really so easy to snip a phone line? The relief I feel as the dialling tone hums against my ears is immense. I lower the handset and press the first 9.

The thudding stops.

The second 9.

The silence is louder somehow than the banging on the glass.

Hesitating, I lower the handset, although I still hold it tightly in my hand as I edge back out into the hallway. Has he gone? It's too dark to properly see. Pressing my spine against the wall I edge towards the front door, pausing after each step.

Waiting.

Listening.

All I can hear is my pulse booming in my ears. I'm close to the window now. The phone reassuringly solid in my hands as I crouch down and awkwardly shuffle forward thinking I'm invisible in the shadows. Under the windowsill, I take a second to steel myself. I raise my head, almost an inch at a time, until my eyes are peeping out of the misted glass.

A shadow shifts.

There's a split second where I can't move. I can't breathe. I can't do anything except let terror crash over me, my eyes bewitched by the movement, but it's the branches of the tree outside. It's nothing but the tree. Gingerly, I stand, cup my eyes and press my face against the glass.

There's nobody there.

But that doesn't mean he has gone.

THURSDAY

Chapter Nine

The clock chimes midnight, and the sound jars me into action. My need to see if the man has gone overrides everything else. Still clutching the phone I tear around the house, flooding every room with light, scooping back the curtains, lifting the bottoms of the blinds. The back garden swarms with brooding shadows as the moon casts a soft glow onto the trees that guard our fence. Out the front, lamp posts dot the street. The council has recently turned off every other bulb and the shady space between them seems vast. Most of the other houses are shrouded in darkened sleep. Whoever was banging on my window has vanished, and it seems fruitless to call the police now, but I don't want to be alone. From the kitchen I pull a carving knife from the block, its blade glinting reassuringly as I stalk to the front door, where I grip the key so tightly my fingertips tinge blue, but I can't bring myself to turn it. To make the short bolt to Jules's house. Too afraid to leave until daybreak, I settle on the sofa instead, determined to stay awake. *Just in case.*

My head jerks upright, as though I'm a marionette and someone has tugged a string. Squinting at the brightness of the room I wipe the drool from my mouth with the back of my hand. I'd thought I couldn't possibly sleep, but I must have nodded off for a few hours, and now it feels there is nothing quite as lonely as 5 a.m. It's quiet. Still. There is no one banging the glass and yet I'm left again with that jittery feeling. Standing, my knees feel exhaustion-soft and I have to gather my strength before I can move. My heart kicks against my ribs as I peer out of each window, waiting for a face to lunge towards me. It doesn't. I pad back into the lounge. It's freezing. I had purposely left the heating off, thinking the chill would keep me alert, but my hands and feet are ice. Kneeling, I lay kindling and criss-cross wood in the grate of the wood burner, before I strike a match and ignite the firelighter. Vibrant flames happily dance their hello as I heap on wood, and I don't feel quite so alone.

My heart lifts a little as I calculate I can collect Branwell in a few hours. I've missed him so much. For such a small dog he has a huge personality. Every now and then I take him into work to see the residents – some of them have found it more of a wrench giving up their pets than their homes. The utter joy on Mrs Thomas's face as Branwell settled on her lap and she stroked him with her arthritic hands was such a pleasure to see.

The plug-in air freshener hisses out vanilla, startling me and, as I turn my head to glare at it, I catch sight of the pink, floral storage box on top of the bookcase. Like a magnet it pulls me forward and, although I don't want to, although I know what I am about to do might be torturous, I can't stop myself from lifting down the box, easing off the lid.

My eyes mist as I stare at what I do not want to see. My history is spread out before me in glossy 6x4s. I'd clung onto the faint possibility that my life might be split into two almost – a glass divide – and the faces of my memories relating to before all of this might still be intact and it would only be now, and what happens after, that is affected. I was horribly, horribly wrong. I pluck a loose print out of the pile. For years I've been meaning to buy albums and stick them in, the way Mum used to. That's partly what kept me going after she was no longer here. The hours I'd snuggle up with Ben and we'd flick through the pages of our past. Sharing the things we remembered: roasting beef spitting in the oven on a Sunday lunchtime, Yorkshire puddings golden brown. The things we didn't want to forget: warm drinks before bed, stirring hot chocolate until the milk frothed and bubbled. And in sharing that way, the colours in my mind hadn't faded the way they had in some of these older shots in the box in front of me. My mum would never become a black-and-white version of herself. I'm for ever thankful that in those times photos weren't stored somewhere on a cloud, password protected and impossible to access. Lost for ever like the person who had lovingly taken them. I think that's why I print mine out. 'Old fashioned' Matt used to say, as I picked up another Snapfish delivery from the doormat. 'Now get your pinny on and get your arse back into the kitchen, woman' he'd joked as he swatted my bottom. He always made me laugh like no one else.

We're laughing in the photo I'm holding. Not Matt: Chrissy, Jules and I. It was Jules's thirtieth birthday and we were wearing bright pink T-shirts, our names emblazoned in chunky black letters. Chrissy and I have our heads together, our strands of long blonde hair entwining. I wish she was here. Tomorrow I must replace my mobile so it's easier to keep in touch. Ben has already cancelled my bank cards.

At the thought of Matt, I rifle through the box, the aching in my chest unable to force my fingers to keep still.

Most of our wedding photos are still at the house – I call it *the* house as I can't quite think of it as ours still and I can't bear to call it his. The images are larger than the ones here, glued into a brown leather album, protected by tissue paper interleaves that turned out to be stronger than my delicate heart. I know I have a couple of spares here. It's the flowers that catch my eye. The yellow roses in my bouquet hanging by my side as vibrant as the beaming sun. You can't see our faces and I'm longing to pretend nothing has changed, but of course, it has, and I am charged with emotion as I study the image. We're stepping off the pavement carpeted with pastel confetti, into the ribboned car, tin cans tied to the bumper. Matt's hand is on the small of my back and for a split second I think I still feel it there, warm and reassuring. Later, those fingers undoing my zip, unhooking my stockings. I lift the box, sniffing hard, and angrily drop it onto the floor as though it is responsible for all that has happened.

The photos jumble and, as I go to slam on the lid, I notice her – Mum – and not only do I notice her, I *recognise* her. The sight of her is like stumbling across a bottle of water in the Sahara. Instant relief, cool and calming. I drink in her face, her smile, her eyes. She looks exactly the same. Looking away, I snap my eyes back to her face, trying to catch myself out almost, but it's still her. It's still Mum. Rummaging through the box I dig out every photo of her I can find, propping them against the TV, on the bookshelves, slotting them into the silver frames Chrissy had hung on the wall housing arty black-and-white landscapes. Everywhere I turn I see her and, deep inside of me, hope flutters its fragile wings and I wrap my arms around myself as though I can keep it inside. Although Dr Saunders said I might recognise

one in a thousand people and not to get my hopes up if I
did, there's a chance, however slim, that I might be getting
better. And it is this thought, not fear, nor loneliness nor
anything else I have felt throughout the night, that carries
me through until dawn breaks, the sun chasing away the
darkness, streaking the sky lavender and pink. Gentle colours
that gradually soften the hard edges of my memories of
last night, until I question whether anything bad actually
happened at all. And as the colours grow stronger as the day
gathers strength, somehow I feel stronger too.

Ben rings me from his car on the way to Edinburgh, the
crackle and hiss from his hands-free system making him
hard to understand. I reassure him I am fine, although we
both know I'm not, and I promise to call him if I need him.

'I worry about you on your own,' he says, and I tell him
I won't be alone for long. I've arranged to pick Branwell up
from Matt's at eleven.

James is standing in his doorway, feet bare, signing for a
parcel, when I swing open my front door.

'Morning, Ali,' he says, and I raise my hand in greeting
without looking at him as I start to cut across the patchy
lawn, car key poised in my hand.

'Did you hear anything last night?' he calls, and I stop
in my tracks and spin around.

'Like what?'

'Some idiot thumped on my door about midnight.
Woke me up.'

'Probably someone pissed on their way home.' The postman shakes his head and laughs. 'We've all been there. That's what comes of having a pub down the road, I suppose.'

As I carry on walking I can't help but feel relieved. It wasn't Ewan, and I'm so glad I didn't call the police. The whole street had probably been disturbed the way James and I had been and that makes it easier to believe the wind could have lifted the lid on the bin, battered my bouquet. Against the drab grey concrete driveway my feet pound the rhythm to the words, *it's over-it's over-it's over*.

I have almost, almost started to accept this until I squeeze past the line of trees that carpeted my car roof with leaves last autumn. As I near the front of my car I notice my wing mirror is cracked and hanging dolefully from the driver's side. Edging forward, my head swims as I know it likely isn't over at all. It's only just beginning.

And I know this from the blood thickly streaked across my now-cracked bumper.

Chapter Ten

The shock on your face is priceless as you stare at the blood covering your car, and I wish I knew what was racing through your mind. You really can't remember anything at all, can you, Ali?

But I know what you've done. And I'm watching you. Waiting for the right time. Waiting to hear you beg.

You will remember everything. I'll make sure of it. It will all come back to you and when it does…

You'll really wish it hadn't.

Chapter Eleven

I can't quell the feeling of panic as I stare at the blood, and although I don't know where it came from, I am hit with a fierce, sudden desire to wipe it away. I can hear James say goodbye to the postman and close his front door, and I dash inside my house and fill a bowl with hot, soapy water. As I scrub my car, possible explanations roll around my mind. Under the cover of darkness muntjacs often venture out of the woodland on the cliff road. I could have clipped one. That would be enough to cause the damage, the blood, wouldn't it? But still, I put my hand on my chest and press against it, trying to slow the frenzied pounding of my heart.

It's another forty-five minutes before I reverse my now-gleaming car onto the driveway at Matt's house. My house. Keeping the damage to the front of the car as hidden as I can, my eyes automatically flicker to the bedroom we shared. The curtains are drawn, and I wonder if Matt is actually up. Usually the first thing he does every morning is sweep them open, scooping them into their tie backs. The first thing Matt *did*, I remind myself. I don't know him anymore.

My windscreen has streaked as it dried, and through it now I can see Mr Henderson wheeling his bin through his immaculate front garden. The brown cord trousers he always wears when he's not working faded at the knees, his white shirt hanging out of his waistband on one side. Already, I am learning to focus on what people are wearing rather than their features.

He's lived in this house longer than anyone else on the street. Seen his son and daughter born here, his wife pass of cancer in her late forties. He's incredibly lonely, I think. He's only in his fifties but he doesn't seem interested in meeting someone new. He seems more isolated than some of the residents I look after and they're all at least twenty years older than him. He works from home as a therapist, using hypnotherapy, and also lectures at the local university on psychology. When we first moved here, often he'd catch me as I came home on a Friday and we'd pass the time of day, over the fence. Before long I'd pop in for a cup of tea at the weekend. There was nothing specific we had in common, but the conversation always flowed as he poured tea into china cups, a strainer catching the leaves, and cut large slabs of fruit cake 'not as light as Jeannie used to make'. He mentioned her infrequently and when he did I could tell it was always painful for him. He'd clam up when I asked about his children whose faded school photos still hung in a gilded frame over the three-bar gas fire, offering nothing more than 'they live abroad'. It suited me, I suppose. I didn't want to talk about my family either, except Ben.

'Ali. It's me,' he calls, as I climb out of my car and I know Matt has told him what has happened.

'I know.' I force myself to smile although it's the last thing I feel like doing.

'My eleven o' clock cancelled this morning,' he says.

'That must be frustrating,' I say but I'm edging slowly up the driveway, not wanting to be caught in conversation.

'It happens. Not everyone is ready to be honest about how they feel. It can be hard. Expressing yourself. Are you back? I've missed our chats.'

'Just picking up Branwell, I'm afraid.'

'You should be at home with that husband of yours. It's not safe out there.'

'What do you mean?' I feel my features stiffen.

'With what happened to you…'

'What did happen to me?' I'm curious. What has Matt been saying?

'You…' He's flustered now. Toeing the kerb. 'You had an accident.'

'Sorry, I…' I'm distracted by happy yapping: Branwell is bouncing at the window. 'I have to go.'

And I'm glad I haven't yet got the hang of reading expressions so I can't see his hurt as I rush towards my warm welcome.

I have my key poised, but Matt opens the front door as though I am nothing more than a visitor. Branwell dances around my ankles, licking my hand, as though he hasn't seen me in forever, and I suppose, in dog time, he hasn't. Crouching on the doormat, I bury my face in his neck, scratching his belly as he balances his front two paws on my knees. It's a comfort. It's a delaying tactic. Matt's already in the kitchen, clattering the dog crate closed, gathering bowls and toys. There's been no whoosh of the tap or click of the kettle. I'm not welcome. Still not welcome. My head injury has been a huge wake-up call, and although I had lain in hospital daydreaming of a reconciliation, it seems that Matt's feelings have not changed and being here, remembering how we fell apart, I'm now not sure if it's Matt I really want, or I'm just frightened of being alone. It's all become mixed up in my head.

Our relationship had deteriorated over a period of months. Matt became increasingly distant. The Friday night bouquets and cinema trips petered out. The house became devoid of the Terry's Chocolate Oranges he'd hide in random places, behind the cushions, in the sleeve of my coat. '*Just because I love you, Ali*'. Our weekends spent with him hunched behind his laptop, eyes bruised with tiredness, snappy and uncommunicative. He found it increasingly hard being self-employed, balancing business and pleasure. If I urged him to take time off he'd accuse me of nagging, the same if I mentioned expanding our family, and that stung. Last year we'd decided the time was right to try for a baby, but he gradually stopped wanting me. Sometimes my fingers stretched towards him in the still of night, but he'd roll over, breathing deeply as though he was asleep, while rejection flicked its pointed tail and fed off my humiliation.

Our marriage was slowly unravelling but still I tried to bind it back together with threads of patience, love and home-cooked meals. One Friday Jules and her husband, Craig, had come to dinner, as they often did. Before they arrived Matt had let slip that Craig was having an affair.

'You're not seeing anyone, are you?' That was my instant thought and, as uncomfortable as it was, it would explain a lot.

'No.' One lonely, exposed word I wanted wrapped in 'of course I wouldn't' or 'there'll never be anyone else for me but you'.

'How long have you known about Craig?'

He shrugged. 'A few months.'

'You've been lying to me?' It rocked me to my core. It was as if I didn't know him anymore. Couldn't trust him.

'I've got to tell her,' I said. 'She's my best friend.'

'Your loyalty should be with me,' Matt said. 'What about the business?' Craig was his biggest client. Before I could answer the doorbell chimed.

The whites of Jules's eyes were streaked pink, and she sniffed as she trailed me into the kitchen. 'I found condoms in Craig's coat pocket when I was looking for some change. I haven't confronted him yet. I wanted to talk to you first. Do you think he's having an affair?' I'd hovered on the crossroads of truth and lies but my hesitation told her all she needed to know. She dissolved into tears and I led her to a chair and held her as her body shook, while the Beef Wellington charred in the oven. Sitting at the kitchen table, she'd drained a large glass of wine, while I falteringly told her what I knew, and shortly after she'd snapped at Craig that they were leaving. The front door slammed a whirlwind of fury; Jules's scorching anger as black as the pastry I'd lovingly rolled out.

'How could you?' Matt rounded on me. 'You'd better not have lost me my biggest client.'

'If you're more worried about your business than you are my oldest friend, you're not the man I married,' I shouted back.

'Perhaps I don't want to be,' he yelled.

'What? That man or married?' I stood, hands on hips, smoke still pluming from the oven.

'Both.'

The fabric of our relationship hung looser after that night. Gaping holes where loyalty and respect should be. Jules discovered Craig's affair had been going on for almost a year, and she moved in with James, who uncomplainingly packed away his Star Wars paraphernalia and moved into the smaller bedroom, leaving Jules with the master. She filed for divorce; Craig, furious with me, withdrew his business and wouldn't take Matt's calls. Matt barely spoke to me. It was hard to bite my tongue when he barked another one-word answer to a perfectly reasonable question; yet, incessantly, I soothed, supported, did everything a good wife should, but there was an impenetrable barrier between us. I became more and more miserable, until Chrissy suggested some space would do us both good and offered me her spare room.

'I'm moving out for a while,' I said as I stared intently at Matt, wanting him to read my thoughts, know it was the last thing I wanted, but I'd been at a loss to know what else to do.

'Perhaps it's for the best,' he said, not meeting my eye.

Hearing this made my throat close to a pinprick and I had to force out: 'I'll go and pack' but even to me it had been apparent that my resolve was weak and ready to crumble if only he'd asked me stay, but he hadn't. Silently, I had clung on to my pride, slippery in my palm, and trudged upstairs to gather my things.

It's been four months now. We've settled into a fragile status quo, still sharing Branwell, sharing the mortgage, but never sharing our thoughts. Our feelings. I don't know if it's too late to fix us. I don't know where to even begin.

Branwell's paws click-click-click against the laminate floor as I follow Matt into the kitchen. I lean against the worktop I once chopped vegetables on for dinner.

'Are you okay?' He may not look like Matt anymore, but his voice, with the gravelly edge, still makes my stomach flip. Concern bubbles under every word.

'Yes,' I say, but what I really mean is no, and he knows me well enough to understand this. He takes a step forward, but hesitates, his arms hanging helplessly by his sides.

'Do I look? Do you?…' His voice rises, and I know he's putting himself in my shoes. Trying to imagine how he'd feel if I was the one who looked like a stranger. I shake my head.

'But…' He trails off, but I know he wanted to say 'it's me' and the undertone is there. How can you not recognise me? Frustrated, he rubs his fingers over his chin in that Matt gesture I know so well, although it's been years since he had a beard. Familiar. He's still familiar to me. And this is the first positive thing I've felt for days. The urge rises to bury my face in his neck. He'd still smell of spice. Not everything is lost.

'What happened?' he asks.

'I'm not sure.' I touch the lump on my head. 'I think I fell.' I tell him what he wants to hear, what I want to believe, because the alternative is too much for either of us to bear. Another man might have put his hands on me. Another man who I shouldn't have been out with in the first place.

'I wanted to visit. Ben said you weren't up to seeing anyone?'

'No. I was worn out. Still am. I've been signed off work for two weeks but the doctor said he might extend it after that. It depends what the specialist says, I think.' The yawn I'd been stifling breaks free.

'Sorry. You look shattered. I'll load up your car. Let you get off home.' The word home spears me and I clutch at my stomach as though I've been impaled. This is home. I want to say. Here. With you. But the words are as dry as dust on my tongue and I face the sink and splash water into a glass, and when I turn around again he has gone.

I allow myself a few more moments of self-pity before following him. Standing on the step, I flick through the pile of mail Matt had pushed into my hand before he headed outside to set up the dog crate in my boot. Mr Henderson is resting his forearms on his wheelie bin as he watches, and I know at least one person will miss me. Matt squeezes past me to collect Branwell's toys and there's a moment where our bodies touch. Matt pauses, just for a second, and that pause tells me the emotions that zing between us are not mine to bear alone. I'm suspended in the hoping, the wanting, the bird in the cage of my chest fluttering to be free, but, instead of speaking, Matt gathers Branwell's things and heads out to the car once more, and I am left standing in the hallway of this place I once called home.

The slam of the boot tells me it's time to leave but I take my time climbing into the car, locating my keys, snapping my seatbelt closed. When there's nothing left to fiddle with I start the engine, and Matt says, 'Take care of yourself, Ali,' as he taps my boot.

Disappointed, I pull away.

As the distance between us grows and grows, it's as though the elastic binding us is tightening around my neck, and rather than drawing us closer I know it will stretch and stretch until one day it will snap. Really, I don't know what I'd expected when I came here today, bruised and frightened and desperate for comfort, but I'd hoped for compassion and understanding. And love. I'd hoped for love. Tears spill and I stretch and pull open my glovebox for a tissue, and it's there. A Terry's Chocolate Orange: '*Just because I love you, Ali.*' I tell myself not to read too much into it. The gesture could have been born out of pity, from a place of friendship. It shouldn't feel like a beacon of hope. But somehow it does.

The journey passes in a flash, and I'm almost home when I hear it, the alert tone on my phone, and it's a relief – I must have dropped it in the car – I no longer have to replace it. That's one less thing I have to do today.

Eager to catch up with my messages, my foot squeezes the accelerator, colours blur as cars rush by, until, at last, I screech into my driveway, the car at an odd angle, but I cut the engine anyway. My hand stretches under the seat, fumbling around for my phone, and I find my clutch bag that I had on Saturday night.

The screen lights up as I press the home button on my mobile. There's only six per cent of battery left. There's a string of notifications but it's the last one that catches my eye and, as I read it, I feel a sharp stab of fear. It's from Instagram. A comment on one of my photos, although I know I haven't uploaded one for ages.

WTF have you been up to, Ali??

Chapter Twelve

After Branwell has been outside for a wee, he reacquaints himself with the lounge, nose twitching into every nook and cranny. I plug my phone into its charger and open my Instagram account once more, ignoring the messages asking what I've been up to, and study the strange photo uploaded instead. It was posted on my account in the early hours of Sunday morning, presumably by me. It's dark and grainy, a complete contrast to the Saturday sunshine brunches and shades of autumn dog-walking pictures I used to post, Matt and I crammed into the corner of the shot, grinning at the phone held in his outstretched arm. Scrolling through my account I can't see anything else I don't recognise among the endless photos of the chameleon sea; grey and angry, mutinous clouds bunched overhead; blue and sparkling under a clear blue sky. My favourite photo is perhaps the message Matt carved into the damp sand with a stick Branwell had found:

I Love Ali

I'd had to step backwards to see it clearly, crunching blackened seaweed underfoot, the wind whipping my hair. Saltwater stinging my eyes. Branwell yapping at the roaring waves, paws damp as he darted forwards and backwards.

Matt's arms around my waist, my head resting back on his shoulder. Feeling utterly loved. Utterly content. The perfect day. I can't quite bring myself to delete my account but it's too painful to look at, and that's why I find it hard to believe I have posted this photo. I double tap it, frowning as it fills my screen.

There's not much to see. There are shades of grey at the front of the photo that fade to a choking blackness. There's a rectangle to the right of the screen that's a different contrast to the rest of the shot. Something looming ominously towards me. I draw the phone closer to my eyes. I think it's a building. What could be inside? Or who? Fear prickles in my stomach along with something else, a hint of recognition. Did I take this photo, and why did I post it with such a cryptic caption?

dark things happen on dark nights

No wonder people are curious. Desperate for answers I call Chrissy. '*Sorry, too busy being fabulous. You know what to do.*' But when I try and leave a voicemail a mechanical tone tells me her inbox is full. I rattle off a text instead.

I've found my phone! Are you having a good time? Where are you?

Frustrated, I open Facebook and, ignoring my notifications, search Chrissy's name to see if she's posted anything that might lead me to her. As her page loads I notice she's changed her header photo. Previously, it was us at Jules's birthday barbecue, James flipping burgers in the background, wearing an apron designed to make him look like a woman in suspenders and stockings. Her new image has *choose love not hate* in swirling pink letters. And I roll my eyes, wondering who she's choosing to love this week but then I see it and there's a sharp ping in my gut.

Add friend.

We're already friends, aren't we? Except, according to Facebook, we're not. I scroll. Most of her posts are set to private, but the latest one, the only one I can see, was posted around the same time as my Instagram photo. It's an image of a dark and choppy sea with the quote:

There comes a time when you have to stop crossing oceans for someone who wouldn't even jump in puddles for you

Feeling winded I sit back as though I have been pushed. Why has she unfriended me? Or had I unfriended her? What *happened* that night? My questions cause a memory to materialise. Shouting, crying. But I can't tell whether I'm the one shouting or whether I'm being shouted at. As quickly as it appears, it's gone and I'm left staring once more at the 'Add Friend' icon. I press it with my thumb, watching as it turns to 'request pending', and I hurriedly shut the app. 'A watched pot never boils', Mum used to say.

Instead, I double tap *Inside, Out*, the dating app I'd used. I open my private messages.

Ewan.

At the sight of his name, a memory. Sipping drinks. Loud music. Overpowering aftershave stinging my throat. He's leaning in. Green tweed jacket. Thighs touching. Lights flash-flash-flashing. Rising to my feet. *I'm not ready for this.* An uncomfortable knot in my stomach. The room spinning red, yellow, green. Blurring until it's gone and I'm back in my lounge, clutching the sofa as though I'd float away if I loosened my grip.

My eyes find one of the photos of Mum dotted around the room. She's unaware of the camera, hunched over my birthday cake piping lilac icing. Twelve pink and white spiral candles rest on the work surface beside her. I think that was probably the last time she was truly happy, and it seems so precious now, those ordinary moments we take for granted at the time. That was the last birthday cake I ever had. I never could bear them after that day. Even the smell of a Victoria sponge rising in an oven brings it all back. The table upended. The silver 'Happy Birthday' topper snapped under trampling feet, the screaming, the shock. My life in shreds, like the violet voile that was covering the table until the men burst in and everything came crashing down.

Scanning through my exchanges with Ewan, I can't see anything that triggers alarm, even with hindsight.

He seems normal. Ordinary.

I don't usually tell anyone I love fishing. They'd think I was really boring but it's calming. Peaceful. Gives me space to breathe. To clear my head.

The sensitive type! I'd replied.

I could pretend to like rugby if that would help you agree to a date…

And I had tucked my phone into my pocket like a secret, again avoiding his question. I didn't want to date anyone, of that I was absolutely sure, but a small, stupid part of me was flattered by the attention. The next notification was as though Ewan was sensing my reluctance.

If you want me to leave you alone I will but I like you Ali and I'd love to take you for a drink, as friends. No pressure. I promise I'm not an axe murderer or anything.

Would you tell me if you were?

But it hadn't been fear of who he might be that had stopped me, it had been fear of who I am.

I had spun the gold band on my wedding finger. Had Matt and I given up too easily? All at once I had felt lost. Hopelessly, irretrievably lost and longing for clarity. If there was a smidgen of a chance my marriage could have been salvaged, wasn't it worth a shot?

Confused, I had then jumped into my car and drove slowly across town, wheels skidding on black ice. The house was in darkness. Frost patterning the path, snow dusting the fir trees. I rapped sharply on the front door, berating myself for not bringing my key, before crunching over the lawn to the back door. The kitchen was dim except for the red glow of the clock on the hob. I stamped my freezing feet as I called Matt's mobile.

'Hello.' At least he doesn't reject my call.

'I need to talk,' I blurted out, my breath steaming in the frigid air.

'It's not a good time, Ali. I'm just burning dinner.'

'You're cooking? At home?'

'Microwaving,' he said. Lying. He was still lying. 'Is it important?'

Yes, it's important I wanted to say. *I'm* important but, instead, I said nothing. Not even goodbye.

Back at my car Mr Henderson was tipping warm water over my windscreen.

'It's icing over already,' he said. 'Didn't think you'd be long. Matt's not home.'

'Do you know where he is?'

'Sorry.' Mr Henderson hesitated, as though weighing up whether to speak again. 'He's out most nights.'

It was like a punch to the gut. I had no idea where my husband was. *Or who he was with*. 'Please don't tell him I've been here.'

'Of course not.' Mr Henderson wiped his damp hand on his cords. 'I can keep a secret.'

I kissed him on the cheek before driving away, my house growing smaller and smaller in the rear-view mirror, and only when it had been swallowed by the darkness, the tears came. Pulling over, I rested my forehead on my steering wheel, letting out my grief, my frustration and, once drained of emotion, I tugged off my wedding ring, the line from the poem I would never be able to forget, 'The Owl and the Pussy-Cat', circling:

"Dear Pig, are you willing to sell for one shilling your ring?" Said the Piggy, "I will."

Had Matt traded me for something else? Someone else? Tugging open the glovebox I toss my ring inside, and, pulling out my phone, once more I typed one word. *Pig*.

But before I could send it, I changed my mind and send something else entirely. To someone else. *Yes*.

And I did not know whether I had agreed to go out with Ewan out of anger at Matt, out of the loneliness that pulsed inside my heart, or if I genuinely liked him.

Fabulous. He quickly replied. *Did I sway you with my charm?*

Sniffing hard I joked: *That and your promise not to be an axe murderer*.

*

Only now it doesn't seem so funny. I think about the possibility of him hurting someone else and I click on the 'compose a new message' icon. I am informed that Ewan is no longer an active member, and a quick search confirms his profile has been deleted. My heart sinks. There's no way of tracing him now, but perhaps I should let the police be the best judge of that. My conscience still nags at me to do the right thing.

There's a chill in the air. I tug the yellow and pink squared blanket that reminds me of a Battenberg from the back of the sofa and cover my knees. It's one of the few things I have from childhood. After school one day I had pulled a crumpled letter out of my navy book bag and thrust it into Mum's hands. It was an invitation to knit squares at home and hand them in to our teacher, where we'd sew them together in class, making blankets for charity.

'I'll dig out my needles and whip a few up,' Mum had said.

'Teach me,' I had begged, and after our dinner of mini sausages buried in mashed potato, a moat of beans spilling over the side of the plate, we'd sat, side by side, on the creaky wicker furniture in the conservatory which Dad called a lean-to. The wind battering the Perspex sheeting. 'You're clearing up, Justin,' she'd said to Dad, as I'd plucked balls of wool out of Mum's craft basket picking out the colours of my favourite wine gums: yellow, orange and green.

Mum cast on before passing me the knitting needles, which felt long and awkward in my hands. Patiently she recited 'in, round, through, off' over and over, until a second row followed the first, and then a third. We had sucked sweets as we looped wool around the needles, crochet blankets draped over our knees as the storm howled outside, the apple tree in the garden bent almost in two. The apples had been thudding into next door's garden like stones, and I had known the next day our neighbour would be lobbing them back onto our lawn, shouting we should cut the bloody thing down. One had hit Ben in the face once and insults had been tossed over the fence like a tennis rally; Mum and Dad hadn't spoken to the neighbours after, but despite the feud I'd felt so content, so cosy. Visions dancing through my mind of hand-knitting jumper dresses, scarves so long I could wrap them around my neck three times. Ben had been in bed, small arms clutching Ollie the Owl to his chest, and from the kitchen ELO's 'Sweet Talkin' Woman' had drifted from the radio as Dad washed up the tea things. The gentle sloshing of water. The rhythmic click-click-click of Mum's needles, her fingers moving so fast they blurred. She was already on her third square.

'Oh.' I'd swallowed my wine gum along with my disappointment. 'Look at my square, Mum?' To call it a square had been both optimistic and mathematically incorrect. It sloped, narrowing into nothing as the stitches had become tighter and tighter. I'd been so afraid of dropping a stitch I'd pulled the wool tautly to me, almost afraid to let it go, scared it would all unravel.

'Sometimes you have to relax. Trust. Have faith it will all work out,' Mum had said, and I had tried again but still I couldn't relax. Still couldn't trust.

And I feel that way now as I clutch my secrets to me as though they are that ball of wool. I'm so, so, scared it's all going to unravel. And although I long to have faith it will all be okay, I know that faith in myself would be misplaced. I don't deserve it, not really.

'Karma,' our snotty neighbour had sniffed after everything happened and at that time I was too young to understand what she meant, but now I do. *Dark things happen on dark nights.* Payback. You can never escape the things you've done, no matter how hard you try. I'm tangled in each and every lie I've told, and somewhere along the way I've dropped a stitch. What goes around comes around they say, don't they? What's happening now can't possibly have anything to do with what happened then, can it? *Enjoy the date, bitch?* However bad this gets I'm frightened it's divine punishment, of sorts, and I've only got myself to blame. And as scared as I am about what's to come, in some strange way I welcome it, because as much as someone out there seems to hate me, it's not as much as I hate myself.

It's still chilly. Stretching my arm over the back of the sofa I press my palm against the radiator. It's pumping out heat. There's definitely a draught coming from somewhere, snaking around my ankles, turning my toes to ice. I peel my weary body from the sofa, every muscle aches and I think I should perhaps run a hot bath. Throw in one of the bath bombs Chrissy loves that fizzes as it hits the water, colouring it yellow, overpowering the house with the zing of citrus. A bang slices through my thoughts. Branwell's ears prick up.

'What was that?' I ask as though he can answer. Stepping out into the hallway, I am hit by a cold blast of air. The front door is swinging open as though someone has just gone out.

Or someone has just come in.

'Chrissy?' I call cautiously, although there's no handbag looped around the bannisters, no shoes kicked off on the mat. No 'Honey, I'm home!' as is her way.

I bend to restrain Branwell, but, before I can grab him, he races outside, and I fly after him, frantically calling his name, as I replay coming home in my mind's eye. There's no way I'd have left the front door open, let alone unlocked. I see myself dashing towards the house, Branwell's lead in one hand, mobile clutched in the other. I remember how desperate I had been to study my phone properly and have to admit there is a possibility that perhaps in my haste I didn't lock the door. Didn't even close it properly and it has swung open in the wind.

Branwell hasn't got far. He's a few metres away being fussed over by a man. Paws trip-trapping over black trainers, tail wagging.

'Thanks,' I mutter as I grab Branwell's collar and lead him back towards the house.

Kicking the front door closed behind me, I release my hold on Branwell and lock us in.

I am almost back in the lounge when I hear it.

The noise coming from my kitchen.

Chapter Thirteen

I'm poised in the hallway, scarcely breathing, as the noise comes again. It's a man's voice, closely followed by the screeching of a guitar – nails scraping down a blackboard – a wailing vocal. Joan Jett's 'I Love Rock n Roll'. A strangled laugh escapes my lips. The radio. It's nothing but the radio. But my relief is fleeting. Who switched it on?

Somebody is here.

Branwell speeds ahead of me and slips through the small space where the kitchen door is ajar.

'Branwell.' I stage whisper his name, desperate to leave the house, but there is no happy clack of claws on tiles. Instead, barely discernible over the music is a knocking sound and instantly I am transported back to last night. The insistent thudding on my window. The expressionless face staring in. My legs are shaking now. 'Branwell.' I try again but my voice is a croak, my mouth desert dry.

Slowly, cautiously, I inch towards the kitchen door. The knocking is methodical, and I can't work out if it's footsteps. If someone is pacing the small room. I swallow a whimper and my throat aches. For a split second I can feel hot hands squeezing my neck, my lungs are fire and then the feeling is gone. My fingertips push the door and I have to steel myself to step inside. My eyes scan the room. Branwell is devouring his breakfast, his nose repeatedly clanking his metal bowl against the kick board of the sink. On the windowsill is the digital radio. Despite its pretty Orla Kiely print it feels menacing.

'Shut up!' I yank the plug from the wall. Branwell studies me, his head cocked to one side, gravy dripping from his white chin.

I didn't feed him.

Going mad-going mad-going mad cackles that acerbic voice but I am convinced someone has been here. Even if the radio had somehow switched itself on accidentally, it wouldn't have played the 80s station; last night I distinctly remember retuning it to Classic FM. *Whoever is toying with me could still be here.* I scoop up Branwell and run.

My heart is in my mouth as I race towards the front door, fearful someone will spring out from the lounge, the coat cupboard, Branwell leaden in my arms. I shift his weight as I reach the front door, my pins-and-needles hand fumbling for the key. It slips from the lock. *Fuck.* Crouching, I swipe for the key. Branwell is still now, muscles tensed, ears pricked. Has he heard something? *Someone?* I'm staring up the hallway as my shaking hand jabs the key in the lock. Did the lounge door just move? My vision is hazing. Adrenaline making my head spin. Branwell whimpers and I'm not sure if it's his fear he's feeling or mine. At last, I manage to unlock the door and fling it open, rushing towards the daylight like I've spent a thousand nights in the dark. Branwell's nose nuzzles the dip between my neck and collarbone as I keep my finger pressed against Jules's doorbell as though my life depends on her answering and, in this moment, it feels like it does.

*

'There's definitely no one in your house.' James clatters my keys onto the coffee table.

I don't reach for them, keeping my hands wrapped around the mug Jules gave me, but, despite the heat from the tea, the blanket I've pulled over my knees, I can't stop shaking.

'Your back door was unlocked though. You should be more careful.'

'It wasn't…' I begin, but was it? I'd let Branwell out in the garden as soon as we arrived home, and in my rush to plug my phone in and read my messages there's a chance I could have left it open. I might not remember feeding Branwell but often I do that on autopilot, like unplugging my hair straighteners or switching the dishwasher on.

'But the radio.' I lean my exhaustion-heavy head back against the sofa.

'It can happen,' James says. 'Do you normally switch it off at the plug or leave it on standby?'

'Standby.'

'There you go then. It was just a power surge. Nothing to worry about.'

'Would that change the station?' I'm doubtful.

'It could have reverted back to the last station it remembered before the surge.'

'You've checked every room?'

'Even under the beds. Unless it's a ghost.'

'James!' Jules lobs a cushion at him.

'Sorry, that was a joke. Look, I'm smiling.' He points at his unfamiliar mouth.

'I can't read expressions that well yet. Sorry,' I say, although I've nothing really to apologise for.

'I can't imagine how you're managing,' Jules says.

'I don't think I am,' I say, truthfully. 'I'm avoiding going out unless I really have to but it's a nightmare when I do. Men are the hardest to differentiate because so many have similar short hairstyles and often dress the same. Jeans. T-shirt. Trainers.'

'But you can tell I'm me because of my long hair?' Jules asks and, although she's formed it as a question, there's a certainty to her tone that, of course, I'll know her. It's almost impossible to explain; I'm still making sense of it myself.

When I was about five I had woken up one Christmas morning and pulled a Mr Fuzzy from my crimson stocking, embroidered with my name, hanging from the foot of my bed. Although I got bigger, more expensive gifts, it was Mr Fuzzy that enthralled me for hours. I'd press the magnetic pen against the plastic covering his face and manipulate iron filings into place, creating hair, a moustache, lips that arched into a smile, or a sad face with a lined forehead and straight mouth. Whenever I'd finished I'd hold my masterpiece carefully between two hands, taking long, slow strides to show Mum or Dad. No matter how hard I had tried to keep it still, the slivers of metal still shifted and the faces always looked different by the time I reached my parents. The features never remained the same.

'I know it's you because I'm seeing you in context but put you somewhere outside these four walls and I'd have no idea. Millions of women have long dark hair. Take away someone's eyes, nose, mouth and leave the hair and it's almost impossible to identify who it belongs to. Have you heard from Chrissy?' I change the subject.

'Yes,' Jules says, a little sharper than needed. She passes me her phone.

Are you okay? She had texted. *We're worried about you.*
I'm fine. Catch up with you at work next week x

It is just me she is ignoring then. I feel sick. I'd been telling myself she hadn't accepted my FB friends request because her battery was flat, she'd forgotten her charger. Anything, apart from the fact she didn't want to reply.

'Lucky cow. I wish I'd gone away while the shop's closed for refurbishment. Not that I could afford a week away.' Jules and Chrissy work together in the swankiest boutique. It's where the green dress I was wearing on my date came from. Despite Chrissy's staff discount it still cost a fortune, and yet I know I'll never wear it again.

I hand her back her phone, straining to recall whether Chrissy said anything about taking a break, but there are so many things I can't remember. Things I'm not sure I want to remember.

'Your memory…' Jules tails off, and I sense rather than see her exchanging a look with James. 'Ben said you think your date hurt you? But you haven't reported him?'

'Not yet. I can't give them anything to go on other than he's called Ewan and he's deleted his profile. I wish I could remember what he looked like. The doctor said my memory might never come back.' A thought occurs to me. 'Perhaps I should speak to Mr Henderson.'

'Your old neighbour?'

'Yes, he's a hypnotherapist.'

'It's dangerous to let some amateur delve about in your mind. I was reading this article on a girl who had hypnotherapy and suffered from False Memory Syndrome afterwards. She believed…'

As Jules talks I allow myself to drift. My energy is still low and the painkillers make me sleepy. I must have dozed off because when I open my eyes again Jules and James are tiptoeing around the kitchen and the lounge has fallen into darkness. Yawning, I peel myself from the sofa and pad towards the sound of their hushed whispers. I catch Chrissy's name, and a spark of paranoia ignites. Do they know something I don't?

'Stay for dinner?' James asks.

I'm tempted for a minute. He's a really good cook; we often share a Sunday lunch before digging out the Monopoly board, where Jules will buy everything she lands on, I'll wait for the colours I like, and James will let me off paying rent whenever I'm running low on money. But I can't stay here for ever because I'm too scared to go home, and I know this constant feeling of fear won't go away until I've reported Ewan to the police. I'd never forgive myself if he hurt somebody else.

'Sorry, I can't.'

'Coffee tomorrow morning?' asks Jules.

I nod as I slip my feet back into my shoes and head towards the front door. Branwell at my heels, scared of being left behind.

Jules and James close the door behind me; I hear the soft click of the Yale latching as I carry Branwell back down the path, not wanting him to dart onto the road. He's hard to spot at night, his white markings barely visible against his shaggy black fur. My breath billows in front of me, my fingertips tingling as I push against the freezing iron of the garden gate. Although it's not yet teatime, the sky is popping with stars against a darkened backdrop. Midnight blue, I think you'd call it, and the ELO song fills my head as their albums once filled my childhood home before shock and shame crept into the places happiness once sat. It's odd, I think, that sometimes I can't remember what I've done the day before and yet I can still remember lyrics I haven't heard for twenty years and now, as the track replays in my mind, I feel a connection with it which I haven't before. The loneliness. The longing. I picture Mum, spinning around the kitchen in her apron, whisking batter for Yorkshire puddings, singing. Always singing. In those days she wanted to. In those days she could. And as I head towards my empty house I so wish she was here so I could talk to her. She, more than anyone, would understand how it feels to suddenly be without a husband. To suddenly feel alone.

Deep in thought, I don't notice the box on the step until my toe kicks against it. Instantly anxiety wells. I throw a glance over my shoulder before snatching up the parcel. It's so light I wonder whether it contains anything but air.

The hallway is black as I step inside, my hand running across the smooth plastered wall until I locate the switch and flick the light on. I talk in a loud voice to Branwell; what I fancy for dinner; I'm dying for a cup of tea. *I am not alone – I am not alone – I am not alone.* The kitchen is exactly as I left it. I toss the parcel on the worktop. I can't bring myself to look at it. I may have felt calmer when I was with Jules and James but now I'm here again my nerves are jangling. Before I call the police, I roll down the blind and busy myself while I wait for the kettle to boil, pulling the tea caddy from the cupboard, rinsing clean my breakfast mug. I'm avoiding looking at the parcel the way I do that religious group who always hands out leaflets in front of the shopping centre, but the box may as well be banging a tambourine and chanting. No matter how hard I try, it's impossible to ignore. I study the three letters scrawled in thick black marker:

ALI

And before I can stop myself, I have grabbed a knife from the block and am slicing off the thick brown tape. Inside nestle the gloves I was wearing that night. The cream wool stained crimson. And a note written in uneven letters.

You don't want to go to the police, Ali. You've got blood on your hands. Perhaps the police will be coming for YOU

I drop the note as though it is as scalding as the water bubbling for my tea and watch it flutter to the floor, almost in slow motion. Branwell paws it before drawing it into his mouth and chewing as though it is a treat. Prising his reluctant jaws apart I fish out the soggy remnants of paper and drop them into the bin, slamming the lid as though I can lock the words away, but they creep out nevertheless. *You've got blood on your hands.* It's a slow dawning when it comes, bringing with it a flood of saliva into my mouth, and I lean over the sink, thinking I might vomit, as though I have taken a bite of that poisoned apple in the fairy stories Mum read me so many years ago. I can't report what happened on Saturday night now. I just can't. I'd assumed the blood on my hands, caked under my nails, had come from the cut on my head, but now my thoughts are veering wildly in a direction I hadn't considered.

What if the blood I was covered in wasn't all mine?

Chapter Fourteen

Switching the radio on was quite subtle, I thought, easily explained away after the initial shock wore off. The same with feeding the dog. One of those mindless tasks it's easy to forget but it will nag at the back of your mind, I know. Did you fill his bowl?

I almost left the gloves on your breakfast bar. Almost. It wouldn't do for you to know I can get into your house though. Not yet. We'll save that surprise for later.

Chapter Fifteen

The kitchen spins and spins; I am Dorothy, whisked away in a tornado. I take deep, shaky breaths as I stuff the bloodied gloves back in the box and thrust it under the sink with the half-empty bottles of lemon cleaner and lavender polish. I slam the door shut on the brown cardboard, which had seemed so innocuous, but its contents might have irreparably changed my life once more. *What have I done?* I weave my way upstairs, shoulder bumping on the wall as though I've had too many gin and tonics, and in my bedroom I fling my pyjamas and toiletries into an overnight bag, before grabbing Branwell and fleeing into the night, not sure if I am trying to escape the box, or myself. Outside I try to calm myself. Where can I go? Jules and James will let me stay, of course, James would probably give up his bed and sleep on the sofa, but they have already done enough today. Ben is in Edinburgh and, after the way Matt dismissed me earlier, I can't bring myself to turn to him. Iris. I click my heels three times. There's no place like home. I bundle Branwell into his crate in the boot and sling my bag on the back seat.

Throughout the journey panic is thick in my throat, my body tense, as though subconsciously remembering that the last time I drove I hit something. *Or someone.* A police car slides past me. Is it an offence to drive with only one wing mirror? I can't remember. To my relief they don't give me a second glance but, still, by the time I pull into the driveway my shirt is stuck to my back with sweat.

*

Walking into my childhood home is like seeing it for the very first, or the very last, time. It seems smaller somehow, or perhaps it is only Aunt Iris who has shrunk. Weight has fallen off her. She's aged, her hands liver spotted and wrinkled like the elderly I care for, and I feel awful I rarely visit but, when I do, a waterfall of memories torrent, snatching my breath, chilling my flesh, as if I've been plunged into an icy river. This isn't where I spent my formative years, of course – it would be even worse to go back there somehow, to the place we were all happy – we moved here when I was twelve and Ben was six. Everywhere I turn I still see Mum.

'Ali. This is a lovely surprise.' Iris proffers her cheek for me to kiss, and I smell the dusting of face powder that coats her skin. I put my arms around her sparrow-thin frame. Her bones dig into me as sharp as my guilt; it isn't fair for me to blame Iris for what happened, but I can. I do.

'Sorry. I should have rung.'

'Don't be silly. You don't need an appointment. It's lovely to see you. Both of you.' She bends to pat Branwell who is pressing his nose against her knees.

She doesn't ask if I'm okay – I'm obviously not – but then she never could deal with difficult situations. I tell myself I'm being unfair. She became both a mother and father to me and Ben and, although her maternal prowess was questionable, she didn't have to take us both on. She bustles around the kitchen, boiling the kettle, warming the teapot, standing in the places Mum once stood, and I feel myself softening towards her.

'Can I stay here tonight? I'm off work and I thought…' I thought I'd feel safer here, but I don't say that out loud.

'This is still your home.' She doesn't meet my eye as she says this and won't have seen the tears in mine.

She pulls open the fridge door, which is yellowing with age, and I remember Ben's unidentifiable drawings being stuck to it with fruit-shaped magnets. I can't believe she hasn't had to replace it, and as I look around at Mum's Portmeirion crockery stacked on the plate rack, at the strip of worktop I'd scorched with an iron, it seems nothing has changed, but of course everything has.

'Do you want some dinner?' Iris asks, and I shake my head. I haven't yet eaten but my stomach is a tight knot of nerves.

There's an awkward pause before she asks 'cake?' and I find myself nodding, wanting to make an effort. Iris reaches on top of the cupboard for the old-fashioned Quality Street tin from before the days when chocolate-wrapped Christmases, bound in bright, crinkly wrappers, came in plastic tubs.

'That looks good,' I lie, peering at the coffee cake, icing hard and crusty, and I make a mental note to bring an airtight container next time I come. Already I'm thinking about my next visit. The events of the last few days have been so turn-my-world-upside-down frightening I'm suddenly grateful for the constants in my life. Iris being one of them.

'Ben brought it.' Iris drives the knife through the rock solid sponge. 'He's so good,' she says. What I take it to mean is that I'm not, and my face stiffens; though I'm thankful Ben was so young he can barely remember what happened.

He's so sensitive I'm not sure how he'd cope with the weight of the memories I carry. I'm not sure how I cope. Sometimes I'm not sure I do.

We sit at the table and make small talk as I force down cake my churning stomach doesn't want. As I bring the fork to my mouth once more my sleeve rides up, and Iris flinches as she notices the bruising on my arms, but she still doesn't ask what happened to me that night or mention my prosopagnosia at all. It's as though, if she ignores it, then it won't be real. She never could handle the truth; instead of seeing this as a fault, which I usually do, this time I try to look upon it as a coping mechanism.

By eight o'clock my eyelids are heavy, and we've exhausted the conversations about the cold snap, the effect it's had on the garden, who won this year's *Strictly*, and I tell her I'm going to bed.

'I'm glad you're okay,' she says, squeezing my hand, as if saying I'm okay is enough to make it so; but instead of drawing away I put my hand on top of hers and thank her for being here. And I mean it.

My bedroom is untouched by time. Walls papered in faded turquoise butterflies. I'd never really made this room my own the way I had at my old house, where posters of Avril Lavigne and Christina Aguilera were Blu-Tacked to my wardrobe and the back of my door, but then I suppose I'd had to grow up almost overnight. My dressing table mirror is clean, and I turn it to the wall, avoiding my reflection as I do so, noticing Iris must still come in here and dust. Branwell stretches across the end of the bed, resting his nose on his front paws.

I sit cross-legged and use my phone to google 'hit and runs' but there are no recent reports, and nothing in this area. I start a fresh search for 'car accidents' but again there is nothing. Blood on my car. Blood on my gloves. *Blood on my hands.* What have I done? My head is throbbing, and I pop another painkiller and, tonight, I know I'll welcome the haziness the codeine brings. I shed my clothes, pull on my pyjamas and there's the familiar creak of the bed frame as I sink deep onto my age-soft mattress, as I slide inside the cold sheets. I shiver, roll onto my side and draw my knees up to my chest, wishing Matt was here, his warm legs thawing my freezing feet. The mattress dips as Branwell shifts his weight and, longing for comfort, I almost allow myself to believe it's Mum, perched on the edge of my bed, opening the book of fairy tales I loved so much.

'Once upon a time' she would begin, and I would feel excitement fizzle inside. I was captivated by missing shoes and pumpkin carriages; spinning wheels and poisoned apples. I'd clutch my heart and sigh deeply with satisfaction as the frog morphed into the handsome prince, clasp my palms together in a prayer of thanks when Sleeping Beauty awoke. Clutch Mum's arm as Snow White fell into a dreamless sleep, as though this might be the time there wasn't a happy ending. At the end of the story, I'd snuggle, talcum-powder clean, under my duvet.

'Tell me about when you met Dad,' I'd ask.

And instead of saying 'again?' Mum's face would light up.

'I was at the milkshake parlour with my friends after school, when your dad walked in. I'd never seen him before but he stood next to me at the counter and—'

'What was the weather like?' I demanded. I always remembered the small details and I wanted them to stay the same.

'It was torrential rain. His hair was dripping wet and his feet had made a puddle on the floor.'

I settled back, comforted by the familiarity.

'"It's such a grey day", he said to me. "It would brighten me up to see a pretty girl smile. Would you smile for me?"'

'What did you say?' I asked, although I knew exactly what she had said.

'I said: "It'll cost you a banana shake". I'd never been so bold before but there was something about him. I couldn't take my eyes off him.'

'Did he buy you a drink?' We both played our parts in this story she told.

'He did. And then we chatted, and he asked, "Besides being beautiful, Marsha, what do you do for a living?" and I told him I was only sixteen, still doing my exams. "I'm eighteen," he said. "If you want a full-time job when you leave school you can always look after me?" I said...'

'Mum!'

'Sorry. He wiped an eyelash from my cheek with his thumb and I knew. I just knew he was the one. I said: "What makes you think I'd want to look after you?" And he said: "Sorry, I thought you believed in love at first sight or—"'

'Should I walk by again?' Mum and I chorused.

That was what I wanted. That love. That knowing. That certainty. That's what I thought I had with Matt. Someone who would look after me the way Dad looked after Mum. In the before, of course. I no longer believe in happily ever after but that never stops me yearning for it.

Almost as though I have conjured him with my thoughts my phone lights up with Matt's name as the handset skitters across my bedside cabinet, vibrating his call.

'Hello.' I am cautious as I answer.

'Hey,' he says and something deep inside of me stirs – hope. His voice is the same, exactly the same, and it forms a photograph in my mind of his face on our wedding day, smiling down at me as a pastel rainbow of confetti arced above our heads. All around us family whooped and cheered. *To have and to hold.*

'I can't stop thinking about earlier. We should have talked properly, but I didn't know quite what to say. How are you?'

'Fine.' I say what I'm expected to say. What I think he wants to hear. But he doesn't believe it for a second.

'No, you're not.'

'No.' I sigh. 'I'm not.' Part of me longs to tell him about the gloves. About the blood on my bumper. Although I can't remember anything about Saturday night, I can't really believe I have hurt anyone, and neither would he. He used to roll his eyes whenever I chased spiders around the lounge with a glass and a coaster, carefully scooping them inside the tumbler before letting them out into the garden. But there's another part, a darker part, whispering *what if you did hurt someone?* And I know I can't drag him into this, whatever *this* is. I'm on my own.

From this day forward.

'I found the chocolate orange. Thanks.'

'It was nothing,' he says, although both of us know it was something. 'Have you eaten it yet?'

'No.'

'You must still feel ill. I can't stop wondering what happened to you. Do you remember anything yet?'

In sickness and in health.

'Nothing,' I say and there's a pause. His breath whispers down the line, in-out-in-out, and I lay my head on the pillow and imagine it's on his chest. His fingers playing with my hair.

'Ali.' One word. Just one word coated with tenderness. 'I'm sorry.' It's the nicest he's been to me in ages.

'It's not your fault,' I say but I don't know whether he's apologising for now or for then.

'Is there anything I can do?'

There is so much I want him to do. I want him to explain why he stopped trying. Why he let me go. But instead I ask him to talk to me and when he asks 'about what' I say 'anything'. I put Matt on speakerphone and rest my phone on the pillow next to my ear. I close my eyes and listen as he speaks, and we fall into a shared memory of when Branwell was a puppy and we'd first brought him home from the breeders. His paws had skidded on our laminate floor and he'd shot down the hallway like Bambi on ice skates. The amazement on his face the first time he saw grass. His confusion at patio doors, batting his paw against the glass as a ladybird scurried up the outside of the pane. Eventually I start to drift and the last thing I remember is Matt saying good night.

Sleep claims me but it is far from restful. I am chased through my nightmares by a faceless man, while my feet squelch through crimson blood flowing a river. He catches me.

With a gasp, I startle awake, my hands springing to my throat to wrench away the fingers I think I feel there, squeezing, squeezing, squeezing.

There's nobody here.

I snap on my lamp and cross the room, the warmth of the carpet against the soles of my feet reassuring me I am awake. Swishing open the curtains I am greeted by the moon casting a creamy glow. Threading through the shadows is a figure. I am paralysed with fear as I wait for him to turn, my face a ghostly smudge reflected in the glass, but he doesn't falter, doesn't look up at my window as he ambles down the street.

It's not Ewan. It isn't.

And yet at the corner of the street he hesitates, and the whispers of my nightmares trail icy fingers down my spine.

Chapter Sixteen

Bad night, Ali? Wait until you get home. I've left a surprise for you.

FRIDAY

Chapter Seventeen

I bounced between sleep and wakefulness as nightmares attacked and retreated with alarming regularity, until I crept downstairs with Branwell at 6 a.m., yawning, as I spooned coffee into a mug. The ancient heating system gurgled to life, as I sipped my drink and waited for the caffeine to hit.

'You're up early.' Iris glides into the kitchen; she looks even smaller, swamped in the dressing gown she still calls a housecoat. 'Are you okay?'

'Yes.' I answer without hesitation because that's what we always do. Avoid the unthinkable, the unimaginable, the unspeakable. 'I'm going home.' I rise from my seat, because I won't find the sense of safety I was seeking here, among the secrets and lies and the tangled, torturous past. Stupid to ever think that I could.

There's a dragging sensation in the pit of my stomach as I drive home. That Sunday evening, back-to-school-tomorrow dread, or returning to work after a sunshine summer holiday. My fears are realised as I heft my bag from the back seat and release Branwell from his car-boot prison and I see it. On the step. A padded brown envelope. I look over my shoulder before scooping up the package.

ALI

Scrawled in the same black marker. The same block handwriting.

Once inside I run my fingers under the seal, bouncing up and down on the balls of my feet like a boxer psyching himself for a fight before I can look inside. There's a small rectangular box. Antidepressants. A neon yellow Post-it note stuck to the outside.

In case you can't live with what you've done. Tick Tock, Ali, time is running out

Time for what? I grip the note tightly in my clammy hand until it crumples, all the while shaking my head in denial, but I know I can't avoid it any longer.

I need to find out *exactly* what happened that night.

I need to find out what I've done.

Mr Henderson answers the phone on the first ring.

'Can you hypnotise me?' My words come out in a garbled rush before I have even said hello.

'Of course, when would?—'

'Today. Now.' My voice cracks.

He barely hesitates before he says: 'I can see you at eleven.'

As I'm shaking biscuits into Branwell's bowl I call Jules to cancel our coffee and, when I tell her where I'm going, she insists on coming with me and I'm grateful. I'm nervous about what I might uncover but I can't stick my head in the sand. If whoever is sending me the notes goes to the police, as they've insinuated, it's better I know what happened, to give myself a chance to think. Formulate a plan. *A lie* says that little voice, and I bat it away.

Mr Henderson's treatment room is stark white, certificates in gilded frames hang in a perfect line. I can imagine him alternating his tape measure with a spirit level. He's so meticulous. I've never been in this space, which was once his garage. It's odd to think our garage, next door, is crammed with Matt's golf clubs, the elliptical trainer I never used, the Christmas decorations. 'Everything but a car,' Matt used to joke. Smoke spirals from an incense stick, jasmine, I think, filling the air and I wonder whether he's lit one to mask the faint trace of damp. I've never known him to burn one in his house. Despite the orange bars of the electric heater blasting out heat, there's a chill emanating from the bricks.

'It's not too late to run,' Jules whispers loudly, staring at the treatment table as though it is a medieval torture contraption. I shush her, aware that Mr Henderson can probably hear her from the hallway, where his footsteps echo and the tea tray rattles.

Mr Henderson kicks the door closed behind him. 'Help yourself.' He rests the tray on the polished-to-perfection mahogany coffee table. The room is sparse but spotless. There's not the thin layer of dust that often coats the photographs in his living area.

He sits on the high-backed chair opposite me, crosses his legs and picks up a clipboard and pen. Today he's wearing a tie, and this is a formal side to him I'm not used to. The dynamics of our relationship has changed, and I take my time spooning sugar into tea, splashing in milk, to mask how uncomfortable I am. I'd thought I'd be sitting in his squashy armchair in the lounge I've sat in a hundred times before, that it would be almost like a social call.

Jules, on the other hand, has no qualms about saying what she thinks. 'I don't believe in all this.' She sweeps her arm around the room dramatically.

'You don't believe in hypnotherapy?'

'Any of it,' she says firmly. 'It's like homeopathy. How can it be that you can dilute something with water and it becomes a cure?' She shakes her head as she stretches for a shortbread. 'Or that reiki thing. Healing coming out of hands. Please.' She leans back, her gaze challenging as she crunches her biscuit, but Mr Henderson's response is calm and measured.

'I can't speak for other therapies, or other therapists, but hypnotherapy is a very powerful tool when used correctly. There are hundreds of research studies demonstrating the effects. I can show you some reports if you'd like?' He addresses Jules, not me, and I think how patient he is. How kind. It's not like this is her session.

'It's okay. I can see *you* believe it.' Jules sweeps crumbs from her lap. 'So you just do what? A session, and Ali is magically better? She'll remember what happened and recognise faces again?'

'Unfortunately, Ali has sustained damage to the temporal lobe of the brain and hypnosis can't repair that. I can't help with facial recognition. But for the memory loss there's no telling at this stage how many sessions Ali might need. Brains are like fingerprints, they're all unique and everybody responds differently. Amnesia is a complex psychological condition. In localised amnesia, which is what you are suffering from, Ali, you're unable to recall the events of that night; although the memories are still in there somewhere, it's a matter of finding them.'

'But I will remember?'

'Possibly. You could remember today, next week, next year or perhaps never. Often, when we experience something so shocking that our mind cannot process it, we either blank things out entirely or pretend they never happened by doing something completely normal.'

'This isn't normal,' Jules mutters loud enough to be heard.

'What do you mean, "normal"?' I'm trying to equate everything he says with my own experiences.

'For instance, there was a case where a woman, after years of domestic abuse, killed her husband, and her children, but rather than killing herself she cooked them a meal, as though nothing had happened.'

'That can't be true.' I am horrified. How can you not know you've murdered your entire family?

'Her mum called round and caught her stepping over bodies to lay the table, the walls splattered with blood. She had no conscious recollection of any of it. You were at a bar?'

'Yes. Prism.' I try to push away the image of that woman, her poor children, what she must have gone through to have snapped like that?

'It's very possible going back to the bar could trigger your memories, or hearing a song that was playing that night, smelling the same perfume someone was wearing, tasting the same drink. We're often transported back to certain events through our senses. The smell of cinnamon, for example, always reminds me of the Christmas cake Jeannie used to make. We'd throw in a five pence piece and make a wish.'

There's a wistful expression on his face and I wonder whether he is recalling his children, wondering what they wished for, wondering if they came true.

'Coconut always reminds me of the beach,' Jules chips in. 'Suntan cream.'

All at once it's as if I can hear the shrieking of gulls. The fabric of the picnic blanket against my skin as we'd lain on the clifftops, outside the crumbling cottage, Matt's hands on my body, firmly massaging lotion into my shoulders, my breastbone which always burns, dipping into my bikini top, brushing my nipples.

'Ali? Are you okay?'

Jules's voice jolts me back to now, my face as blazing hot as the sun I'd imagined I was lying under.

'Is it dangerous?' I ask. If one simple trigger can make me recall, so vividly, the feel of Matt's skin on mine, do I really want to be back in that night? Fingertips bruising my arms, tights torn. My throat raw from screaming.

'No. There has never been a credible report of anyone being harmed through hypnosis. You're the one in control. You won't do anything you don't want to do, and you won't remember anything you can't cope with.'

'But what if she does?' Jules says. 'I find it all really worrying.'

'Ali must be imagining all sorts.' Mr Henderson's words are slow and patient as he addresses Jules, and I want to point out that I am still in the room and I'm perfectly capable of making my own decisions, but I know Jules is just worried about me. 'It's only natural. And sometimes those imagined fears keep shouting for attention until they are prevalent in the forefront of consciousness all the time, impossible to ignore.

The truth will set you free, the saying goes. It's far easier to deal with the black and white rather than the shades of grey lurking in the darkest depths of our minds. Know your enemy as it were.' His eyes meet mine as he says this, and I can't help the shiver streaking down my spine. 'Memories can be dangerous and not just for the person affected.'

'Can we just start?' I say. 'The sooner I know, the better.'

'Unfortunately, I can't just reach into your head and pluck out the memories you want, so you might not find anything out today, but I'll do my best. Jules, if you'd like to wait outside.' Mr Henderson stands and gestures to the door.

'Not a chance,' Jules says. 'I'm staying here to see what you do to her.'

'Jules!' I'm mortified. 'He's not going to do anything to me.'

'You know what I mean. If it's all above board there's no harm in me staying, is there?'

'It's not usual,' Mr Henderson says. 'Having someone else in the room can be a distraction.'

'I don't mind,' I say, as I head towards the therapy table. We'll be all day at this rate.

'Right.' Mr Henderson says and this time there's a tightness to his voice. I settle down on the cold couch and cover my lower body with a fleecy, bottle green blanket. Music floods the room – pan pipes – I can imagine Jules rolling her eyes.

'Are you comfortable, Ali?' Mr Henderson asks. I tell him I am, even though my muscles are tight, my body as stiff as a stick.

'Good. First I'm going to guide you through a visualisation, and you'll go into a trance. This isn't as scary as it

sounds. We go into trance multiple times a day, often referring to it as autopilot. Do you ever drive and find yourself
at your destination, yet you can't remember your journey?'

'All the time.' The blood on my bumper.

'That's a form of trance. We're physically present but our
subconscious has taken over. You'll still be aware of your
surroundings, to a degree, and be able to stop me at any
time. Ready?'

No.

'Yes.'

'Then we'll begin.'

Chapter Eighteen

At first I am self-conscious as Mr Henderson talks me through his visualisation. My eyes are screwed tightly closed but I feel a flush to my cheeks as I imagine him and Jules watching me. Waiting. In truth I'm both scared this won't work, and scared it will, in equal measure. What would Mr Henderson do if I confessed to hurting someone? Would he be duty-bound to report me to the police, morally bound? I'd wanted to ask but I didn't know how. My mind buzzes while in the background I am guided through a garden, down some stone steps, deeper and deeper. Mr Henderson's voice is a soft and soothing balm on my raw and jagged nerves. In spite of my reservations, little by little I feel my body getting heavier, seemingly sinking into the hard surface I am lying on, even though I know it can't be.

'You're walking over to the flower beds now, Ali. Picture the colours. The smell.'

Yellow roses on my wedding day.

The sky is clear and bright.

The warmth of the sun on my skin.

'Feel the ground beneath your feet.'

Grass tickling my bare toes.

It's a gorgeous summer day.

Birdsong.

I drift. Indecipherable words dance around my ears. I feel content. Relaxed. Half-a-bottle-of-wine hazy.

'We're going back to last Saturday. Back to Prism.'

I want to shake my head, but I can't summon the energy. I want to stay in the garden, where it is safe. I want to say no but thirst has dried my lips. Slowly the garden slips away, and it's like the sun passing behind a cloud. I shiver and feel goosebumps spring up on my arms, but my body is heavy and I can't will my hands to pull the blanket up around my chin.

'No. No. No.'

I think the words are in my head, but Mr Henderson gently asks why I'm saying no, and I don't know whether I'm saying no to now, or no to then. Music blasts in my eardrums. A thudding bass. Flashing lights. All I know is that fear has slid into the places where relaxation had nestled moments before. The images keep coming. Dancing. Laughing. Drinking. A sense of wanting to run. Run from what? My date? This session? Back to the garden. Pick a daisy. Pluck away the petals. Let them flutter in the wind like confetti. Will you take this man? He loves me, he loves me not. Not. Matt doesn't love me, even though he slipped a ring onto my finger.

Pussy said to the Owl, "You elegant fowl! How charmingly sweet you sing! O let us be married! too long we have tarried: But what shall we do for a ring?"

'Where are you, Ali?'

Bedroom. Ben's bedroom. Reading to him. Lying on his racing car bed but it's shaking. Shaking. Someone is shaking me. Gripping my arms hard. Too hard.

'Go back to the bar, Ali.'

The garden. I want to go back to the garden, but instead the cold, bony fingers of the past are dragging me back. Dragging me back to where I don't want to go. But I have to. *Tick Tock*, the note had said. I have no idea what the time limit is or what might happen when it runs out. Sand running through the egg timer in Chrissy's kitchen. Sand running through my fingers as I pop the lid off the Tupperware and offer Matt an egg mayo sandwich, sprawled on the picnic blanket outside the crumbling cottage on the clifftop. Focus. Tick Tock, Ali. I can't think! Talking. So much talking – Mr Henderson – I want him to shut up. Shut up. SHUT UP. I'm screaming it in the bar, my voice barely discernible over the pulsing base.

'Ali, who are you with?'

Cold, it's so cold. I'm outside. Rain is hammering down but, even so, the booming music is still audible. The smell of rotting food from the industrial bins is overpowering but it's not that causing my stomach to churn with sickness. The alley is black except for a soft green glow emanating from a fire exit sign and a rectangle of light framed by an open door.

'We shouldn't be out here. I want to go inside.' I turn, but fingers digging tightly into my elbow drag me back and I slip on my heel, my shoulder scraping against the slimy bricks.

'I don't want…' I begin but the light begins to disappear as the brick is kicked away and I am left with nowhere to go as the fire door crashes shut.

I. Don't. Want. To. I am shouting now. Shouting then. Shouting now. Panic gripping me tightly. I. Don't. Want. To.

'Who are you with, Ali. Look.'

'Stop!' A hand on my shoulder. Jules's voice. 'That's enough. Ali, you're okay. You're safe.'

'You shouldn't have woken her,' Mr Henderson says. 'We were on the cusp.'

'Just look at her,' Jules snaps.

I'm blinking. Blinking and crying. Crying and blinking. Back in the room. Back where it's safe. Except it isn't, is it? Now more than ever I know someone hurt me. But I still don't know who.

The engine hums as we wait for the traffic lights to change. I rest my cheek against the window, feeling the tiny vibrations all the way to my toes. Jules taps on her phone. A car pulls up beside us and the driver turns to look at me. *It could be him. It could be anyone.* As we'd left Mr Henderson's he suggested I come back next week to try again. Alone, he'd stressed, and I knew he was annoyed that Jules had interrupted our session, and somehow, I feel I've let him down. Let everyone down. I'm shaken by the indeterminate flashes that had come back to me, but I can't piece them together. The shouting. The anger. Someone must know who I was with.

'Where do you think Chrissy is?' I ask Jules, as I release the handbrake and accelerate, the wheels of the car turning as fast as my thoughts.

'Probably off with some man or other,' Jules says. Since Chrissy revealed one of the men she had dated once was married, Jules has taken the moral high ground.

'It's women like her who break up marriages,' she had said, draining her glass of wine, after Chrissy went to the loo.

Now I wonder if she's glad Chrissy is away so that she gets to be the one supporting me, but that's unfair. No one is enjoying this, least of all me.

I indicate left and pull cautiously out of the junction. 'She's not replying to my texts.'

'Stop worrying.'

'I need to find out who my date was, and she was the only one, other than me, who saw him.'

'Christ!' Jules shouts, and automatically I screech on the brakes. 'Sorry, I thought that dog was going to run into the road. Let it go, Ali.' She touches my arm. 'Move on.'

But I can't. I can't move on. I thought pushing everything to the back of my mind, the way I had before, would help me forget. But not being able to properly remember, somehow that's worse.

'You coming in?' Jules asks, as I slot the car into my driveway. 'James is working from home. He's eager to hear all about it.'

'No. I'm going to have a hot shower.' I'm still shaking with cold. With shock.

After I've eaten and rinsed my plate and cutlery I can't ignore the pleading looks that Branwell is giving me any longer, his eyes pinballing between me and the door. A soft whine escaping his lips. Sometimes I'm convinced he can tell the time. I only work five minutes away and always come home in my lunch break. After I've eaten my sandwich and put my plate in the dishwasher, Branwell tears down the hallway, ears flapping, tongue lolling, turning happy circles, and I have to wait for him to calm before I can snap his lead onto his collar. Although I'm signed off sick I want to stick to the same routine. It seems important somehow, pretending everything is normal even though it so obviously isn't.

Rain is splattering against the window, so I shrug on my waterproof and pat my pockets, checking for poo bags.

I'm ready to go but I'm hesitant. Reluctant to unlock the front door. A cold, sharp fear rooting me to the spot. The hypnotherapy treatment has made me feel worse, not better. The flashes it revealed. Unease has burrowed deep under my skin, tiny creatures hatching eggs.

Branwell cocks his head to one side, hope written all over his furry face, and I know a walk will do us both good, but still I have to take a deep breath before I can step outside.

The wind is bracing. The naked branches of the trees are shadows against an iron sky. Drizzle flings itself in my face and I bow my head, pushing forward as the weather pushes me back. Branwell tugs the lead, racing to the end of the path, turning left and stopping at the patch of turf he always sniffs before having his first wee. Traffic passes slowly. Tyres sloshing through puddles. Headlights slicing through the dreariness. A jogger passes huddled in a hoodie, catching my eye and nodding as he passes. Black trainers slapping against the concrete and as I see those trainers something stirs in my subconscious. I concentrate until I remember the man outside my house, fussing over Branwell when he escaped through my open front door, and I watch him until he rounds a corner. I'm soaked to the skin, paranoia and rain clinging to my clothes. Branwell lurches forward, dragging me over to the bright red postbox, as though it is an old friend, nose twitching, before he cocks his leg once more.

My nose and fingertips are numb with cold. The lead grows slack and I realise we are at the crossing. Branwell is sitting patiently on the kerb, waiting for me to press the button, standing as the beep-beep-beep sounds, his paws click-clacking over the sodden tarmac.

The seafront is deserted. In the summer there's always a throng of tourists, ice-cream smeared children carrying crabbing nets and buckets, dads with lobster pink shoulders, mums fishing coins from purses for the penny arcade that flashes like a beacon, drawing families inside when the sky clouds and showers fall. I rarely come here then. Locals know about the nooks and crannies that visitors don't. The cove that's only accessible on foot; the clifftop walk accessed through a rutted track that doesn't appear on any map. That's where I used to walk Branwell, ignoring the sign that spelled danger, picking my way through the crumbling ruins of the cottage that once stood tall and proud until that stretch of coastline eroded. Mum, Ben and I used to picnic at the cottage, high above the crowded beach. Later I'd taken Matt there and shared my memories, told him what a special place it was, and that was where he proposed. We'd made love inside the old building, up against the bare brick wall. As I think of it, I remember something from the hypnosis. A picnic with Matt at our special place. I feel a pang of something I can't identify deep in my belly, but I push it away. Perhaps when spring approaches and the town bustles once more I'll go back there, but today I stick to the seafront. It's bleak, waves roaring in a pebble grey ocean, the wind numbing cheeks and ears, but I like the solitude. No one takes a holiday at this time of year. I unclip Branwell's lead and watch as he races off on our usual route, ears flapping in the wind. It isn't until I've straightened up, salt spray dampening my face, that I notice someone sitting on the bench, staring out at the sea. It strikes me as odd that someone would sit in this foul weather. Immediately I check out his shoes. Black trainers.

'Branwell!' I call his name as my pace quickens. My black-and-white dog is a speck in the distance as he hares towards the deserted Pitch and Putt and the steps we usually take down to the beach.

'Branwell.' I shout again. His name is snatched away by the wind but, to my relief, he is hovering next to the bench where, in the sweltering summer months, the same elderly couple sit with a flask and a Tupperware of sandwiches, tossing crusts to the seagulls who shriek out their hunger. Initially I can't see why he's stopped but, as I draw closer, I see he's munching on a hotdog someone has dropped.

I look over my shoulder. The figure on the bench has gone. But still, I think, as the bushes sheltering the golf course rustle in the wind, the trees creak, there are plenty of places to hide. I shiver as I crouch down.

'Haven't you heard of the five-second rule?' I mutter as I clip Branwell's lead back onto his collar. There's no way I'm walking along the empty beach. I straighten up, notice what's been left on the bench and everything around me recedes. The roaring of the waves, the rain hurling itself at my face, the pier – it all slides away.

A pair of shoes. My missing shoes. Black pointy heels with a silver bow. The shoes I was wearing that night.

Taped to the slats of the bench is a note, a sandwich bag
keeping it dry.

Two words.

Run, Ali.

Without hesitation, I scoop up the shoes and sprint towards
home.

Chapter Nineteen

I feel a smidgen of pity for you as you stare at your shoes in horror, your mouth opening and closing like a goldfish, and I quickly push it away. Have you ever felt pity for anyone other than yourself, Ali? Have you?

You run, faster than I ever thought you could. Does it drive you harder when you have no idea who you are frightened of? Who you are running from? Is adrenaline coursing through your veins? Your heart racing in your chest?

It's almost comical the way you race across the empty golf course, towards the main road, the dog as confused as you are, your arms windmilling to keep your balance as your feet lose traction on the wet grass, the heels you were carrying tumbling to the floor. You fall heavily on your hands and knees, the dog springing forward, licking your face. You look around as though someone might be watching, and I am, Ali. I am. I wouldn't miss your terrified expression for anything. I can't resist rustling the bush I'm crouching in and your wide eyes seem to stare directly into my hiding place, but you don't spot me. Even if you could, you wouldn't be able to identify me, would you? From this close range I can see your cheeks are wet and I hope it's with tears, as well as the rain.

You scramble to your feet and, without picking up the shoes, set off again, but this time, despite your hurry, your gait is slower, awkward. You're reluctant to put weight on your left foot and

I'm glad you're hurt, Ali. Glad. But you haven't started to suffer nearly enough. I'm only just getting warmed up.

Out on the main road a car backfires and you actually duck, covering your head with your arms, as though someone is shooting at you. As if I'd do that, Ali. Shooting is too quick for you. Too painless.

But still, as I watch you hobble away I can't deny there's a stirring deep inside of me, but you've brought this on yourself, Ali. You really have.

Chapter Twenty

My ankle shrieks with pain as I do an odd half-run, half-limp all the way home, yanking on poor Branwell's lead whenever he lingers. Constantly looking over my shoulder slows me down, but I can't help it. I know someone was watching me at the golf course; my skin feels grubby with the weight of their eyes, but the streets are almost deserted, the rain keeping everyone indoors. I swing open the gate, and it crashes shut behind me as I splash up the front path, my trembling fingers fumbling for the right key, terrified someone will snatch them from my hands, but there are no footsteps, no squeaking of the hinges on the gate, nothing to be heard except the rain bouncing off the porch roof and my racing heart pounding in my ears.

Once inside, I lock the door before kicking off my muddy boots and shrugging off my sodden coat. Branwell shakes splashes of water from his fur, peppering the white walls with tiny, dark dots. He trots after me as I automatically head for the kitchen. I can't stop shaking. Desperate for comfort I rattle off a text to Matt:

I can't walk Branwell

And while I wait for his reply I limp into the bathroom and put the plug in the bath, twist on the tap and slosh coconut bubble bath into the steamy water. While I'm waiting for my bath to fill Matt asks, *Why?*

I hesitate. I don't know what to say, who to trust.

I've sprained my ankle I tell Matt. It's not a lie.
Sorry.

I shed tears of self-pity, along with my clothes, before sinking into the bath, placing a rolled-up hand towel under my neck, lying back. The warm water heating my flesh until the hot throbbing of my ankle is barely discernible. On lazy Sunday mornings we'd sit in the bath, Matt stretched out and me sitting between his legs as though in a rowing boat, my back against his chest. He'd lather shampoo and massage my scalp, until I felt I was melting into him, his soapy hands running over my shoulders, dipping down to my breasts. Now, I scrub at my skin until it is pig-pink and raw, as though I can wash away the loneliness I feel. And as the memory of Matt fades, another takes its place, of the other time I lost my shoes. I must have been about eight. Dad had taken me to a theme park for the day. I'd felt special as we'd zoomed down the road, me sitting in the passenger seat feeling all grown up, watching Mum shrink in the wing mirror. Ben on her hip waving his pudgy arms goodbye. The countryside had flashed past, rolling fields and grazing sheep, as we sucked sherbet lemons and sang along to 'Blowing in the Wind', until we bumped down a potholed lane into the already crammed car park.

At the entrance I held out my arm for the purple 'all rides' band to be clipped onto my wrist, as Dad poured over the shiny trifold map he'd been given with his change.

'C'mon.' He grinned, knowing exactly where he wanted to go, and laughing we'd weaved through the hordes of visitors, eating vinegary chips, aiming telescopic lenses at candyfloss-sticky children, until we reached a rainbow-coloured inflatable, larger than our house.

'It's so high.' I squinted at the inflatable that seemed to stretch all the way up to the sun. Dad stepped forward but my feet were rooted to the glistening tarmac beneath my bright green jelly shoes.

He stretched his fingers towards me. 'You trust me, don't you?' he said, and I nodded. I did. I had. Slipping my small hand into his we clambered up the squishy plastic, sometimes sliding backwards, sometimes stopping to catch our breath, but always, always, laughing. At the top, Dad balanced on the edge. 'Cross your arms over your chest,' he told me. 'And let yourself fall backwards.'

'I can't.' A hard ball of anxiety was ping-ponging around my stomach as I watched the girl in front of us shriek to the ground.

'It's safe. You'll be okay,' he said but I felt anything but okay as I stood on legs that felt too weak to support me, the breeze ruffling my hair like fingers, ready to push. Eventually, reluctantly, I closed my eyes and tipped my centre off balance until I was screaming, falling into nothingness, scrunched fingers clinging onto my T-shirt and blind faith I'd be okay. It seemed to last for eternity – my jellies flying off my flailing feet, the wind whistling in my ears, cheeks wobbling, Dad shouting over and over it would be okay, even though I've never felt so scared – but, in reality, it must only have been a few seconds. I thudded onto the chunky blue crash mat, once more surrounded by the smell of hot dogs, Destiny's Child urging 'Say My Name' from tinny speakers on tall poles. But I hadn't been able to speak. Or think. Even when I stood I still felt as though I was falling, and I linked my fingers through Dad's, wanting reassurance I was safe.

I lost my shoes that day but that fear, that sense of plummeting uncontrollably into nothing, has stayed with me. That's the way I felt when I lost Dad. Lost Mum. It's the way I feel right now but, this time, there's nobody's hand to link my fingers through. No one to tell me it's going to be okay.

My mobile phone rouses me. I'm snoozing on the sofa, Branwell nestled in the curve of my knees, my book has tumbled to the floor. I stretch out for my handset thrumming across the coffee table. It's Ben.

'Hello,' I croak.

'You okay?'

'Shattered. I must have dozed off.' I sit up and yawn. Click on the lamp before checking my watch. It's almost five. Already I'm in fleecy pyjamas, my hair still bath-damp. The co-codamol I'm taking is knocking me out.

'How was Edinburgh? Are you back?'

'About twenty minutes away. Thought I'd call in and see you? I could pick us up a takeaway? Chinese okay?'

'Perfect. See you soon.' We finished the call without discussing what we'll eat. It will be lemon chicken, it always is. It was Mum's favourite and, after what happened, she started to make her own version rather than buying in from a takeaway. Thick yellow sauce. Tender white meat. I gather cutlery, put plates to warm in the bottom of the oven and feed Branwell so he'll be full when our food arrives, although that won't stop him hoping for a prawn cracker to crunch. As I bustle around the kitchen I wonder whether Mum stopped ordering from the Chinese because we could no longer afford it or whether she felt she didn't deserve a treat. I think it was probably the shame of everything that kept her bound to the house at first, and I think, if she knew the worst was yet to come, would she have done things differently? Ran through fields of sunflowers, the sun on her skin, the wind in her hair. Walked head high, shoulders back, through the streets, at the very least. It's one of those things I'll never know. So many things I'll never know. And I'm not sure whether it's the extra time on my hands while I'm not working, or what happened to me last Saturday reinforcing how fleeting life can be, how much we take for granted, that has the past creeping more and more to the forefront of my mind, and I'm trying to hold it back, but like water seeping through a dam, it's filtering through all the same. Maybe my subconscious is trying to tell me I should be running through fields of sunflowers, the sun on my skin, the wind in my hair. Walk head high, shoulders back, through the streets, but how can I? Not when Ewan could be out there. Watching. Waiting.

Forty minutes later there's a rap at the door. I know it must be Ben, yet my heart rate grows faster.

Run, Ali.

I peer out into the murky evening. Although I can tell the man standing on the step is holding a carrier bag with the name of our local Chinese on it and is wearing wire-rimmed glasses just like Ben, I'm still hesitant to unlock the door.

'Hurry up, Ali-cat.' Ben spots me at the window. 'It's freezing out here.'

And, reassured by his voice, I let him in.

*

In the kitchen I serve up lemon chicken, the citrus tang catching at the back of my throat, fluffy rice speckled with yellow egg, bright green peas.

'Glad you dressed up.' Ben's eyes flick over my pyjamas as he shrugs off his suit jacket, loosens his tie, pulling it over his head and stuffing it into his pocket, the way he always did the second he got home from school. And although I can't recognise his features it doesn't seem quite so important anymore. However old he grows I still see the small boy who zoomed plastic cars around the lounge floor, melted chocolate buttons smeared around his mouth.

'My lack of effort proves how much I love you,' I say. 'It's a compliment really. Was your trip successful?' I dump the plastic containers in the sink to rinse and recycle.

'Very.' His voice is flat.

'You must be pleased?' He'd been worried about the losses they'd been making for ages.

'Yes, just knackered.' He pushes his glasses back up onto the bridge of his nose. 'It's such a long drive. I think I'll see if I can get the train next time, run it through expenses. I feel I could sleep for a week.' He pops the cork out of a bottle of wine he's bought, and I start to say I can't drink on my painkillers, but then I think one can't hurt and I reach for two glasses.

We eat our food at the breakfast bar, the kitchen warmed by the oven.

'Remember when Aunt Iris tried to make this for the first time?' Ben asks.

'God, yes. She didn't peel the lemon and you nearly choked. She held you upside down by your ankles while I slapped you between your shoulder blades.' We laugh now but it wasn't funny at the time, Ben's small face beet purple, the helplessness I felt.

'She was useless in the kitchen, wasn't she?'

'It must have been hard for her,' I say, as I dip a prawn cracker into the sauce. 'To be suddenly landed with two children when you've already decided you don't want any.' *I've lost the life I could have had*, I heard her say once, on the phone, shortly after she'd moved in, when she thought I wasn't listening. I had covered my guilt with a thick layer of resentment. 'She did her best.'

'You're sticking up for Iris? That's usually my job. That bang on the head must really have done something to your brain.'

'Ha ha. I went to stay with her last night actually.'

'Why?' Ben puts his cutlery down and studies me.

'I don't know,' I say, although I do.

'Why, Ali?' Ben covers my hand so I can't raise my fork.

'I was scared.'

'Of what? Of who?'

He's not going to let this go, so, falteringly, I tell him, picking out the things I want him to know, keeping hidden the things I don't. He doesn't speak as I tell him about the note on the flowers, the man banging on the window.

'Someone was following me along the seafront today, I'm sure of it.' I don't share the gloves, the blood on my car, my shoes. I don't want to worry him anymore than I have to, and there's a part of me that wants to figure out exactly what I'm supposed to have done without speculation or dismissal from those around me.

'Bastard. And this was the man you had the blind date with? Ewan?'

'It must be.'

'You should have told me. I'd never have gone to Edinburgh.' Ben pushes his plate away, fury radiating from him.

'That's precisely why I didn't tell you. Look, please. Let's change the subject. You make the coffee. Let's sit in the lounge. We can both put our feet up.' I slide off my stool.

The lounge is cooler than the kitchen was with its oven warmth. I click on lamps and press my hand against a radiator. It's barely warm.

The thermostat for the heating is in the hallway, and after I've tweaked it up I walk towards the front door to roll down the blind that covers the small window. The evenings draw in so quickly, sucking away the fading light. The cord is in my hand, the blind lowering, when I notice a shadow move outside. Someone is in my front garden.

'Ben.' My voice urgent.

Instinctively, I flick off the light to stop the window reflecting my own image back at me. As the hallway is plunged into darkness the shape freezes, a face staring directly at me.

'Ben.' I shout louder now.

'You okay?' Ben hurries towards me.

'He's outside.'

Emotions flicker across Ben's face. I think I see shock and something else. Perhaps fear. I can't read his features well enough, but nevertheless, I berate myself for dragging my younger brother into the mess I've made.

Ben darts for the door handle, his mouth a thin, straight line.

'What are you doing?' My voice is high and scared.

'I'm putting an end to this once and for all.' Ben flings open the door. 'Leave my sister alone,' he shouts as he tears outside.

The man runs, Ben at his heels.

I swipe at Branwell's collar to stop him giving chase and usher him safely into the kitchen. Outside, I look left and right but the street stretches long and empty. Fog swirling around the orange glow of the street lights.

Deep inside the darkness, a man screams.

Chapter Twenty-One

The scream came from the direction of the pub, and I pelt towards it, adrenaline dulling the pain in my ankle as my slipper socks pound against the pavement. Frost is forming on the windscreens of the parked cars – later a thick layer of ice will form – but the cold doesn't register as my arms pump by my sides, my thigh muscles fire.

Ben.

Cigarette smoke mingles with the cold air I am heaving in. The path is lighter now. Spotlights outside the pub illuminate hanging baskets, which in the summer trail pink and purple plants that are now brown and decaying. The wind creaks the sign back and forth. Self-conscious, I slow. The pub is Friday-night busy. Smokers leaning against the wall. A woman with a glossy black bob wearing a too-short skirt, legs mottled with cold, shuffles from side to side on impossibly high heels as she smokes. A cluster of men discuss tomorrow's match, clad in denim, T-shirts – despite the temperature – trainers.

'Oi. Oi.' Shouts a voice. 'You come ready for bed, darlin'?'

Conscious of my thin pyjamas I cross my arms over my breasts, keep my head down and, as I stalk past, it occurs to me: one of the men could be *him*, Ewan. I start to shake.

'Leave her alone,' says a different male voice, and I'm grateful, until they continue: 'You look great in those pyjamas but they'd look even better on my bedroom floor.' There's nothing funny about the sound of their pealing laughter. 'I'd show you a good time.'

'She'd need a microscope to see your "good time",' the girl shouts, dropping her cigarette butt into an almost-empty bottle of cider. It sizzles as the red tip turns dark. 'Leave her alone, knobhead. You okay?'

'I'm looking for a man…'

'Look no further!' A guy leaps in front of me, grabbing his crotch.

'Fuck off.' The girl pushes him away.

'My brother,' I say. 'He was chasing someone.'

'Yeah, they shot down the alley.' The girl nods to the right of the pub. I hope she'll offer to come with me, but she totters inside on her spindly heels, the men following like sheep.

In daylight the alley streams with kids using it as a cut through to the local secondary school. At night it gapes like a mouth, ready to swallow me up. At first I can't see anything; I can't hear anything. I take a step forward towards the chip of light at the other end. Another step.

Bang.

I spin around, my heart pounding, but voices drift and I realise it was the pub door swinging shut. The slamming of a car door. The revving of an engine.

A third step.

An unidentifiable sound.

A fourth step.

A movement about halfway down. I narrow my eyes, but I can't quite make it out.

'Ben?'

A groan.

'Ben!' This time I can hear it's him. I rush forward. He's lying on the ground in the foetal position. I crouch beside him, fumble for his hand, my fingertips seeking out his pulse. 'Are you hurt?' It's a rhetorical question, born out of helplessness. It's an effort for him to speak, but when he does he slowly says 'not as much as the other guy,' and my panic begins to abate.

Ben pulls himself to sitting, and then stands, wobbling as he does, slinging his arm around my neck for balance.

'Can you walk?'

'I'm okay,' he says, although he obviously isn't.

We make our way home slowly. Ben leaning heavily against me. My knees buckling as I try and support his weight, trying not to think of all those years ago when I could swing him effortlessly into my arms, his legs wrapped around my waist. Pain shoots from my shoulder into my neck. My ankle throbbing once more – adrenaline has ebbed away. There's no one smoking outside of the pub now; but: two people are heading for the entrance. 'I'll have what he's been on.' Sarcasm sits on my tongue, but I grit my teeth and don't let it out. We've had enough trouble for one night.

*

Once inside the house I settle Ben on the sofa. Branwell lets out a happy yap as I open the kitchen door to fetch a bowl of warm water. From upstairs I lift a bottle of TCP and cotton wool from the bathroom cabinet.

Ben is chalk white. Glasses skewed. Blood staining his white work shirt. A criss-cross graze covering his swollen cheek, a bruise already forming on his forehead.

'I'm so sorry.' I kneel beside him and dampen a cotton wool ball. Dab it against his broken skin.

'It's not your fault. I'm sorry I let him get away.'

'What happened?' I gently press my fingertips against the wound, feeling for gravel, but I think it's clean.

'He took me by surprise. I rounded into the alley and he grabbed me and threw me against the wall. Must have hit my head because I don't remember anything else until you appeared.'

'We should probably take you to the hospital and get you checked over.' I unscrew the lid from the TCP; the smell stings my nostrils.

'I'll live,' Ben says. He winces as the disinfectant seeps into his wound. 'I remember you doing this to my knees when I was small.'

'You were forever falling over.' Emotions rise. 'I don't know what I'd do if anything happened to you.'

'Nothing's going to happen to me. It's you I'm worried about, Ali-cat. I think we should call the police.'

I sit back on my heels, dropping the cotton wool onto the floor, pushing Branwell's nose away as he sniffs at it.

'Did you get a good look at him?' I ask.

'No, I didn't see his face at all. But we should have reported what happened to you last Saturday. Even if you couldn't remember anything, something would have been on record.'

'You know why I didn't want to go to the police.'

'It wouldn't be the same this time. It's not the same situation. Please, Ali. What if he comes back and I'm not here?'

I chew my lower lip, weighing up the options. What about the gloves? The blood? *In case you can't live with what you've done.* I'm so scared. Afraid of what they might find out if they start digging around. Afraid of what I might find out. But as I look at my brother, pale and shaken, his cheek glistening red, I know he'll be worried sick about me if I don't make a statement and it feels selfish somehow to put myself first.

'I'll fetch my phone,' I say.

My mobile is charging in the kitchen. I unplug it from the wall and, as I unlock it, a text alert flashes from an unknown number.

If you want to keep your brother safe don't go to the police, Ali. Imagine how he'd feel if he knew what you'd done, let alone if he sees this.

At first I'm confused. *Sees what?* But then my phone pings with another message, a video this time. There's a sick feeling in my stomach as I press play. The footage is dark, grainy, but there's no mistaking it's been filmed in the lounge, flickering tea lights appear to be the only lighting. From the angle, I'm guessing it was filmed on a phone placed next to the TV somewhere. There's the pastel pink wallpaper patterned with dove grey birds, the faceless angels, the bookcase with my pink floral box on top but I barely register the details, all I can focus on is me. I've my back to the camera, blonde hair spilling down my naked back; the green strapless dress I was wearing that night bunched around my waist. You can see the sides of my breasts bouncing up and down. A man's bare legs are visible beneath me, his trousers around his ankles, his hands gripping my waist as he drives himself deeper inside me as I thrust my hips backwards and forwards. He's looking directly into the camera, his face in shadows, and even if it wasn't, I wouldn't be able to identify him. I can't show this to anyone else. It must have been taken last Saturday but I don't remember, and although I don't look like I'm protesting, I know I wouldn't have consented to sex with a virtual stranger, I just wouldn't. I feel dirty. Violated. Instantly ashamed. There's another alert. Again, those four words:

Enjoy the date bitch?

Bile, hot and sour, floods my mouth and I hunch over the sink, the lemon chicken rising in my throat. Sex. I've been filmed having sex. What if Ben sees it? Matt? What if it ends up on the internet? I vomit again and again until my stomach is empty of food, filled instead with rage.

How dare he threaten me. Blackmail me. Bring Ben into this. How fucking dare he.

Another alert.

Who knows what else I filmed that night, Ali?

I can't go to the police now, I can't, but tomorrow I'm going to find out exactly who Ewan is and what he wants, even if it kills me.

I think once more of the video.

Even if I end up killing him.

SATURDAY

Chapter Twenty-Two

Orange and scarlet ribbons streak the sky as the sun begins to rise. In the eight hours since Ben left, my anger hasn't abated, although my determination to track down Ewan is, admittedly, now tempered with fear. Ben eventually accepted my decision not to call the police, putting it down to my reluctance to relive the past. Of course I couldn't tell him about the video, the bloodied gloves, the damage to my car. The threat that I might have done something terrible and been filmed doing it. Although it may seem foolish to want to track down a man I know is clearly dangerous, I can't just sit and do nothing. After last night's attack on Ben it seems personal in a way it hadn't before – again I feel that red hot burn in my veins when I think of the bruising on Ben's face – and I almost, almost wish the blood on my gloves is Ewan's. That I have hurt him. This idea takes shape until its edges are pointed and sharp. Perhaps that is what happened? Perhaps Ewan attacked me and I fought back. Fought back hard. Perhaps all this is nothing but hurt pride intent on scaring me. If so he'll get bored soon, surely. He has to. I tell myself this, but it doesn't ring true. The video doesn't show me protesting and again I wonder if I was drugged. Feeling dirty once more as I think of the footage, I shower for the third time since watching it, and dress.

*

I am chiselling two slices of bread from the loaf out of the freezer when the doorbell rings. I hover in the doorway, knife still in hand, when the letterbox rattles.

'Ali,' shouts Matt, and instinctively I pat my hair as I hurry to let him in, as though that will make me more presentable.

'This is a surprise.' I'm not sure what to say. Matt has never come here before. Branwell squeezes between my legs, tail wagging so fast it's a blur.

'Thought I'd better come and walk him with your ankle and all.' He crouches down, and Branwell rests his front paws on Matt's knees as he licks his face. 'I've had a wash, thanks.' Matt holds him at bay as he raises his head and, flustered, I step back and pull Branwell's lead from the cupboard along with his treats and some poo bags. I can't bring myself to look at Matt, almost as though he'll be able to read my expression and know I've had sex with another man. Regret crawls across my skin.

'Are you okay? Have you remembered something?' Matt asks, as he snaps the lead onto Branwell's collar.

'Why does everyone keep asking me that?' I say, sharper than intended.

'Okay.' He straightens up. 'Perhaps a coffee when I come back then?' he says and, embarrassed by my brusqueness, I offer to have a cooked breakfast waiting.

*

Sausages and bacon sizzle as I think how odd it is the way things work out. Matt is being nicer to me than he has been in ages. I slice mushrooms, quarter tomatoes – an edible version of the olive branch I am offering – and I've just laid out plates when Matt returns. He washes his hands and drops bread into the toaster, buttering the slices after they pop.

'You've become domesticated,' I say to fill the space between us.

'Don't believe everything you see!'

We fall into an awkward silence once more when I don't answer. I can't. I can't believe anything I see.

It feels odd to have Matt here, and I think he feels as uncomfortable as me as he sips from the mug of tea I have pushed towards him and makes a face, looking around for the sugar I have forgotten to add.

'What have you been up to then?' he asks, and my guilt rises before I realise he is fumbling for conversation too. We're both at a loss to know how to be with each other. Who to be with each other. 'Silly question,' he says, filling the silence when I don't. 'How are you feeling?'

'My head's still sore but I'm getting better. The painkillers make me woozy though. I keep napping.'

'And your memory? The proso thing?'

'No change.' I stab at a mushroom. 'An appointment letter came this morning, though, for the research pro-gramme into prosopagnosia at Stonehill University, for next Thursday.'

'That's great, although it's a bit of a trek. What happened to your car, by the way?' Matt asks. 'I didn't notice the damage at the front when you picked Branwell up.'

I chew slowly while I formulate an answer. 'Someone clipped it in a car park.'

'Probably not worth an insurance claim but you shouldn't be driving with only one mirror. I'll take it in and get a new one, and get the bumper replaced.'

'You don't have to.'

'I want to. You need looking after, Ali. Keeping out of trouble.' He nudges me with his elbow to prove he's joking, but the bacon sits greasy and heavy in my stomach. I push my plate away. Why now? Why is he being so nice when I've slept with somebody else and potentially ruined any chance we might have had at getting back together? Momentarily, I consider whether I should tell him, but then I think how I'd feel if I knew he'd touched someone else and I know this is a secret I must keep. Another one.

Matt mops up the last of his egg yolk before he stands and pulls on his coat.

'Stay.' One word, though there are a thousand 'I'm sorrys' and 'I need yous' hidden under the surface.

'I can't. I've somewhere to be.' He doesn't elaborate. 'Where are your car keys?'

I fetch my spare set and drop them into his outstretched palm, and as my finger brushes his, a jolt of electricity shoots through me.

He drags his heels as he ambles down the hallway, as though he's reluctant to leave, and he turns to face me when he reaches the door, and I am sixteen again with first-date-first-kiss flutters.

'Matt, I have something to tell you.' My words fall out in a gibbering rush. 'I've been thinking since the hospital and—'

'Me too.' I fall silent and study him but his expression is unreadable. 'I could have lost you. I mean properly lost you. Alison.' My name is warm and soft as it falls from his tongue. My heart racing again but this time it isn't through fear. Matt takes my hand in his, kissing my palm before drawing me against him for a hug. His body is still familiar to me and I allow my rigid frame to relax into him. My head fits perfectly in that hollow between his head and shoulder. I feel the warmth of his arms wrapped around me, and despite the shame that crashes over me in sickening waves every time I think of that video, I am disappointed when he lets me go.

'We'll talk soon, I promise, Ali. There's things you should probably know.'

'What things? Why can't we discuss them now?'

'Because I have somewhere I need to be. Sorry.'

I feel a pricking sensation at the back of my eyes and I will myself not to cry as he leaves. He's *still* not putting me first. In the kitchen, I carry our plates over to the sink to wash up and find a Terry's Chocolate Orange next to the taps, and I don't know what to think, but I don't have time to dwell. I need to get changed. It's exactly a week after my date.

Mr Henderson had said: 'It's possible going back to Prism could trigger your memories.'

That's exactly what I'm going to do.

Chapter Twenty-Three

Normally if I'm going out on a Saturday night I take care over my make-up, my hair, my outfit, checking out my reflection from all angles. Tonight, I've pulled on plain black trousers and a long-sleeved T-shirt that covers my bruises. I can't bear to look in the mirror still, but even if I could, I wouldn't be contouring my cheeks, darkening my brows. The thought of another man even looking at me, let alone touching me, makes me feel sick to my stomach. The taxi beeps its horn outside, and I wish I had my car so I could make a quick getaway if tonight gets too much for me.

I lock up and hurry down the path, tell the driver I won't be a minute, and I stride towards Jules's front door. She must have heard the horn. Through the lounge window I see her and James. She's gesturing with her hands as she speaks, and her voice is raised, but I can't hear what she's saying. I rap sharply on the window and point at the cab behind me.

'Sorry.' She's breathless, seconds later, as she opens the door, slams it shut behind her.

'Where's James?' He had said he'd come with us.

'He has a migraine.'

I glimpse through the window again, he's sitting with his head in his hands. I feel a lurch of trepidation. I'm apprehensive about returning to the bar – having James there would have settled my nerves.

'Look, Ali,' Jules still hasn't moved, keys dangle from her finger, 'do you think this is really a good idea? Especially as James can't come now?'

'I don't know what else to do.' I shrug. 'It's exactly a week later, so I'm hopeful the bar staff will be the same. Somebody must have seen me. Remember me. Maybe know who Ewan is.'

'It's turning into an obsession. I don't mean to be blunt, but so what if you find out who he is? He's hardly likely to tell the truth about that night, and it's all over now. Can't you just move on?'

'No.' I don't elaborate. I can't tell her about the gloves, the car. My vague, amorphous suspicions that I might have done something terrible and Ewan might have filmed me doing it. She'd definitely try to talk me out of going then, and in this game of cat and mouse I'm sick of being the mouse.

'What if he's there?' she asks. 'You wouldn't know him if you saw him. He could—'

'He won't.' I cut her off, already nervous enough. 'Besides you'll be by my side all night. Please, Jules. I'm going with or without you. I'd rather you came.'

She sighs. 'Okay but I'm getting bladdered and you're paying.'

It crosses my mind that if I was honest with Jules about all the things Ewan has done she might not drink, remain vigilant, but then again she might change her mind about coming with me and I don't want to be alone. I stride towards the taxi, telling myself that even if she doesn't know the full story there's safety in numbers, but even before that thought has properly formed I know I am deluding myself.

*

The freezing air stings my lungs as the taxi drops us off outside Prism, but as soon as we step inside heat hits me. There's a girl handing out leaflets for cut-price pitchers, and I study her but I've no way of knowing if I've seen her before. I remember the tips Dr Saunders gave me and I search for distinguishing marks, tattoos, distinctive jewellery, but last week I probably wouldn't have been looking for any of those things and she remains unfamiliar to me.

'Was she working last Saturday?' Jules asks. I shrug help-lessly and notice Jules raise her eyebrows as she too begins to realise how fruitless this could be.

'Have you seen me before?' I ask the girl as I take a leaflet.

'No,' she says, but she's barely glanced at me.

Two bouncers flank the double doors leading into the bar.

'Do you remember me?' I ask one. He shakes his head.

'Ooh is he your baby's daddy?' asks the other, and I feel a flush creep around my neck as I scuttle through the entrance. In front of me, bodies: a couple writhe to the music, alcohol loosening stiff joints and inhibitions.

'Drink?' Jules shouts over the music and, although I don't want one, I need to talk to the bar staff and so I nod. Jules orders me a spritzer and herself a double JD and Coke, which she downs before she's paid. 'God it's depressing being single,' she says as she signals to the barman for another. 'I feel too old for places like this.' She doesn't usually drink much, and I wish she'd slow down. I've enough to worry about tonight without adding her to the mix.

'Were you working last Saturday?' I say, as the barman sloshes another shot of amber liquid into Jules's glass.

'Yep. I work every weekend. Got to pay my way through uni somehow.'

Jules throws back her second double and asks for a refill.

'This is an odd question,' I say. 'But do you remember me being here last weekend?'

'Had too much to drink, did you?' He flashes a smile. 'Got up to something you shouldn't? With someone you shouldn't?'

Why would he say that? The features stiffen on my face as I try to keep my tone light.

'Just trying to piece together a few things. You know how it is.'

'You look kind of familiar. Did I serve you?'

'You can serve me.' Jules slaps another twenty on the bar. 'Another two doubles. What?' She catches my look. 'It saves queuing.'

'I was here with a man. And my friend, blonde, about my build. Chrissy.'

'Oh, I know Chrissy!'

'Doesn't everyone?' Jules mutters under her breath.

'I remember seeing her. Not you though. Or the guy. Sorry.' He turns to serve someone else.

Dejected I carry the white wine spritzer he poured for me over to the booth in the corner. As I slide onto its sticky, plastic seat I've a strong sense of déjà vu. *A thigh pressed against mine, a hand on my knee. A prickly, uncomfortable feeling.* I scan the room. There's a man leaning against the bar watching me. I tear my gaze away, and see another man awkwardly moving his body to the beat, and he stares in my direction. Panic wells as my eyes flit back to the bar. The man has changed position, standing tall now, and I think it's not the same person, looking my way, or is it? It's impossible to tell. His features have rearranged once more.

'I think I'm being watched,' I say to Jules, discreetly signalling with my eyes. Trying to appear casual as she steals a glance, I pick up my drink and pretend to take a sip, but my hands are shaking and wine trickles down the side of the glass. Two men hover by our booth, one whispers something to the other and he looks at me over his shoulder before turning back to his friend. They take a step nearer.

'Jules.' My heart is galloping now.

'Ali, it's a meat market. What did you expect, two women out alone on a Saturday night? Men are going to look. Usually that's kind of the point.'

My eyes scan the crowd. You'd think it would be easy to identify people you know by their clothes, their hair, the way they carry themselves but it's our features that make us unique. Recognisable. Take those away and it's like pebbles on a beach, too many similarities, and it takes patience and time to tell them apart. I don't have much of either.

'We shouldn't have come.' The music grows louder in my ears. Despite the fact I probably know a good few people here tonight, everyone is a stranger. It's busier now. The drinks half price until midnight.

'I'm sure if Chrissy was here you'd be having a good time.' Jules knocks back her fourth double. There's a slur to her words.

'What does that mean?'

'It means that ever since you moved in with her you've dumped me.'

'I haven't!'

'Even tonight you're looking for her.'

'It's odd we're not Facebook friends anymore. I want to know why. I'm worried about her, Jules. Aren't you?'

'Not particularly. You drinking that?' She nods towards my wine and when I shake my head she picks it up. 'She'll turn up Monday, when the shop reopens, and regale us all with some big adventure.' She tips her head back and drains the glass.

'Steady,' I say. There's a tension between us I don't quite understand and part of me wishes I hadn't coerced her into coming.

'Why?' Jules says and there's confrontation in her tone. 'I might want to get pissed and shag a stranger, the way Chrissy does.'

'Just because Chrissy had a fling with a married man once doesn't make her a slag.'

Jules snorts.

'And just because Craig slept around it doesn't mean you have to.' The words are out of my mouth before I can stop them.

'*Slept around*? I thought there was only one? How many?' Even in the green and red flash of the lights I can see the colour has drained from her face.

'I don't know.'

'How many women, Ali?' She thumps the table with her fist.

'Honestly, Matt didn't say…'

'Matt's a tosser too.'

'Don't call him that,' I say quietly.

'Why?' She studies me. 'Fuck. You're not thinking of taking him back, are you?'

I am forming the word 'no', but I can't bring myself to say it.

'Christ, Ali. Seriously. After the way he's treated you?'

'It's been hard, yes, but marriage is hard, isn't it? We've been talking, today. What happened to me has been a wake-up call to us both. He's been different since I was in hospital. Nicer.'

'Fucking brilliant. So you think couples should work through their problems? You hypocrite. You lost me my husband and now you're...' The bitterness streams from her lips, where it sits on the table between us, toxic and thick, while I cut in, my voice shaking with anger.

'I didn't "lose" you your husband. You left of your own free will when you found out he was a shit.'

'At least he was *my* shit. You go around ruining lives.'

'Ruining whose life?' I'm shouting now. Again I can feel eyes on me but this time I don't care.

All of a sudden it's as if someone has deflated her. 'Sorry. Sorry.' She starts crying. Rubs her nose with the back of her hand. 'I don't feel good, Ali.'

'You shouldn't have mixed your drinks. You always were a lightweight.'

'I didn't mean it. I just miss Craig. I miss being married. You understand that, don't you?' She's crying harder now, and I slide around her side of the booth, put my arm around her shoulders and make soothing noises that I do understand, but inside I am reeling. Alcohol coaxes out the truth, Mum used to say. The truth is she is lonely. The truth is she blames me.

It's almost midnight and we're more than ready to go home. I'm coming out of the toilets, a wad of loo roll in my hand for Jules. All the emotions she's felt since she found out about Craig's affair have tumbled out tonight, and there's a taxi on the way to pick us up. Before turning left to head back to the main section I glance to my right. At the bottom of the darkened corridor the fire exit sign glows a dull green, and the sight of it stops me in my tracks. That was what I'd remembered during my hypnotherapy session. *I don't want to*. Being dragged outside. The rain. The cold. The door slamming shut. Every cell in my body is screaming at me to walk away but, tentatively, I take a step forward, and then another. I'm shrouded in fear but I can't turn back. I have to know if it will trigger more memories. The corridor is longer than I thought. The music fading behind me. *Shut up. Shut up. Shut up.* My skin is crawling with recognition now, I'm almost at the door. Another step. I stop. Stretch out my fingers and touch the cool metal bar.

'I've been looking for you.' Hot breath against my neck. The hairs on my arms stand on end. Slowly, slowly, I turn around.

'Leave me alone,' I say to the man in front of me. My eyes flicker to the right. My hands ball into fists.

Run.

My feet pound but before my mind registers I'm moving I'm being yanked backwards by the strap of my handbag. I fall against his chest.

'You're coming with me.' Onions on his breath. Fingers clamp around my elbow. He drags me further into the blackened corridor, away from the crowd, where no one will hear me scream.

SUNDAY

Chapter Twenty-Four

The DJ announces midnight and like Cinderella I am trying to make my escape.

'Let me go!' I wrench my arm away from the man, stumbling, as he releases me. I find my footing, thinking I can run for the exit – the taxi should be waiting outside – but before I can move he blocks the corridor with his sheer bulk.

'What do you want?' he growls, and I rub my elbow where I'd banged it on the wall.

'What do *I* want?'

'You're a copper, ain't you? Coming into my gaff. Questioning all my staff.'

'God, no! I was in here last weekend with a man. A blind date.' I study his face, as I speak, for signs he believes me, while I deliberate how much I should tell him. He isn't likely to want his bar associated with an attack. 'I really liked him.' I tilt my head to one side and twizzle a strand of hair around my finger the way I've seen Chrissy do a hundred times before. 'I can't quite remember what he looked like. You know how it is.' I giggle in what I hope is a girlie way, although to me it sounds too high. Too scared.

'You were pissed.'

'Yeah – well it was two for one on the shots. Look, I don't suppose you could help me? Let me look at the CCTV.'

He stiffens. Turns away.

'Wait!' I pull out my work ID from my purse. 'Look, I'm not police, I'm a care assistant, for the elderly.' I pass him my card.

'My nana's in one of them 'omes.' He taps the card against the back of his hand while he thinks. 'Okay. I'll help you. Because it's good. You looking after old folk. Cleaning up their piss and shit. This can be my good turn.'

'Thank you!'

'For a price,' he adds.

*

'God, I feel rough,' Jules says for the millionth time. She's wearing dark glasses despite the lack of sun and clutching a bottle of Lucozade, her go-to hangover cure.

'I'm not surprised. Thanks for coming with me.'

'I owe you one. Sorry I was such a bitch last night.'

'It's all forgotten.'

'I still don't think you should do this though,' Jules says, but I've already pressed the buzzer on the door. 'It could be dangerous.'

'It's broad daylight and we've got each other. Safety in numbers. Carl's bark was definitely worse than his bite,' I say but there's a brittleness to my voice and I can't force my mouth to curve into a smile.

'I don't mean that sort of dangerous,' Jules says. 'I mean, what if you remember?'

'That's kind of the point.' My breath clouds in front of me as I press the buzzer again, stamping my feet to keep warm.

'But what if it's too much for you to cope with? Too horrible.'

'We went through this last night. It can't be worse than the things already running through my mind.'

'But this time it's costing you money. You're handing over £500 to a complete stranger on the off-chance that the CCTV recorded you last weekend. And what if it did? What then?'

Before I can answer, the door swings open, and I feel almost victorious as I recognise Carl with his height and width, bulging muscles, sleeveless T-shirt despite the sub-zero temperature, black hair slick with gel.

He slowly appraises me from my head to my toes and back up my body, his gaze lingering on my breasts, before his eyes meet mine. I can feel my cheeks burn hot as I pull the lapels of my coat closer together.

'You came back then?'

'No shit, Sherlock,' Jules mutters, and I poke her in the ribs.

I step forward but Carl angles his body, blocking the entrance, palm outstretched, eyebrows raised.

I fish around in my handbag for the roll of notes I'd stuffed there earlier.

'Are you sure about this?' Jules asks. 'I think you're wasting your money, Ali.'

'You're wasting my fucking time,' Carl growls, and I quickly press the money into his hand.

'Come on then.' Without waiting to see if we follow, he turns and strides past the sweeping staircase leading to what used to be a second bar that hasn't been open for months. Sometimes there are barely enough bodies to fill the downstairs.

Everywhere looks so shabby and old without the mood lighting, the softening haze of alcohol. The toilet doors are propped open, a whiff of bleach overpowers the lingering smell of urine. Jules and I both stop dead as we step into the main space that always seems so tiny but now stretches long and wide.

There's a bored-looking girl, jaw energetically working gum, dark roots morphing into a sharp blonde bob, swishing a mop over the floor which I'd never noticed before was parquet, and suddenly I'm transported back to a memory. Mum and Dad perched on too-small grey plastic chairs at the back of the school hall, me a Wise Man, draped in an old sheet, a tea towel covering my head, trying not to scowl at Melanie, who was playing Mary. She cradled a plastic baby Jesus who actually weed when you squeezed his tummy. A chubby Ben bounced on Dad's knee, clapping in all the wrong places. Pointing and squealing my name over and over, while Joseph made his impoverished plea for a room for the night.

'Ali?' Jules places her hand on my arm bringing me back to now, where, instead of coat hanger tinsel stars, there's a lonely disco ball twirling. 'Are you having a flashback?' Her forehead is furrowed in concern.

I shake my head. I'm not. Not in the way she thinks anyway.

Carl pointedly checks his watch, and I hurry forward again, peeling my shoes off the sticky floor. We pass the booth in the corner and I feel the same uncomfortable feeling wrapping itself around me like ivy. Instantly, in my mind's eye, the lights strobe, music blares.

As we pass the bar Carl tosses the roll of banknotes I'd given him at a girl who is chucking empty bottles into a green plastic grate. Jules grimaces at the sound.

'Pay the supplier in cash when he comes. Stop him fucking whinging,' Carl says.

'What about?…' The girl starts but Carl has already turned a hard left into the corridor, and as we pass the fire door I begin to shake. *Please don't. Please stop.* I touch my cheek, expecting my fingertips to come away wet but I'm not crying, not now anyway.

We push through a door marked 'Staff Only' and descend a set of grey, concrete stairs, a draught nipping at my ankles despite the lack of windows. Carl enters a darkened room. There's a flicker. A humming. The fluorescent tube clinging to the low ceiling springs to life, and I blink in the glare.

Even with only three bodies the 'office' is full. Carl squeezes past me, and my spine presses uncomfortably against the gun metal filing cabinet, but still his skin brushes against mine and I try to relax my features, knowing my face has twisted into a grimace. He leans over the battered desk, one drawer is missing, and fiddles with a small TV until it fizzes with static. I turn my head away from his armpit. Body odour and danger. An inked cobra wrapped around his bicep, a roaring tiger on his forearm and, touchingly, the word 'Sharon' on his wrist in uneven letters, the 'r' higher than the rest. I wonder if she's his girlfriend or daughter.

'The quality is shit.' He fiddles with a dial until a fuzzy image appears of the edge of the bar, timestamped Saturday. *That* Saturday.

I sink into the faux leather chair, not caring it's ripped and stained, orange stuffing spilling out like intestines. This could be it. The moment I find out the truth.

'Most of the cameras don't work,' he says but I can't tear my eyes away from the barman, shaking cocktails, making pitchers. Was one of those drinks for me? Did somebody slip something in it?

'There's hours of footage. I'll be upstairs when you're done.'

Without an extra body the room feels even colder, and Jules picks up a kettle and tests the weight for water. 'Start without me, I'll make us a cuppa.'

'I can hardly start without you, can I?' I say, sharper than I intended as my eyes flit over the fragmented picture. I begin to doubt even Jules will be able to pick me out. 'I'll make the drinks.'

The rims to the mugs are chipped, insides yellow, matching the nicotine stains on the ceiling. I pick out the two cleanest, ignoring the bare breasts pictured on one and the 'fuck you' slogan on the other and spoon out coffee.

'Here you go.' I set Jules's mug on the desk. 'I wouldn't recommend drinking it, but you can warm your hands, at least.' I slide into the chair next to her and study the ghostly faces on the screen. 'Am I there?'

'No, but this is giving me some idea of how you must feel.' Jules turns to me, sympathy in her eyes. 'Everyone looks the same.'

'They do but I'm learning to pay attention to what people are wearing, how they speak, their mannerisms. Ben's quite distinctive with his silver glasses. You always speak with your hands.'

'Me? I don't,' Jules says. Pointedly I look at her hands: she had raised them to her chest as she said 'me'.

'Okay. I'll give you that.'

Without natural daylight I lose all sense of time. My back twinges in protest as I fidget on my seat. Jules's eyes are glazed as drinkers shoulder bop at the bar to a song only they can hear, as the barman pours yet more shots. I'm reminded of the black-and-white shorts Dad used to watch of Laurel and Hardy, light and shadows, static and silence. I'd sit on his knee, and every time he shook with laughter, I'd giggle too, only this time nothing is remotely funny. Lost to my thoughts I almost miss it.

'Jules!' I lean forward, peering at the screen, 'Is that me?' A pale figure in a strapless dress, long white hair glowing under the spotlight.

'Christ, I'd almost nodded off.' Jules wipes her mouth with the back of her hand and fizzes open her Lucozade.

'Is it me?' I ask again. It's hard to tell without colour but, despite the grainy image, I can see the dress is the same style as my green one. 'That's my choker!'

'It's you,' Jules says. 'I'll rewind it.'

'Play it in slow motion.' I'm determined not to miss anything. The tape whirrs backwards before playing once more. I'm standing at the bar waving a note. A man slips in the space next to me. I turn my head, lips mouthing words I cannot hear. Neither of us smiles.

'That must be Ewan! It looks like I know him, doesn't it?'

'It's impossible to tell.' Jules is frowning as she studies the screen.

'Wait. Pause it.'

Playing the tape again we're joined by a third person at the bar. Light hair, about the same size as me. She speaks, waving her arms for effect. She looks worried and pulls my arm. I break free. Put my hands on her chest and push her. She grabs me again and leads me away from the bar, and before I disappear out of the sight of the camera I say something else to the man as I leave.

'Is that Chrissy?' I ask although instinct tells me it is. Why would we be arguing though? We never did before.

'Yes.'

'And the man. Do you recognise him?' I can't stop staring at the before-all-of-this me. My heart cracking that I can't warn her somehow of what is to come.

My question is met with a painful pause, until eventually the silence seems to buckle under the weight of just one word.

'No.'

Tearing my eyes away from the grainy image I turn to look at Jules. It's freezing but sweat sheens her skin.

'Honest,' she says, but she can't meet my eye and there's a catch to her voice.

She's lying.

Chapter Twenty-Five

'Carl.' I shout again up the stairs.

Frustration simmers in my veins. I've found the footage I need but I still can't identify Ewan. I wouldn't even have been able to identify me and Chrissy if it weren't for my dress. My choker.

'It might not even be him,' says Jules. 'It could be some random you've got chatting to.'

It is him. I'm certain. The jacket. More formal than the other men in their T-shirts and jeans. Recognition nips at my skin with sharp teeth.

'You done?' Carl fills the room once again with his hulking frame.

'Can you print out a photo of him?' I point to the monitor.

'What do you think this is, fucking CSI? We're hardly state of the art 'ere, darlin'.'

If I don't have something to take away the whole day has been a waste of time. I unlock my phone.

'No photos.' Carl stands in front of the desk. 'I'm doing you a favour. You've seen what you wanted. Time to shift your arses.'

With a last, lingering look at the screen, I trudge back upstairs, and we're ushered outside into the bitter cold.

'Are you sure you didn't recognise him?' I ask Jules.

'Positive.' She's fishing in her bag for something, and even if she looked up I wouldn't be able to read her.

'Shall we get the bus?' I'm lost without my car.

'I've a few things to do. You'll be okay getting home?'

The thought of being out on my own is terrifying but she's already given up most of her weekend for me. It hardly seems fair to ask her to stay.

'I'll be fine,' I say and my nerves knot inside my stomach as I watch her walk away, mobile glued to her ear.

The app on my phone tells me that with Sunday service there isn't another bus for ninety minutes. It's too cold to hang around the bus station. Usually I'd plump for Starbucks, on the market square, but the staff might recognise me and think I'm ignoring them. It saddens me to think I might always feel this embarrassment. Dr Saunders warned me that the majority of sufferers of acquired prosopagnosia develop social anxiety and depression. He said it's important not to avoid social situations as that further reduces self-confidence, but it's difficult to mix when I feel set apart from everyone else. At the theme park Dad and I had spent ages in the House of Mirrors. I'd found it disconcerting that the mirror-Dad had morphed into someone too short, too tall, too fat, too thin. His features distorted until he looked like someone else entirely. He had roared with laughter at our reflections; still, it unsettled me, this different image I was presented with. Uncertain, I'd kept throwing sideward glances his way, seeking reassurance that he was still the same person. Still my dad. That's how it feels now. I'm stuck in a House of Mirrors but, no matter how many sideward glances I throw, I'm never reassured.

*

Buying a coffee is something so small, so normal. But I have to brace myself to push open the door to an independent coffee shop, the bell announcing my arrival as I step inside this ordinary world where I feel anything but ordinary. It's packed. Tub chairs full of shoppers weary from their exertions. Multicoloured plastic bags adorned with 'SALE' crammed under their tables.

Taking a deep breath of cappuccino and freshly baked rolls, I try and calm myself, sensing eyes on me. I tell myself I'm paranoid, but my gaze is pulled left by a loud tutting sound and blood roars in my ears, along with the sound of hissing machines heating milk, frothing cappuccinos. A face stares at me, and my heart stutters. Is it him? A sharp nod of the head tells me he is tutting because I am still holding the door open, a blast of icy air against the back of my neck. In my panic I let the door crash shut, and there's a split-second lull in the hum of conversation as almost everyone turns my way. Behind me, the door is pushed open again and a young mum, swinging ginger ponytail, manoeuvres her pram over the small step, and I am forced forward so she can close the door behind her. Sound swells around me. The walls are edging in, the sense of being trapped overwhelming, but as I look over my shoulder, out of the window at the throng of shoppers, it seems more terrifying out there than it does in here. 'If you act like a victim people will treat you like a victim,' Iris said all those years ago, and at the time I'd thought her cruel and heartless, but today her words resonate with me in a way they couldn't when I was twelve. Pulling back my shoulders, belying a confidence I don't feel, I join the queue, my toes tapping with nerves inside my boots as I wait. My eyes constantly scanning the crowd. Apart from the girl in the crimson coat and the man wearing army fatigues, it's like a uniform almost – black winter coats, black boots, black trainers, blue jeans – an army fighting the elements, the harsh winter weather winning the war.

A hand on my shoulder. 'It's your turn,' says the woman, rocking the pram, as inside snowsuit-covered legs angrily kick off a blanket.

'Sorry.' I stutter out my order, a toffee latte and, as an afterthought, I add a piece of rocky road. Normal. I can do normal. I give my name for the drink and after I've paid I carry my plate to a table already occupied by a family of four. Mum and dad, and two small boys roughly the same size. The woman smiles as I sit and raises her eyebrows slightly, as though waiting for me to speak. I glance at her children again. They could be twins for all I know and perhaps she's waiting for a comment about how identical they are. Miserably I pick a lump of pink marshmallow from my cake and pop it into my mouth. It feels like cotton wool clogging my throat as I swallow.

Grateful to hear 'Alison' yelled from the counter, I fetch my drink, taking a sip as I carry it back to my seat. The coffee burns its way down my throat. I try to relax, but it's hard not to watch the men in trainers, one scrolling through his phone, the other reading a paper.

I pull my phone from my bag to stop myself from staring. There's a text from Ben telling me he needs to talk, and I phone him, but the call diverts to answer service. There's another text, from Matt, and my thumb hovers over his name, second-guessing what he might say. Whether he enjoyed our breakfast as much as I did.

I'm having a clear out. Do you want the green glasses?

His message brings a sharp, cruel, moment of realisation. It's over.

We bought those glasses on our honeymoon in Marrakesh. In our apartment we filled them with bubbling champagne and toasted a future that looked as bright as the blazing sun. Matt hooked open the doors of the balcony and we lay, naked limbs entwined, watching the sky turn from cornflower to lavender, until we dozed, wrapped in dusk and dreams, waking so late we missed dinner. Now he wants to discard the glasses, as though they are nothing, as though I am nothing. Something shifted lately, I had thought: the late-night phone chats, the Terry's Chocolate Oranges. My black-and-white thinking had whispered he wanted me back, but pity is grey and cold and lonely. I wonder whether my condition is the last straw. Is it too hard to have a relationship with someone who couldn't pick you out of a line up? Can't follow movies. Ignores friends and family if seeing them out of context? It shouldn't be, should it? Not if it's love? *If.*

I've deliberated so long over what to reply to Matt that it's almost time for the bus, and I think I'll nip to the loo before I leave. Stepping out of the toilet cubicle I am stopped in my tracks. Unprepared. At home the mirrors are covered, but here I am faced with my reflection. Tentatively I step forward. My fingers hovering in front of the glass. I trace the lips that tremble with the effort of not crying, the eyes that are wide and glistening with tears. Leaning forward, my forehead rests against the forehead of the mirror-me that shouldn't look like someone else entirely but somehow does. I feel a wrenching pain in my chest. Despairingly I think I will never get used to this.

The door swings open, and I straighten up, my face has morphed into someone else again. My knees feel weak as I steady myself against the basin for support. The girl stands next to me and snaps open a compact, brushes powder over her nose blotting the shine, something I used to do at least three times a day, and there's something about the way she stands back, her mouth curving into a smile as she appraises her appearance, that breaks my heart. Tearing my gaze away I pump soap into my hands and rub them together and, when the girl shuts herself in a cubicle, I slam my palms against the mirror and smear oily, green soap all over the glass, as though I can make myself disappear. Only when I am nothing but a ghostly smudge do I allow my arms to drop back down to my sides. In the periphery I can still see the reflection of the cubicle doors, but I am gone, and it is as though I have never existed at all, and I find this thought strangely comforting.

*

Back at the table I shrug on my coat and wind my scarf around my neck. Outside, dusk is gathering. The family has gone, under the seats where the children sat, a scattering of splintered crisps.

It isn't until I pick up my cup to drain the last dregs of my now-cold latte I notice it. The black X that now crosses out 'Alison'. The single word that has been written in its place, and that word is enough to cause the cup to slip through my fingers, caramel-coloured liquid pooling on the floor. *Going mad-going mad-going mad*. I must be mistaken. I can't tear my eyes away from the cup as it rolls. Desperately hoping that once it stills I will see that, of course, my name is still there. My mind playing a trick on me. But it isn't. The cup wedges against the table leg, and it's still there. That word. I bolt for the door, snagging a table, the sharp corner digging into my hip, tea sloshing onto a saucer. I stumble, my hand automatically grabbing the arm of the person whose drink I have spilled, but the second I have gained my balance, I'm weaving towards the exit again. I don't stop to apologise, to offer to mop up or replace the tea that is now dripping onto the floor. Panic shimmers dark at the edge of my vision. The voice of the past whispering its cold, sour breath into my ear.

Sarah

Sarah, written in thick black letters on my cup.

Sarah

And suddenly everything that's happened doesn't feel quite so random anymore, because I can count on one hand the number of people who know that Sarah is my birth name. Alison came later. Much later. After everything that happened when my family moved away to try and escape both the past and ourselves. As I rush out of the café I steal a glance back over my shoulder, scanning the sea of faces, desperate for a glimmer of recognition, a clue as to who is persecuting me, but everyone's a stranger.

Sarah.

Except they can't be.

Chapter Twenty-Six

Ali. I'll still call you Ali. It's almost impossible to think of you as Sarah, and by the look of shock and panic on your face I think that over the years you've almost convinced yourself you are not her. You are someone else. Someone good. But that's a lie you tell yourself so you can sleep at night. How many things you've blocked out. How our minds try to protect us from the things we cannot cope with, but the reality is always there, under the surface of half-truths that are as brittle and easily broken as you.

There was a moment when you pelted into my table, lost your footing and grabbed my arm to stop yourself falling, I thought it was all over. No matter how much research I've done into your condition, it's unfathomable to me that you could be so close and not recognise me, but you didn't. You genuinely have no clue who anyone is, and I felt a pang of sympathy for you as I realised just how frightening and uncertain the world looks to you right now. How vulnerable and scared you must feel. That was before you released your grip and sped away without an apology. Without offering to clear up the mess you had created.

That's you all over, isn't it?

I watch as you fling open the door and hare out into the street, frantically looking left and right. Seeking comfort from faces who shift and change every time you look away. I bite the

last of my toasted teacake, melted butter oozing down my chin.
You turn left. I wipe my greasy fingers on a napkin. Thanking
the lady behind the counter – I still remember my manners – I
hurry out into the street and follow you.

Chapter Twenty-Seven

There's a sense of hysteria in the last hour before the shops close, wallets, thick with the first payday since Christmas, shoppers desperate to bag that last bargain, or perhaps it is only me who is hysterical as I fight my way through the shifting sea of people.

Sarah. It's been so long since I was called by that name I'd almost forgotten who I was, but the two syllables stroke me with their familiar fingers as the past slams into me. My cheeks are stinging with cold and tears and I'm not sure if I'm crying for who I am now or who I was then. The whoosh of traffic sloshing past on the wet road has muted to nothing more than a whisper, while the voice in my head screams my lost name over and over. *Sarah, Sarah. Sarah.* Except I'm not her, I'm not. I'm Ali. But as I catch sight of my reflection in a shop window I don't look like Ali. I don't look like Sarah. I don't know who I am anymore. The pressure inside my head mounts and a shard of memory drives itself into my consciousness. Shouting. Screaming. *I know. I know what you did.* Crying. Begging. *Please.* Hands on me. Pain. Blackness. *You deserve everything you get.* And the hope that Saturday night was an accident, or even a random attack by a stranger, turns to ashes. *You have blood on your hands.* Oh God, what have I done? What have I done again?

I turn left into the pedestrianised part of town. A busker strums his guitar. At his feet, his rolled-up sleeping bag glistens with rain. A few bronzed coins in his sodden cap. 'Will you still love me tomorrow?' The lyrics stop me in my tracks. My dad loved that song. Crooning it to Mum, his arms wrapped round her waist as she washed-up after Sunday lunch, soapy suds up to her elbows, the kitchen smelling of roast beef. Did she still love him after what he did? It pains me that I'll never know. All around me shoppers stream, sidestepping the busker, swinging carrier bags and avoiding eye contact with him. I fumble for my purse and pull out a ten-pound note. Hesitantly, I hold it out, not wanting to place it in the cap, where it will be tossed in the wind along with my memories and my pain. He stretches out his hand. His eyes meet mine. *Will you still love me tomorrow*? Our fingers touch and something passes between us. A question? An understanding? Automatically I back away. Suddenly aware this could be him. Ewan. The man who hurt me. Who thinks he knows me.

Sarah.

I spin and thrust myself into the centre of the crowd, as though, if I stand shoulder to shoulder with them, I will not be any different. As though I will not be utterly lost and utterly alone. As if I pretend enough, I can be like them and sometimes pretending is enough. It has to be. I've been doing it for years, but it's all beginning to fall apart. Just like I am falling apart after the almost impossible task of stitching myself back together.

I'm only ten minutes from the bus station when I become aware of them through the hustle and the bustle. The footsteps matching mine step for step. I turn a slow

360. My eyes raking through the charcoal gloom. Why does everyone cloak themselves in darkness in the winter? Black coats. Black boots. Black trainers. So many black trainers. Pounding the pavement, marching towards me, an army of shoes, and I can't tell the difference. Who's good. Who's bad. Who was following me. As I spin, features rearrange. I'm shaking, shaking, shaking, like I shook my Etch A Sketch all those years ago. Images falling away, to be replaced by something new, something different. Nothing ever looking exactly the same. A tidal wave of panic crashes down on me, adrenaline flowing fast through my veins, chilling me to the bone. Everyone's a stranger and yet someone isn't.

Sarah.

I stop spinning and wait for the pavement to settle beneath my feet. 'Give it time and you'll find your sea legs' Dad used to say whenever I felt nauseous travelling in the car, but I'll never get my sea legs. I'm bobbing, endlessly bobbing, in that boat with the owl and the pussy-cat; the honey and plenty of money and time is the one thing I don't have.

Enjoy the date bitch?

Someone is out to get me. The sky is crushing down. Clouds vacuuming air. A pain stabs my chest, radiates down my arm and I think I must be having a heart attack. Feet. I turn and scan the feet once more, and there's a pair directly behind me. Black trainers. Walking away from me but I don't think that's the man from the coffee shop. His jeans are black, not blue. I am becoming more observant, the small details. Remember the small details. Except I don't want to. Not here. Not now. ***LET. ME. GO.*** My eyes flit once more and stop. Widen with horror. Black trainers. Blue jeans. Beanie. Standing still, so still. Watching, waiting. Backing away I inadvertently shake my head. *No. Please don't hurt me*; but if it's him, he already has. His expression is impossible to read.

There's a sudden, sharp pain to the back of my head. My jaw clamps shut, my teeth slicing into my tongue. Coppery blood fills my mouth. At first I think I've been hit but, as I turn, I see I've walked into a lamp post, and I feel a thousand curious eyes on me as I whimper. The pain in my chest comes again. Throwing a glance behind me, he's gone, but leaning against the wall, waiting for the cashpoint is another man, blue jeans, black trainers but no beanie. Is it him? *Going mad-going mad-going mad.* Is it the same man but without a hat? He takes a step towards me. I don't hesitate for a second.

Run.

My feet sloshing through puddles. My thin jumper damp with the freezing air and sweat. My open coat billowing behind me, my breath rising like steam. I cut through the car park. Here the crowd has thinned along with the bright shop lights and the streetlamp. The gathering dusk shades the sky. My pulse is drumming in my ears but I daren't slow. I daren't risk a look behind me. As I pelt towards the road I see a cab approaching; the warm honeycomb glow of the taxi light signals safety. Waving my arms I step off the kerb. A horn sounds. Brakes squeal. I don't move. Can't move. Waiting for the impact. Welcoming it, almost. But there's the humming of an engine. Warmth on my thighs. The now stationary car almost touching my legs.

I placate the driver with apologies and an offer of double fare if he takes me where I need to go. There's only one place I want to be. Need to be. I rest my head back, close my eyes and I don't open them again until we are there.

Chapter Twenty-Eight

Once as I child I caught a butterfly in a jam jar and I sat, cross-legged, under the blazing summer sun, and watched the insect frantically beat its delicate wings, driving itself into the glass again and again, with fear. With confusion. It knew it had been cornered, trapped, but it had no idea why; yet it retained a desperate belief that there had to be a way to escape the nightmare it found itself in. The frantic fluttering grew slower and slower until it lay, folded in on itself, its spirit broken. Springing to my feet I unscrewed the lid and took it over to the violet buddleia, where I tipped it gently onto the flowers it favoured. I chewed my lip as I waited for movement. I hadn't wanted to kill it, or hurt it, even. I only wanted to watch, to see how it would react. When it stretched out its wings and rose into the clear blue sky I felt a rush of relief. See? I'm not a bad person. I'm not.

You remind me of that butterfly as you dart through town. Dazed. Not knowing exactly what is happening or why, only that it is horrible and frightening and seemingly senseless. And you have a primal, desperate desire to escape. And that's what I want for you. To see your spirit broken. To see you lying folded in on yourself. Defeated. Only I won't be showing you the same compassion. You, I want to hurt.

The busker draws your attention and suddenly you are still. From this close range I can see your lips moving along with the words, 'Will you still love me tomorrow', and I don't think you're even aware you're doing it. You pull out a note from your purse and again I feel the same pang I felt at the café. That niggling feeling that perhaps you don't deserve all of this. And shortly after there's that split second when you jump in front of the cab – I think it's going to hit you – and I almost, almost, yank you back onto the path. Afterwards, as I watch you climb into the back seat and the tail lights disappear, I tell myself I almost saved you so I could be the one to destroy you. Not because I still feel anything for you. Not anymore. But I'm not sure I believe that now.

There's another cab approaching but I make no move to flag it down. To follow you. After all, it isn't as though I don't know where you live, is it? We'll meet again soon.

Chapter Twenty-Nine

If Iris is surprised to see me, she doesn't show it.

'Did Ben tell you to come?' she asks. I shake my head.

'I need to find something.' I mount the stairs to my childhood.

'I'll put the kettle on,' she says. 'Let's have a chat when you're ready.'

As soon as I read my real name, Sarah, written on the cup, everything I had fought so hard to become slipped away. I was twelve again – guilty, frightened and ashamed. Filled with an intense longing to feel close to Mum and Dad once more. Now, in my old bedroom I kneel on the floor and pull everything out of my cupboards until I find it: the old Clarks shoebox that once housed sensible lace-up school shoes but now contains the remnants of one of the worst days of my life. Not the worst day, of course, that came later. The age-brittle elastic band anchoring the lid snaps as I stretch it. Out tumble birthday cards, most of them pink, some embossed with 'Daughter', 'Sister', 'Niece', all of them announcing 'twelve today'. I don't know why it had felt so important to keep them, but it had. Almost as though, if I pretended everything was normal, it may have become that way and I could have displayed my cards, opened my presents. Be a child again. Despite their age the cards are still stiff, unbent by time. We never did stand them on the mantelpiece, like other birthdays, until the balloons deflated and the last of the cake was eaten. I trace my fingers over the largest card. A panting puppy wishes me a 'Yappy Birthday'. Inside, the white space is yellowing through time, but the writing is clear and springs out at me.

> *Happy Birthday to our precious girl, Sarah. Lots of love Mum & Dad*

I rock forward, bending at the waist, trying to ease the stabbing pain the words have caused that's as real and as raw to me as the wound on my head that throbs and throbs, as the memories of that day become impossible to ignore.

*

I'm twelve! I can hardly believe it!

Loitering on the landing, I strain to decipher the fierce whispers drifting from my parents' bedroom, but I can't catch more than the odd word. Mum seems furious with Dad for something he had promised to do, and Dad is shushing and reassuring her he will sort everything out. It goes quiet for a bit and I think I can hear Mum crying. Miserably I wonder whether anyone even remembers it was supposed to be my special day. Mindlessly, I scratch the bannisters with my thumbnail, watching the gloss paint flake and crumble onto the flattened carpet that is rough beneath my bare feet. The sound of *Scooby Doo* floats upstairs, and I can almost picture my little brother, arms folded tightly around Ollie the Owl, enraptured as Fred and the gang predictably unmask the

janitor. Until recently I longed to be part of Mystery Inc.
Daphne was my heroine. Mum laughed and called it my
'purple phase'. Long after I should have been sleeping, I'd
lie in bed, twisting my fine blonde hair around my fingers,
willing it to fall into soft waves by the morning, longing
for the day I could dye it red. It all seems so babyish now.
I've outgrown cartoons although I do sit and watch them if
they're on, which they often are in this house. Still, it's not
as if I'd choose to. Melanie Peeks said anything animated
is for losers and I'd nodded along. Shaggy still makes me
laugh though, he's such a scaredy cat. Not that I'd admit
it to Melanie, of course. 'I'm more sophisticated now,' she
had said after her birthday, and we had crowded around
her desk admiring her nail polish, her black wristbands
that were exactly the same as Avril Lavigne's. The thick
black eyeliner our teacher made her go to the toilets and
wash off *immediately young lady*. Her mood ring. Not that
she needed one of those, I privately thought. She only had
one mood – mardy. But she is so beautiful. We all want
to be just like her. I'd begged Mum to buy me a bra and
then I stuffed it with toilet tissue and strutted around the
playground, giggling, and it worked! Melanie chose me to
be part of her group, and they'll all be here for my party
this afternoon. I can't wait.

There is a packet of pink balloons on the kitchen table
waiting to be inflated and a stack of silver paper plates and
napkins. I had told Mum not to embarrass me by making a
jelly or anything. I only want cool food. Pizza and fries, not
the chunky chips Mum buys at Iceland. The skinny ones
that Melanie says she ate in America. Mum's made a cake,
as usual, I saw the Tupperware on the top of the fridge; I

hope she doesn't expect everyone to sing. Melanie says that's for babies. At her party she had a pile of cupcakes and no candles. I wish Mum and Dad would hurry up and come out. I've finished my cornflakes and got dressed and I still haven't opened any presents.

I hadn't wanted a party at home. I'd had a bit of a strop, actually, and I still feel bad about that now. The way Mum's face fell. The guilt in Dad's eyes as he explained they couldn't quite stretch to hiring out the community centre and a disco. Since he lost his job we've had to 'tighten our belts', and at first I thought this meant our clothes would become loose because we couldn't afford to eat, but it actually meant something worse. There were no trips to the cinema, or swimming or anything. I told Mum I'd rather go without the fruit she makes us eat every day and the vegetables she says are expensive and go to the ice rink instead. She'd said 'nice try' and shook her head, but I thought secretly Dad would rather be skating than eating broccoli. We're not doing half the things we used to together. He's out most nights, and he's never home to read me a story anymore. If I wake him up before I go to school he's grumpy, and he smells funny too. Mum says he'll 'pull himself together' when he gets another job, as though he has fallen apart like the little wooden horse he'd won for me at the fair. I'd spent hours pressing the button underneath, watching the horse flop to pieces, only held together by string and hope, springing whole again when I released my thumb. I don't think Dad's like that. He just needs a shower and some 'bleeding luck'.

'A party at home will be fun. Don't you trust me?' he had asked, and I had nodded. I love Mum to bits but I love Dad just that teensy bit more. He's the one who lets me stay up past nine o'clock and have 'just one more' biscuit that always turns into three.

'Write a list of what you want,' he had said. 'Anything.' And Mum had shot one of her looks at him he calls 'her lasers'. Excited, I'd sat at the kitchen table, glass of milk in front of me, and thought long and hard. Make-up was top, of course, the big set from Boots that Melanie has, with twenty-two different coloured eyeshadows. Twenty-two! Glitter. The hairspray that streaks pink but washes out.

'Can I have an iPod? Melanie has one and it's so cool?'

'If that's what my girl wants,' Dad had said.

'I'm getting an iPod and I'm having a make-over party,' I'd told Melanie airily, as though it was what I wanted all along, and I actually saw a spark of admiration in her eyes. Everyone else in our year has had a boring disco at the community centre.

I wanted a new dress. It had to be from Top Shop and short and stretchy. 'We're rock chicks,' Melanie had said, her arm jangling with the bangles. Melanie wore shoes with heels, even for school. I'd tried walking in Mum's when she was in the bath, but I'd turned my ankle. I've asked for some of my own, and if I open them soon I've time to practice in front of my mirror, swinging my hips like Melanie. At the bottom of the list I'd added a Bratz doll. It's not like I'll play with it or anything, but I think they look really cool. I'll keep it hidden in my wardrobe until Melanie goes home though, just in case she laughs.

At last my parents' door creaks open.

'Happy birthday, princess!' Dad lifts me up and swings me around as though I am still five, and although I like it I tell him not to do that later. 'Afraid I'll embarrass you, eh?' He showers kisses on me, and I turn away from his smelly breath.

'Happy birthday, darling.' Mum smiles but her red-rimmed eyes don't crinkle around the edges and she can barely look at me. She won't look at Dad at all. I wrap my legs around his waist like a monkey and peer over his shoulder into their bedroom, but the space on top of their wardrobe where they always keep presents is empty.

'I'm going to pick up your presents once I've made you pancakes and maple syrup,' Dad says, as though reading my mind. Mum fires him one of her lasers, and I think it's because she doesn't approve of sugar for breakfast. Dad crouches down and I wrap my arms around his neck as he piggybacks me down the stairs.

The house smells of garlic bread. Mum clatters in the kitchen. *Let Go* spins on the CD player in the lounge. Melanie bought me it; although Izzy whispered to me she had nicked it from HMV. As I'd unwrapped it Melanie had said she'd show me how to put it on iTunes and transfer it onto my iPod, and I'd caught the way the corners of her mouth twitched into a half-smile as I'd told her my present hadn't arrived yet, as though I'd been lying.

Melanie brought her make-up kit with her and is being the beautician. I wanted to try but she'd batted my hand away from the brushes and told me she had the most experience, and I suppose she has. Her mum subscribes to *Cosmopolitan* and at breaks we pass it around. Some of the articles make me feel hot and funny but the clothes are way cool. Lauren hasn't arrived yet but she's always late for everything.

'Clear the table, food's ready in ten,' Mum calls, and I start to stand, but Melanie grabs my wrist.

'I've nearly finished.'

Splaying out my fingers again I watch as Melanie slicks blue varnish over my thumbnail. Izzy scrunches up discarded wrapping paper and tosses it into the bin.

'Where's Dad?' I ask Mum for the umpteenth time. She balances my cake on a rosebud stand on the table covered with violet voile. A silver 'Happy Birthday' sign is stuck in the frosted lilac icing. Twelve pink and white spiral candles dotted around the edge.

'He'll be here soon,' she says again, as she bustles back into the kitchen, but I am not reassured. He's been gone for hours, and my throat feels all tight and swollen. He has never missed a party of mine before, even when he had a full-time job. Where is he?

'All done.' Melanie screws the lid back on the polish. 'Aren't you going to blow on them so they dry?' She raises her eyebrows and, feeling stupid, I huff air onto my nails, until the front door slams.

Dad bursts into the lounge, wild-eyed, his face pale and slick with sweat. He is empty-handed.

'About time,' Mum shouts from the kitchen.

'Dad? Where are my presents?' As soon as I ask I wish I could take the question back. I can't pinpoint why I am scared, but as he meets my eyes, I feel a thousand apologies pass wordlessly between us, and I want to say I don't care about the presents, I don't care about anything except the fact that he is here, but before I can speak there's a thudding at the front door.

'Lauren!' I rush to answer, pleased she's made it before tea. I don't think Dad calling my name really registers, and it isn't until I swung open the door I realise I've made a horrible, horrible mistake.

'Justin Crawford?' One of the policemen says. He is almost as tall as the freaky substitute teacher we'd had for science last week. I have to shade my eyes from the sun as I look up at his stern face.

'He's in the lounge.' Shock makes my voice a squeak. The men thunder down the hallway, and I rush after them. As I pass the kitchen, Mum wrenches her hands out of the sink, soapsuds floating to the lino as she grabs a tea towel. Her mouth in an 'O'. I am not sure why the police want to talk to Dad but my stomach feels all funny and I know it is bad. Very bad.

'Justin Crawford,' the policeman says again, and my guilt at having let him in is nudged aside by relief as my eyes scan the room. Dad isn't there and there's a split-second moment when I think they'll leave. That everything will be okay. Mum will bring out the pizza and after we've eaten barbecue chicken and pepperoni slices, melted cheese stringy between our fingers, I can blow out the candles and will wish the police would never come back. But that's before Melanie opens her pink glossy lips and says, clear and true, 'he's hiding behind the sofa'.

The memory plays as though in slow motion.

Furniture upended in the struggle. Dad fighting to break free, shouting his innocence over and over. Mum, fisted hands pushed against her chest, knees buckling as she screamed 'No!'. The cake wobbling and crashing to the floor, sponge scattering, the snapping of candles and, seeing this, I began to cry. If I didn't have twelve candles I couldn't make a wish and that's when I knew, with certainty, they were taking Dad away and things would never be the same again.

My brother huddled in the corner, clutching his owl, rocking backwards and forwards, tears dripping down his chubby cheeks. Avril Lavigne singing 'Complicated'. The smoke alarm screeching. The smell of burning garlic bread filling the room. But perhaps, more than the hurt, the shame, the humiliation, it was the scathing look in Melanie's eyes that stayed with me and, inexplicably, despite it being Dad who had done something wrong, it was her I hated.

*

'Ali?' Iris taps on the door. 'Are you all right?'

I am scared, lonely, regretful – all of these things and more – but I tell her I am fine and that I'll be down in two minutes. I pack the birthday cards and my shame tightly in the box where they can't be seen and, as I cross the hallway, I pass Ben's old room. The door is ajar and his bed by the window is pooled in moonlight. And although I know it is empty I can almost see him kneeling at the window in his Thomas the Tank Engine pyjamas. Ollie on his pillow.

'Same moon?' He'd point solemnly with his chubby finger at the sky, at his book.

'There's only one,' I'd say.

Hand in hand. His brilliant smile lit up his face as he slipped out of bed, rubbing the tiredness from his eyes. *On the edge of the sand.* His small hand in mine. *They danced by the light of the moon, the moon, the moon.* Spinning in circles, pyjama clad and barefooted. *They danced by the light of the moon.*

*

In the kitchen Iris sits at the table. A red knitted cosy covering the teapot. Ben bought her a Tassimo machine for Christmas, and I don't think she's ever used it. She picks at a piece of fraying wool as if taking the time to choose her words.

'I've something to tell you,' she says, careful and considered. 'Show you, I suppose.'

From out of her apron pocket she pulls a letter and slides it across the table. Despite not seeing the handwriting for years, it's looping, cursive script instantly triggers an outpouring of guilt, sorrow, rage, and something else.

Fear.

Chapter Thirty

Although it has been years since I have seen Dad and my tainted memories are no longer clear and sharp, certain things have stayed with me. His handwriting is one and the sight of it brings other memories to the forefront of my mind. The smell of Polo Mints he always sucked that did little to mask the faint trace of tobacco that clung to him, even though he insisted he had given up smoking, and later, to cover the alcohol he drank when he could no longer cope with the mountains of bills piling up. Sometimes I catch sight of men who, from the back, look like him, dark brown hair brushing against the neck of a black leather jacket. It's impossible, I know, he's not free to walk among us and, even if he were, he'd likely be greying now. Balding perhaps. Every now and then my cheek tingles and I raise my palm to it believing I can still feel his scratchy beard as I lean back on his lap, his face close to mine as he enthralls me with yet another tale of handsome princes, beautiful princesses. Until I was twelve, Dad was my absolute hero, who instilled a belief in romance and roses, and happily ever afters. But that belief turned out to be small and slippery and impossible to hold on to. I don't know if I'll ever forgive him; even now there's an aching in my chest when I think of him. I miss the man he was, not the man he is now, of course, for he is a stranger to me. Try as I might I just can't equate the dad who used to play horsey, letting me hold onto his ears as I balanced precariously on his back, my knees digging into his ribs – giddy up – long after I grew too big and too heavy, with the dad who stalked into the post office with two others, balaclavas covering their faces, demanding cash – though it wasn't money they took, but a life. For a long time afterwards, I blamed myself. If I'm honest there are times I still question whether it was my fault. Was I too greedy? Too demanding? Too everything I shouldn't have been? Although I try to bury it. Ignore it. There's always a yearning to confront the twelve-year-old girl I was and shake her, hard. Tell her presents don't matter; who cares whether you have an iPod when your dad can no longer be there to capture the image of you blowing out candles – not that I've had a birthday cake since. Not until Chrissy bought me one, and the sight of the frosted icing, the smell as she struck the match, had caused the whole dirty truth to come tumbling out. I'd told her everything I hadn't talked about since I first fell in love with Matt, and she'd sat in stunned silence as the flames crackled and flickered before the candles burned themselves to darkness, but it didn't matter. I had long stopped making wishes.

Mum said it was really nothing to do with my birthday; they'd fallen behind on the mortgage payments and every-thing had got on top of Dad. It was a chain of circumstances that led him to do something stupid. But stupid is leaving the milk out of the fridge on a hot summer's day, forgetting what level the car is on in the multistorey. Stupid isn't armed robbery, even if you are not the one carrying the gun. I don't know what he was thinking, my sweet and gentle father, and I've never asked him. He never came home again after the day I willingly let the police into our home. We'd learned about Judas at school and that is how I felt. How I still feel, if I'm honest. Dad isn't the only one I'm ashamed of and that's why I keep it all bottled up inside. Ben was six at the time, too young to remember the details but I'd sat him down when he was older and told him the truth before he found out via Google. We'd both cried as he gripped my hand fiercely and told me it wasn't my fault, that he'd have let the police in too. Once, as adults, I had wondered aloud whether we should visit Dad, and Ben had looked horrified and I suppose in a way it was like suggesting he visit a stranger.

Sometimes I try to share childhood stories, wanting to spark Ben's memory almost so he has some recollection of the before Dad. The Saturday afternoons Dad would wrestle with Ben and always let him win. The Friday nights he'd let me style his hair until it was spiky stiff with gel. Our Sunday swims, Dad diving under the water, nibbling our toes, making us screech with fear and laughter. Ben's never interested though. 'If he loved us that much he'd never have done what he did,' he says, his face closed, but I always think it was *because* he loved us he did what he did. 'We had the best mum in the world,' Ben said, and we both teared up as we remembered Mum, as we always did. 'She adored us. And that makes up for everything.' And that's true, to an extent, but it still pains me to remember my last words to Dad were 'where are my presents?' and not 'I love you', because I did.

But now, it's hard not to hate him. Not to blame him for everything that came after. It's hard not to think of him at all, but I try; in much the same way as I try not to think of the poor woman who wanted a book of stamps and ended up paying for it with the highest price imaginable. The gun went off accidentally, apparently, but that doesn't make it any easier to live with. Even though I wasn't there at the time, the scene played endlessly in my head every time I closed my eyes. The crack of the gun. The woman crumpling to the floor as her two young children, a boy and a girl, watched. Did they scream, I wondered? Cry. Or were they frozen in shock, splattered with blood and brain and disbelief? Every time I think of them my heart aches. We'd all lost parents as a result of that day, although it's incomparable, I know. Their loss was through no fault of their own, and mine? My faults are tangled behind a spider web of shattered memories, regret and recrimination. And nightmares. The endless, endless nightmares.

It started soon after Dad's arrest, the blame, and I think in a way we invited it. Felt we deserved it. The bricks through the window. The graffiti etched into the paintwork of our car, sprayed on the garage door. The hate campaign grew, as did the media coverage. Two children had witnessed their mother's murder, and the local news tirelessly reported it. Ben and I were children too, but we didn't seem to matter. Emotions ran high and the nationals picked the story up. Dad and his accomplices a perfect representation of all that was wrong with Britain. After Dad's prosecution we thought it would die down. Dad's sentence was harsh. He hadn't pulled the trigger, but he was made an example of nonetheless; we were still spat at in the street, had dog shit pushed through the letterbox. Eventually, after someone set our garden shed on fire while we slept, Mum told us we had to leave Tanmoor. She packed her Portmerion, Dad's vinyls and the fragments of our shattered childhood into boxes and we drove silently away from the house where I was born for the very last time. My throat was thick with tears as I gazed sadly out of the back window, whispering goodbyes to my princess canopied bed in my pastel pink bedroom, my tree house, and my name. Mum let me pick a new one and I'd always liked Ali. She let me choose Ben's name too and, in a way, it felt like an adventure. A fresh start. Except it wasn't. Things were about to get a whole lot worse and, although Mum told me over and over it wasn't my fault, somehow it felt like it was. I blamed myself for it all, and sometimes I wonder whether Dad blamed me too. Whether afterwards he hated me as much as I hated myself. And I sometimes wonder if I could go back to that day, with Melanie streaking my nails blue, Mum shaking frozen chips onto a baking tray, the smell of garlic and anticipation as I waited for Dad to come home, if I could go back and save Dad, knowing a woman had died, two children had been left motherless, would I still have opened the door? Let the police in? It pains me to know that I would.

For some moments I am lost between past and present, unable to anchor myself in either as I stare blankly at the envelope but only seeing the images in my head that tumble together, blurring at the edges, one fading only to be replaced by another: the snapping of handcuffs onto Dad's wrists; the look of blind panic in his eyes; the policeman's hand resting on the top of Dad's head as he climbed into the police car; Dad tossing pancakes so high they almost stuck to the ceiling; the way he met my eyes with such love as he drizzled maple syrup over my breakfast. The look the policeman gave as they found him cowering behind the sofa; disappointment, disgust, triumph. That's one face I wouldn't mind forgetting.

I try to push the letter back to Iris. 'I can't.'

She covers my hand with hers.

'You need to see it, Ali,' she says firmly.

I don't want to.

I'm scared of what it might say. I'm scared of how I might feel. Nevertheless, my trembling hand pulls the paper from the envelope and I begin to read.

Chapter Thirty-One

Dear Iris,

This is a difficult letter to write. But then I'm sure it's a difficult letter to read. You've probably already guessed from the absence of the prison postmark that I'm out. It's been six months and I really should have contacted you before, but I wanted to have something positive to tell you, to offer, other than empty promises and the thousand apologies you've heard before. My Prison Welfare Officer urged me to get in touch before I was released, family support is vital she said in keeping prisoners on the straight and narrow. It gives us something to live for apparently, stops us reoffending, but there's no chance of that. It was a one-off. A stupid, stupid mistake. The first, the only, illegal thing I've ever done and somehow, even as I stood in the dock, I thought the judge would see who I really was inside, let me go.

Strange, but I think it's only since I've been handed back my freedom I've started to think of myself as a criminal rather than a victim. The extra time I had added on to my sentence for being involved in an incident where another prisoner was set on fire and killed felt horribly unfair; after all I was trying to prevent it, not take part, and I was terrified I was a target too. But now I understand. Every action has a reaction. If I hadn't done wrong in the first place I'd never have been in that position. I have hurt people. And now I'm out it seems realer than it ever did inside. People look at ex-cons a certain way. Treat us differently. And the world is a very different place to the one I left. I wasn't the victim at all, was I? I tried not to be bitter about my sentence. I tried not to let it change me, but it has. It was inevitable it would. I want to build a new life. A good life. A month before I was released I wrote to Sharon's family, the woman who died. Who we murdered, I suppose. I might not have pulled the trigger, but I've got blood on my hands nevertheless. Everyone involved has and we've all paid the price. We're still paying the price. I wasn't allowed their address but the prison said they'd post it on for me and I had hoped they'd reply before I was released. They didn't. I told her family how sorry I was. How sorry I am. I told them I was getting out and promised I'd spend the rest of my life trying to put right all the wrongs I had caused.

My probation officer found me a room in a halfway house, a job in a factory. It's odd that, before I had no job and couldn't pay the mortgage, now I've work and cash in my pocket. The first day off I had I took the bus back to Tanmoor. The post office now a Tesco Extra, the maternity wing the babies were born in is now a Costa Coffee. But the house. The house is exactly as I remembered it. There was one of those Little Tikes red and yellow plastic cars in the front garden and a swing around the back, and it broke my heart that I couldn't slip my key in the door to find Marsha weighing raisins for spotted dick or hear the theme from Scooby Doo. Do you remember the New Year's party we had when I popped the cork from the champagne and it dented the coving? Marsha and me would always laugh about that afterwards. Cuddle on the sofa in the evenings and say 'do you remember the day we raised the roof'. I cupped my hands and peered through the lounge window to see if that coving was still there. It isn't. Everything has changed, hasn't it? Everything important, gone.

Even now I can't get my head around what happened to my darling Marsha and that is my biggest regret. That I wasn't there for her. Part of me wants to ask if you blame me but it doesn't really matter. I will always blame myself. A man is supposed to protect his family, isn't he? Instead, I destroyed mine. Thank God she had you, Iris. And the kiddies. I don't know what would have happened to those poor little mites otherwise. Taken into care, I expect. I wasn't there, and I should have been and for that I am truly remorseful.

I want to see them, George and Sarah, although I suppose I should call them Ben and Ali, shouldn't I? They're different people now though, aren't they? They've been through so much but finally I can hold my head up and say I've a job, a roof over my head. Somewhere they can visit. I don't suppose Ben remembers me really. All those nights I spent driving him around in the van, in the dark, until he was asleep. Carrying him inside and laying him in his cot. He'd always wake as I had one foot out the door, little bugger. I'm a stranger to him now. And Ali, my precious girl. Every time I close my eyes I see her look of horror as the police dragged me out the door, and I can't imagine how that felt knowing she was the one who let them in. I want to see her face-to-face. To find out how she really feels. To let her know how I feel. I asked Marsha not to bring them in, to move on, to forget about me, but now it feels like the wrong decision. Of course I didn't know what was to come. I didn't know that she wouldn't be able to take them anywhere. My poor, darling wife. But

the children. I want to know who they are. I want them to
know who I am.
    I want them to remember.
    Yours
    Justin

                              *

It isn't until Iris squeaks her chair across the kitchen floor
next to mine and presses a tissue into my hand that I am
conscious I am crying. After I've wiped my eyes and blown
my nose I remember Iris asking me when I arrived whether
Ben had told me to come. I ask if he is aware of the letter
I am still clutching tightly in one hand, almost afraid if I
loosen my grip it will slip through my fingers and it will be
like losing Dad all over again. Over the years I've tried to
convince myself that I don't care, that I'm better off without
him, but the hot searing pain in my chest tells a different
story entirely. My feelings are conflicted. On the one hand
I want nothing to do with him; a woman died, and I can't
look him in the eye knowing that he was at least partly
responsible. But there is another part of me unfurling that
is desperate to see him once more.

'I told Ben when he rang last night,' Iris says. 'We've
talked it through and he's decided he doesn't want to see
him.' Ben has always been closer to Iris than I have, ringing
her without fail twice a week and visiting at weekends. He
was such a sensitive child, distraught once Mum had gone,
and I convinced myself I was the one who had to be brave.
The eldest. Ben needed a mother more than I did, he was
only nine and I was fifteen, but that was a lie I told myself,
because it doesn't matter how old we get, how big we grow,

we all need a mum, don't we? But now, with the soft hum of the fridge behind us, my head resting on Iris's shoulder, I feel for the first time I can have that bond with her too. She brushes my fringe away from my forehead, soft fingers stroking my skin, and I realise how much she loves us.

Later, after we've eaten something unidentifiable out of the freezer I call a cab. I'd love to stay but I have to get back for Branwell. As we hug goodbye it feels real and solid and, for once, I am not the one to pull away.

Once home, I climb out of the taxi half-expecting to see the windows ablaze with lights. Chrissy back, ironing a blouse, getting ready to return to work in the morning, but the house is shrouded in darkness. Cloud blankets the sky and it's pitch-black as I trudge up the path, my legs leaden with the emotion of the day. The outside light doesn't come on and I feel a sense of foreboding. Hurriedly, I switch on the torch of my phone. The light illuminates the door and instantly my heart jumps into my mouth.

Blood.

Crimson letters spread across my door.

MURDERER

MONDAY

Chapter Thirty-Two

'Thanks for helping me,' I say again to James. My hands are pink and raw in the bitter morning air, stinging from the turps that is seeping into the cracks in my dry skin. I'd scrubbed at the door late last night, but 'murderer' had been sprayed in paint, not blood, and hot, soapy water couldn't wash it off.

After a restless, disturbed sleep I'd woken from a nightmare at 5 a.m., pyjamas drenched in sweat. I'd switched on my light to reassure myself blood wasn't streaming down my walls, as it had in *The Amityville Horror* I watched last year through splayed fingers, Matt's arm heavy and reassuring around my shoulders. I'd made a mug of hot chocolate and huddled back under the duvet, Branwell at my feet, the photo of Mum on my lap. Her face my anchor in this unfamiliar world I've tumbled in to. I'd traced her features and tried to second-guess what she'd have thought of Dad's letter. His release. Would she have forgiven him?

*

The period after he was arrested, or 'went away' as Mum called it, was difficult for us all. Mum wafted from room to room, clothes hanging from her ever-shrinking frame, the shadows under her eyes so pronounced it looked as though someone had punched her. The guilt I felt clogged my throat, burned behind my eyes and, little by little, I was disappearing inside myself, until, one day, I might have vanished if it hadn't been for Ben. He was only six and too little to understand what was going on, let alone express how he felt, but it was apparent from his behaviour that he was hurting just as much as we were. Rather than playing for hours, as he used to, building brightly coloured Duplo towers, racing around the garden on his bike, short legs pumping, stabilisers wobbling, he'd trail Mum or me around the house. Ollie the Owl scrunched in his tiny fingers, a fearful expression on his small, pale face. It was as if he was scared we would leave too. The sound of him whimpering at night floated down the landing and I'd lie quietly, waiting for the creak of Mum's footsteps, but increasingly the house lay still and silent and it was me who'd comfort Ben. Folding myself into his narrow racing car bed. Brushing his damp hair away from his forehead as he cried. I'd read the nonsense poem he loved. 'The Owl and The Pussy-Cat' and as he drifted off I'd whisper soothing words, sometimes speaking of nothing, sometimes pouring my heart out. Because despite trying to be strong for Mum – for Ben – I was aching for all I had lost and scared of what was to come. It became our nightly ritual, these one-sided chats, and after Ben had fallen back into an uneasy sleep and his pillow was saturated with my tears I'd try to extricate myself from his room. Inching closer and closer to the door, all the while watching him for signs of stirring. Sometimes I wouldn't make it back out onto the landing before his wailing sliced through the heavy night air but, more and more, it was me he cried for, not Mum, and I was happy to pitch in. Do my bit. Thinking it was only temporary until Mum felt better. Stronger. I hadn't known then, of course, that my childhood wasn't on hold. Effectively, it was over. I hadn't known then that the worst was yet to come.

*

Still undecided as to whether I should reply to Dad or not, first light had shimmered at the edge of my curtains, the black sky turning gloomy grey. Shaking myself out of my thoughts, I had slipped into a tracksuit and banged on James's door, wanting something to clean away the graffiti.

But already we've been rubbing at the paint for forty-five minutes as it dissolves painfully slowly, grateful for the tree shielding the house from prying eyes.

'Sorry, I can't help,' Jules calls over the fence, dropping her keys into her bag. 'Can't be late for our grand reopening.'

'Can you talk to Chrissy?' I ask. 'Find out why she's ignoring me.'

'We're not kids, Ali. Can't you ask her yourself?' A note of irritation has crept into her voice.

'I will when I see her.'

Jules must catch the quiver in my voice because she sighs and tells me she'll do what she can, before she waves goodbye.

'I don't think this is strong enough.' James holds his cloth over the neck of the bottle and tips it upside down, before once more rubbing at the fading letters staining my front door. 'I'll nip to B&Q later, see what they've got. But at least you can't read what it says anymore.'

The scarlet accusation has transmuted into a pink smear but 'MURDERER' still doesn't have to be sprayed across the white uPVC for me to see it. It's carried in the sharp, frigid breeze; drummed by my heart that's beating too fast.

Murderer.

'Hey.' James lightly touches my shoulder, and I realise I've been staring vacantly into space. 'Don't worry about it. It will have been some pissed-up tosser on his way home from the pub last night.'

'What if it's…?' I trail off.

'What if it's what?' James urges me to carry on.

'What if it's not some pissed-up tosser?' But what I really want to say is: what if it's true? Would he still be standing by my side then? Would anyone? But James doesn't know about the bloodied gloves, my damaged car and, although I'm desperate to confide in someone, my trust has splintered. The less people who know the better.

'Coffee?' James asks. I'm about to say no when he says: 'I can hardly feel my hands anymore.' Making him a hot drink is the least I can do. He's been standing outside, on this viciously cold morning, for over an hour now and it acts as a reminder that some people are genuine and kind.

We carry our drinks through to the lounge, Branwell close at James's heels, and as we perch at either end of the sofa, an awkwardness settles around us that wasn't there before. I can barely look at James, and he is stiff and uncomfortable in my company, not sprawled back on the cushions, the way he would have been before.

'Who are the photos of?' he asks scanning the lounge.

'My mum, Marsha.' I watch as he crosses the room and studies her.

'You can see the resemblance. You've her eyes. She's beautiful too. Is it…' He fumbles for words. 'Is it different looking at a photo? Do you… you know?'

'Know who she is? Yes. But not because it's a photo, features are still jumbled in pictures. With prosopagnosia you can sometimes recognise about one face in a thousand. For me, it's Mum. I'm not likely to recognise anyone else but…' I fumble for the right words as James sits back down, crosses his legs, more relaxed now we're talking. 'If there is only ever to be one face that makes sense to me, I'm glad it's her.'

'Because you love her more than anyone else?'

I think about this carefully before I answer.

'Because she's not here anymore, I suppose.'

'You never talk about her.' It's a statement, not a question.

'No.' A knot forms in my chest. I never talk about Dad either; and even though he's been at the forefront of my mind since the letter, I'm definitely not telling James about *him*. 'Fancy another drink?'

'I'll make them. You're still supposed to be recuperating. Shall I whip up some sandwiches for lunch?'

'Please.' I hold out my cup for James to take, and when he's clattering around the kitchen I keep my gaze fixed on Mum. Remembering why I never speak of Dad, the knot tightens.

*

There was a period of adjustment for us all, living without Dad. 'Children are resilient' was an overused phrase muttered by Iris, our teachers, the kindly family therapist who kept referring to us as 'victims', spending every session kneading a tissue as though she was the one who might collapse into tears at any moment, and it was true, partly. We'd moved to a new house, new school, used our new identities, tried to pretend we were a normal family. Ben bounced back, as though he were made of rubber; although, at home, he was still my shadow-me, and the relief on the faces of the professionals who, other than offering platitudes and too-bright smiles seemed at a loss to know how to help us, was clear. 'You see? We told you!' And I was brushed under the carpet, along with the dust and the decomposing spider with stiff, stick legs, at twelve still a child but not quite. 'If you act like a victim, people will treat you like a victim,' Iris said, and I tried to be the girl I was before, but it was impossible. Mum wasn't the same either, irritable and tearful. She seemed to forget Ben and I were there half the time and, far from time healing, she seemed to be getting worse.

Life felt like the neon yellow spinning top Ben had with the zoo animals on, whizzing faster and faster until you could no longer see it clearly and were longing for it to stop. Mum wasn't coping, increasingly tired, frequently waking in the night. The doctor prescribed antidepressants for stress but she stopped taking them when her headaches became frequent and fierce. She'd press the heels of her hands against her temples as though trying to push the pain away. One night she pulled the tray from the grill with her oven-gloved hand and stabbed a fork into fishcakes with more force than was necessary. The clatter as the grill pan hit the kitchen floor caused my head to snap up from my homework.

'Mum,' I slid out of my chair, 'have you burned yourself?'

Mum dropped to her knees but made no move to clear up the mess. Instead, she lifted the bottom of her black-and-white butcher's apron, buried her face in the fabric and cried uncontrollably, shaking off the hand I rested tentatively on her shoulder. Silently, I led Ben into the lounge and flicked on *Cartoon Network* for him. Back in the kitchen I helped Mum onto a chair, before I carried the bucket, speared with a mop, from the utility room and swished warm citrus water over the golden breadcrumbs and flakes of fishy mashed potato. The kitchen was clean and tidy, but Mum was still in a state and so I scraped alphabet spaghetti into a plastic bowl and, while it spun circles in the microwave, I buttered toast and made a cup of Ribena. It was only when Ben was settled on the sofa, his tea on a plastic tray on his lap, I could turn my attention once more to Mum. She was still crying, her face red and blotchy, her breath hiccupy gasps.

'Mum?' I crouched to her level, as she used to do when I was little, and I clasped her hands in mine. 'Mum.' But she was still sobbing. Lost to me. Everything spinning again, faster and faster; Ben's top. Elephants into giraffes. Rhinos into kangaroos. Nothing making sense. My socked feet slipped on the wet tiles as I turned and ran, skidding into the hall, snatching up the phone and jabbing numbers so forcefully the tip of my index finger stung.

'Auntie Iris.' Now it was me who was crying. Me who couldn't catch my breath. 'You have to come. Something's wrong with Mum.'

And it was at that point my already fragile world irrevocably transposed into something else.

Something worse.

Chapter Thirty-Three

'Mum had motor neurone disease,' I blurt out, as soon as James has one foot over the threshold and, as though shocked by letting the words escape, my throat constricts to grain-of-sand small and is just as dry.

'Oh, Ali.'

James puts the tray down and kneels in front of me, resting his hand on my knee. 'How old were you?'

'About twelve when it started.' It's hard to pinpoint the exact timeframe. For such a long time Mum's odd behaviour was attributed to stress. It took almost a year to get a firm diagnosis and, during that time, MND was something her and Iris whispered about from behind closed doors but, unlike Ben, I was old enough to understand. To google. On the school computer I'd read accounts of how bad it could be, how bad it would get, with a sense of rising panic. I'd fled the library, squeezed through the broken fence at the bottom of the sports field and pelted home, my satchel banging against my thigh as I ran straight into the kitchen, into the arms of Mum, where, for the first time since Dad was sentenced, I cried and cried and allowed her to comfort me like the child I was but pretended not to be. Iris was in denial, even when Mum was finally diagnosed. I remember walking into the house that day sensing a change. The threads of the fabric holding our family together unravelling.

'She'll be fine. She's a fighter,' Iris had said, refusing to believe her younger sister would do anything but get better. But I knew. I knew from the websites I'd read at school. I knew from the weighted feeling on my chest. Mum was going to die. Despite Iris's denial, the way she always told Ben that Mum was 'under the weather' but she'd be fine, she moved in with us that same day; so I suppose on some level she must have accepted the inevitable.

'So Ben was?' James mentally calculates. 'Six?'

'Yes.' Too small to understand why Mum gradually stopped taking him to the park, running around the garden.

'He's too young to be told, Marsha,' Iris had said firmly when Mum suggested it was better to prepare him. but I think not only was Iris protecting Ben; she was, in her own way, trying to protect us all, Mum included, as though if Mum didn't acknowledge her condition out loud, it wouldn't be true.

'And your dad? How did he cope?'

The pain in my heart is searing. 'Three hot meals a day and nothing to worry about,' Iris had scathed. But he had written 'even now I can't get my head around what happened to my darling Marsha', and I think for the first time how hard it must have been for him, inside, feeling helpless, not knowing we were feeling just as helpless on the outside. 'That is my biggest regret. That I wasn't there for her. Part of me wants to ask if you blame me but it doesn't really matter. I will always blame myself', and I wonder if he knows we blamed him too. If perhaps he'd have welcomed the vitriol Iris spoke of him.

Once, we went to a support group, in a community room, in a medical centre where decay and depression seeped through the dank and dreary walls. Open-mouthed we'd listened to numerous cases where MND had developed after a particularly stressful episode. 'Of course you'd have to already be genetically predisposed,' the chairman had said, 'but many of us here believe that stress could be a contributing factor.' We'd sat, mute with shock, unable to rip our eyes away from those in motorised wheelchairs, unable to move, speak, communicate, learning about the vastly different experiences of the families there. The varying rates of progression of the disease which would ultimately rob us of our mother. Sometimes speech was the first to go. Sometimes movement. Sometimes the ability to swallow. Despite the brave face Mum tried to put on – her cup rattled so hard in its saucer, tea drenched her wrist – it had all sounded so hopeless.

'Stress,' Iris had muttered under her breath at the end of the evening when we gathered our belongings along with our blame and our hate for our father and swept out of the centre. 'I knew it was his fault. I just knew it.'

'That's just a theory,' Mum had said. 'I don't believe it. Don't you either.' She had squeezed my arm. I'd known Iris was being irrational but I 'd understood why. It was hard to rage against a disease, against science, against God. Dad was a living, breathing person and it was easier to channel our frustration, our despair, our hurt onto him. I think it's human nature to want someone to blame, because if we start to believe for a single second that there are circumstances out of our control, life becomes a brutal enemy rather than the gift it is.

At home, Iris had scrunched up the leaflets we'd been handed and tossed them in the bin. 'We'll never go back there,' she had said. 'We're not like them. We're not.'

But we were.

'Dad was… He wasn't around.' Is the best that I can tell James.

'I'm so sorry,' James says. 'About everything you've been through.' I put my hand on his, and Branwell runs his rough tongue over my fingers as though he too wants to offer his comfort, and we sit like that, quiet. Unmoving. Until a thick skin has formed on the top of the cooling coffee and the doorbell causes us both to break apart as though we've something to feel guilty for.

I meet his unfamiliar eyes.

As if he can sense my trepidation, James unpeels himself from the floor. 'I'll get it.'

My guilt isn't alleviated when I hear Matt's voice in the hallway, the footsteps heading towards the lounge. I smooth down my hair, my top, as though I've something to hide.

'It's Matt,' James says, something underlying in his tone I can't identify. 'I'd better go. Thanks for the coffee, Ali.'

He's out the door before I can answer. We never did eat our sandwiches.

'I brought your car key back.' Matt spins my key ring around his forefinger. 'It's all fixed. What's happened to the front door?'

'Dad wrote to Iris.' The words slip from my tongue. It's been so long since I talked about my parents, today I can't seem to stop. 'He wants to see me.'

'How do you feel about that?' Matt asks.

'I don't know.'

'Not everyone leaves you because they want to. Sometimes it's because they have to.' There's a subtext to his words and the room is filled with the things he doesn't say.

'You should go.' I stand. I can't cope with this today. The toing. The froing. He inhales sharply, as if there's something else he wants to say, but instead of encouraging him I walk towards the door, pull it open and welcome the rush of cool breeze against my hot skin.

I'm still thinking about words left unsaid when the doorbell rings again. Matt's changed his mind and scenarios whip through my mind. What he might say. How I might respond. I arrange my features into an expression of nonchalance as I open the door wide. The sight of the police uniforms before me causes reality to fall away, my fingers wrapping themselves around the doorframe for support. All I can think about is Dad. I'm back at the theme park. Back in the Fun House. Clinging on to the handrail as we navigate the shifting floor. My left foot moving forward. My right backwards. Unable to coordinate my movements to do anything other than stand frozen with uncertainty. The safety of the solidity beneath my feet nothing but an illusion.

'It's okay,' Dad had murmured behind me. 'I've got you. I've always got you.' And his words had sounded as sweet and comforting as the sticky pink candyfloss we'd feasted on, nothing like the lie they were.

Now I feel the same sensation: of moving while standing still. Of falling.

The policeman's lips form words I cannot, will not, listen to. 'Justin Crawford?' He had barked in the past. But that was another time, another policeman, I think, although I can't be sure. I'm transfixed by his sharp, white teeth. My stomach rolling. The excitement of crunching through hard toffee. The disappointment of the bland, white, apple I was left holding, on a stick. His eyebrows furrow as he speaks again but my ears are full of the past. Music almost deafening. Cher urging me to 'Believe'; kids, shouting 'hurry up', eager to climb through the revolving barrel. 'You're safe.' Dad's mouth against my ear. Mustard-and-onion hotdog breath against my cheek. 'Let go.' And I had. Scrambling through the rotating drum, whooshing down the slide, arms raised, screeching my delight. That sense of freedom.

Let go.

Now, I allow my fingers to uncurl.

'Mrs Taylor, are you all right?' I am asked, and I give the answer I am expected to: yes. I take the ID handed to me and study it intently as though I would be able to discern a fake. As though I would be able to tell whether the face in front of me matches the one on the card. My hands are shaking violently, and I tell myself whatever Dad has done this time won't affect me, but inside I am the same twelve-year-old girl watching her birthday cake tumble to the floor, to be ground into the carpet by black-booted feet.

'Mrs Taylor,' says the policeman taking back his wallet and by the slight rise of his eyebrows I know he has noted my shaking hands. I stuff them into my pockets. 'I'm PC Hunter and this is PC Willis.' He gestures to the woman next to him, with a long, dark ponytail. 'Is it okay if we come in and ask you a few questions?'

'My dad isn't here.' There's a break in my voice as I utter the words I perhaps should have said all those years ago but didn't.

'It's you we want to speak to.' He takes a step onto the doormat, and I feel the blood drain from my face. *You don't want to go to the police, Ali. You've got blood on your hands. Perhaps the police will be coming for YOU*. And I realise they are not here for Dad, after all.

They are here for me.

Chapter Thirty-Four

Silently, I lead the way into the lounge and sit, gesturing for the police officers to do the same. The part of me that remembers my manners wonders if I should offer them a drink, but I don't think my trembling legs can carry me into the kitchen. Sweat is already prickling under my arms and I don't yet know what it is they want.

'You've had some trouble?' I am asked.

'Sorry?'

'Your door? Graffiti?'

'Oh that. A hazard of living on the same street as a pub, I'm afraid.' I try, and fail, to keep my voice bright and breezy. 'Is that what you're here for?' I allow myself one indulgent moment of hope.

'No.' I think how apt PC Hunter's name is, as he stares unflinching at me as though I am his prey. Again, I am transfixed by his pointed canines. Uncomfortable, my eyes shift to the female officer. She smiles as she bends to stroke Branwell, her ponytail falling over her shoulder. I angle my body towards hers, as though she can soften the news they have come to tell me.

'Oh God. Is Ben okay?' The thought something might have happened to him strikes me with such force I cross my arms over my contracting stomach.

'We're here about Christine Young.'

'Chrissy?' The pause is filled by the tick-tick-tick of the radiator behind the sofa and I wished I'd turned the heating down. It's stifling in here.

'She's been reported missing.'

'She's not missing, she's…' *Not here*, I finished the sentence in my head but even to me it sounds ridiculous. I start again. 'She had a week off work last week and went away for a few days. She texted Ben to let him know.'

'And Ben is?'

'My brother. Who's reported her missing?' My tone is more defensive than I intend. I should have been more concerned when she said she needed space.

'I'm afraid I can't tell you that.' Again, a beat. My eyes dart wildly around the room, as if willing Chrissy to appear might be enough.

'We'd like to ask you a few questions and then we'll conduct a search of the house.'

'My house?'

'This is Christine's property, isn't it?'

'Yes.' I take in the angels on the bookcase, wings spread 'they bring good luck' Chrissy had said. 'Of course, it's fine for you to search.' It's not like I have anything to hide. Not here anyway. 'Do you think?…' I try to stop the question before it tumbles from my lips. 'Do you think she's okay?'

'Christine is classed as a vulnerable person.' PC Willis's tone is soft as she tells me this, as though I, too, need special care.

'*Vulnerable?*' I can't help repeating but the Chrissy in the kitchen singing along to the 80s music she loves, zombie dancing to Michael Jackson's 'Thriller', seems anything but vulnerable.

'Are you aware Christine is on medication?' PC Hunter's pen scratches against his notebook. 'Antidepressants.'

'No.' Two high spots burn on my cheeks. Depression. How can I not have known that about her? *In case you can't live with what you've done.* Could it have been Chrissy who had sent the box of pills to me?

'So you've no idea if she has taken her medication with her?'

'I've never seen any antidepressants. Sorry.' It's not a conscious decision to lie but self-preservation has taken over, emptying my mind of everything except the desire to rewrite the past few days. Inside, I'm spinning, looping round and round the helter-skelter. Reality blurring and shifting with every spiral. How can I admit now about the notes, the gloves, the blood on my car? I need time to think.

'Can you tell me when you last saw Chrissy?' The questions machine gun at me. I stretch the neck of my jumper; it feels as though it's choking me.

'We went out. The Saturday before last. To a bar. Prism.' I eye the mugs of cold coffee resting on the table. My mouth is sawdust-dry. I'm still reeling from the fact Chrissy has depression. I wish she'd talked to me. I've felt that blackness. That sense of feeling lost and alone. The struggle to get out of bed. To put one grief-heavy foot in front of the other. If I hadn't had Ben to take care of, I don't know what I'd have done.

'Can you confirm the address of the bar?'

I tell him, the images from the CCTV flashing through my mind. Me pushing Chrissy.

'Did anything happen that night I should know about?' I sense his eyes burning into me as I try to stifle the nervous laugh bubbling inside. There's plenty that happened that night that I should know about, but I can't tell him that. I need to get it straight in my head. I relay what I remember, the getting ready, the laughing, the dancing.

'I didn't come home with her,' I say.

'Did you have a falling out?'

'No!' I almost shout my answer. There is something about being questioned by someone in authority that makes guilt crawl through my hair, burrow into my scalp like mites, even if I haven't done anything wrong. Mrs Turner, my old headmistress: 'you can't go around thumping people'. Rage, hot and angry, in my balled-up fists. Chanting kids. 'Your dad's a murderer.'

Like father like daughter.

'And you haven't spoken to her since that night?'

'No, but she's been in contact with Ben and with Jules.'

'But not with you?'

'I lost my phone.' I dive on the truth as though it is a life raft keeping me afloat. *The Owl and the Pussy-cat went to sea.* That scratching of the pen. Itching of my skin. The mat for the helter-skelter prickly and abrasive against my bare legs. The questions are endless. I keep my answers sketchy and vague. All the time trying to piece together snippets of memories that hover just beyond reach. I'm worried, and it shames me to admit I'm not only worried about Chrissy, I'm worried about myself. *Perhaps the police will be coming for you, Ali.*

'Is it out of character for her to go away without leaving an address?'

'She's gone off before, usually with some boyfriend or other.'

'Did she have a lot of boyfriends?' There's judgement in his tone.

'No. I didn't mean that.' Everything I am saying is coming out wrong.

'It's okay.' PC Willis's voice is gentle. 'We're just worried. You must be too.'

'I didn't think. I didn't realise... She posted on Facebook. She must be okay.' I press the heels of my hands hard against my eyes to stem the tears that threaten. I'd been so wrapped up in myself.

'Tell me a little about... Chrissy, she prefers being called? Have you known her long?'

PC Hunter falls silent as I answer PC Willis's softer questions. No; I haven't known Chrissy long. Yes; she'd offered me her spare room when I separated from Matt. No; I hadn't met her family. Her parents were both dead. I don't share with PC Willis that I think that is part of the reason we grew so close, so quickly. We've both experienced loss. Loneliness.

'Does Chrissy have a boyfriend at the moment?'

'She dates but there's nobody serious. She's been out a lot lately, so I think there's someone new, but I don't know who. She told Ben she's with a guy. She's been quite commitment phobic since her divorce. Says she'll only bring someone home if they're "the one".'

'How about her other friends?'

'There's Jules next door.' I think of her pained expression whenever I include Chrissy in our plans. 'They work together and the three of us socialise. I've known Jules for years. There's other girls that work in the shop. The gym. She takes two Zumba classes a week.' I rack my brains but most of the time we stay in, sharing pizza, watching movies and when she goes out I don't always ask her where she's been, and she doesn't always tell me.

It's shameful, when you strip it back, how little I know about her although I call her one of my best friends. But then I'm finding out I don't know myself as well as I thought either. Tasting my answers on my tongue before I release them. Gauging whether they sound honest and plausible. Gauging whether *I* sound honest and plausible. PC Hunter asks me whether there's anything else I should tell him before they start the search and, again, I wish I could read faces. I'm silent as I weigh up my options. I could tell them everything: my blind date, my head injury, the doctors would verify my staying in hospital. They'd question why I hadn't reported it before, and I'd have to explain about my dad, my last experience with the police and the whole sorry tale would come tumbling out. It would be a relief, almost, to share the notes, the veiled threats. The fact I think I'm being followed. But I can't share some parts without the other. The blood on my car, the accusations. *Dark things happen on dark nights.* It crosses my mind that I've hurt Chrissy, but I dismiss that thought before it is properly formed. Besides, she texted Ben and Jules. Posted on Facebook. She's fine. She is. She has to be.

'Ali?' PC Willis prompts and I see her exchange a look with PC Hunter.

'Sorry, I can't be of more help. What happens now?'

'We'll conduct a search in a minute. Depending on what we do or don't find, other officers will be checking the places she normally frequents. Talking to anyone who knows her. Looking into her background and the people who know her.'

'But you can check her phone records? Her bank? She must have been spending money?'

'That's not one of the first lines we look into,' PC Hunter says. 'Only on the TV do we snap our fingers and have unlimited budgets to turn over every stone. It's early days and although we're concerned about Chrissy's mental health we'll take this one step at a time.'

They stand simultaneously, marionettes threaded to an operating cross, Branwell dancing around their ankles.

'Could you shut the dog in the garden so he doesn't get in the way.' PC Hunter doesn't look at me. It isn't a question.

'I'll pop him next door,' I mutter.

Minutes later, when I return, after thrusting Branwell towards a bewildered James, the search has begun upstairs and it is like something out of a film, or out of a nightmare. The blue rubber gloves have been snapped on and it seems to be far more formal than the cursory look around I'd envisaged. They are looking under beds, in cupboards, the places where monsters hide, although I know monsters don't always lurk in the shadows. I perch on the sofa, feeling awkward and uncomfortable in my own home. My stomach's on a spin cycle. Where is Chrissy? I cover my face with my hands and try really hard to revisit that night. To remember the last time I saw her. Instead of the laughing and the dancing I see my hands on her shoulders pushing her away. Hear my own voice rising in pitch. Feel distress slide through my veins. Dark holes nestle where my memories should be. The space where the truth should sit gaping wide and empty. I text Ben.

The police are here looking for Chrissy. Do you think I should tell them about Dad?

OMG why? What's she done? Why is Dad relevant??
I'll come.

No stay at work. Sure all fine. She hasn't done anything
but she didn't turn up at the shop today. I'll call you later x

Ben is right. Dad has nothing to do with Chrissy, and I
know if I tell the police I'm from a criminal family, they'll
look at me differently. Treat me differently. It's happened
so many times before. Smiles tighten, spines stiffen and I'll
be instantly condemned.

Like father, like daughter.

But he wasn't all bad; he had just made one single, awful,
choice. Have I done the same?

'Mrs Taylor?'

My name jerks me back to the present, and as I rise and
head towards the voice I speculate whether or not it's a good
thing I am no longer being addressed as Ali.

I know.

As soon as I step into the kitchen, I know.

Before I have seen the box on the worktop. Before I
have caught sight of the cream gloves stained scarlet with
blood, inside.

'Can you explain these?'

I can't. I can't explain. The click of Dad's camera as I
thudded to the bottom of the helter-skelter. The click of
the handcuffs around his wrists.

'They're mine,' I say slowly. I can hardly pretend they
aren't.

You've got blood on your hands.

PC Willis lifts the gloves.

I am floating, floating, floating high up to the ceiling.

PC Hunter's eyes drill into me as PC Willis drops the gloves into a clear plastic bag, and I know they are taking them away.

Are they taking me as well?

Chapter Thirty-Five

'Why didn't you tell me?' Jules still has her coat and shoes on. She'd arrived home from work just as PCs Hunter and Willis were leaving. They had promised to be in touch shortly which sounded more like a threat than a reassurance, though I can't blame them. My harried explanation about the bloody gloves being part of a Halloween costume sounded heavy and awkward as it hung in the air, as I was desperately trying to convince myself it was true. Perhaps the blood is fake. If it's not, though, I know it won't take them long to find out and they'll be back.

Tick, Tock, Ali.

Jules had hovered on her step, under the pretence of rummaging around for her keys. When they'd left our eyeline she'd asked if I was okay. I'd burst into tears and, even now, half an hour later, sitting on her sofa, I can't seem to pull myself together as I hiccup out everything that has been happening. Branwell lies at my feet, head between his paws, ears down, gazing up at me with such pure love it sets me off again.

'What if I go to prison? Who would look after Branwell?' I'm gabbling now. Mind depicting the worst possible scenarios it can conjure. 'She's catastrophising' the school support officer would say, after Mum reported another incident where I'd found my homework stuffed down the toilet, my ham sandwich covered in mud, 'murderer' etched into my desk, as though I was imagining it all. As though the school didn't have a responsibility to keep me safe. It was a relief to move away. Start again. But however far I run I can't escape myself.

'I would look after him.' James tries to pass me my coffee but takes one look at my shaking hands and sets it down on the table instead. 'You know I think the world of him. And you.'

'James!' Jules snaps. 'Don't be a dick. It won't come to that. Ali hasn't done anything wrong.'

'I know that but…'

I let their voices fade as I tap away on my phone, before a thundering fills my ears and I rock back and forth wanting it all to stop.

'Breathe.' Two hands on my shoulders forcing me still. Eyes meeting mine. 'In and out. Slowly.' Gradually my lungs stop fighting for air and I'm aware of the whimpering I had been making. 'It says,' my heart is hammering painfully in my chest, 'you can be convicted of murder without a body. If there's enough circumstantial evidence.'

'Who says?'

'Wikipedia.' I'm scrolling again.

Jules gently slips my phone out of my clammy hands. '*Wikipedia* is bollocks, and what's all this talk of murder? No one is accusing you of anything, although someone clearly has it in for you. We just need to figure out who.'

'It's my date. It has to be. The gloves. The blood on my car. The antidepressants. The Facebook post. I'm being set up. He must have done something to Chrissy and he's framing me.' It seems glaringly obvious, now, that everything that has happened this past week has all been building to this. I just couldn't see it before.

'It might not be. There's no evidence,' James says.

'You don't need evidence. People have been convicted for less. Weren't you listening?' Hysteria has crept into my voice. 'Oh God. Chrissy. What's happened to her?'

'Nothing that we know of.' Jules is slipping off her coat off, settling next to me and stroking my arm as though I am a frightened animal that needs soothing, and, I suppose, in a way, I am.

'But she didn't show up at work?' I already know the answer.

'No. Nobody called the police though. That's a bit extreme for one day off. We all take the odd duvet day. Who do you think reported her missing?'

I open my mouth, but clamp it shut again when Jules says: 'Please don't blame that on your date too.'

'I've got to tell the police everything. Let them look at the CCTV from Prism and put out a photofit for Ewan.'

'Won't that look more suspicious? You should think about this properly. They'll wonder why you haven't reported it before and you've just said you haven't got the note from the gloves, or the flowers, and you left your shoes in the park. What if they think you're making everything up? It doesn't make you sound very credible, does it?'

And I have to admit it doesn't.

'I don't think I can wait until next Friday.' I pace the lounge as I talk. My ankle still twinges but it's healing.

Eight strides from the sofa to the TV.

'It's only three days since we first tried hypnosis, Ali,' Mr Henderson says. 'Do you feel ready? You were quite distressed after Friday's session?'

A hiss of vanilla from the air freshener.

'I have to—' A lump in my throat traps the rest of my words.

Twelve paces from the window to the far wall.

'Has something happened, Ali? You know you can talk to me. I'm here for you.'

'The friend I went out with that night is missing. The police are looking for her. I *have* to remember anything that might help them. I'm worried sick about her.' And about myself, although I don't say this; it sounds horribly self-indulgent to be thinking of myself when Chrissy is God knows where.

The doorbell chimes, and I edge out into the hallway, phone clasped to my chest.

Six steps to reach the front door.

'It's me.' Matt's voice floats through the letterbox.

'I've got to go, Mr Henderson. Matt's here.' I cradle the handset between my chin and cheek as I open the door.

'Are you getting back together?' It's an innocuous question but there's hope in every word. 'I feel I've lost a friend without you next door.'

'He's here to walk Branwell.' I mouth 'Mr Henderson' to Matt. 'Bye.' I end the call.

Without small talk, I pass Matt Branwell's lead.

'Are you okay?'

'Why is everyone asking me that today?' I snap.

'Whoa.' He holds up his hands. 'You look pale is all. I care.'

'Do you?' But without waiting for an answer I tell him to enjoy his walk and stalk into the lounge. I slam the door behind me, and the photos of Mum I have propped on the bookcase flutter to the ground, and as I pick them up I think I see something in her eyes.

Worry? Accusation?

When Matt comes back I don't invite him in.

Somehow, I have gone through the motions of cooking a meal, then moving food I cannot taste around my plate, and now I am getting ready for bed as though this is just another ordinary day. I hang my shirt on a hanger and think of all the small things we take for granted. Being able to choose what we wear each day, what we eat, who we spend our time with and I think how impossibly hard it must have been for Dad to have his identity stripped away, along with his freedom and his family.

I perch on my dressing table stool, my navy scarf with swallows dipping and diving drapes the mirror. I unscrew the lid from my face cream and hover the pot under my nose, breathing in deeply. Roses. In a split second I am transported. Cross-legged on the bed in my parents' room, watching Mum tug cotton wool from a roll and ball it between her palms.

'Always make time to look after your skin.' She'd blobbed cream onto the tip of my nose and I had squealed at its coldness.

I'd rubbed it into my cheeks, sniffing my fingertips when I'd finished. 'It smells of flowers.'

'Roses,' Mum had said. 'My mum used the same brand and promised me if I used it twice a day my skin would be petal soft. Yours too.'

'Will this make me as beautiful as you, Mum?'

'You already are, sweet girl. Inside and out; although I'll let you into a secret – it's the inside that really counts.' She'd picked up her brush that was oyster white and shimmered in the light and ran it through my hair, slowly, methodically, while I counted to one hundred.

Towards the end, Mum was almost unrecognisable from the woman she once was; stress and illness had aged her terribly. Her body weak, muscles wasted, but she was still beautiful to me as I would be to her now, even if I can no longer see it myself. But what if the inside is dirty and tarnished? What if a person has done something so terrible, so unforgivable, only ugliness remains. What then?

Tick, tock, Ali.

Time is running out.

Chapter Thirty-Six

It's all escalating rather quickly now, isn't it, Ali? What was your overriding emotion when you opened the door to the uniformed officers? Fear, I hope. How quickly did the penny drop, hard and solid? Your friend is missing. You hadn't cared enough to report it yourself. The small pieces of evidence that piece together to form something larger and impossible to ignore.

They can't have uncovered everything yet, but they will.

Tomorrow's another day.

Enjoy sleeping in your own bed tonight, Ali. It might be the very last time. This can't go on much longer.

Chapter Thirty-Six

TUESDAY

Chapter Thirty-Seven

My phone trills an unknown number, and my stomach lurches in response. Is it him? My date? My tormentor? Picking up my handset I am poised to reject the call, when it crosses my mind it might be Chrissy and, hesitantly, I press the green accept button with my thumb, hoping to hear her voice floating down the line. 'Ali, you'll never guess what's happened.' And she'll have a story to tell, an adventure to relay, and I'll tell her what a fuss she has caused, and one day we'll laugh about the time we all thought she was missing.

'Hello?' There's a hopeful note to my voice.

'Mrs Taylor? It's PC Willis.'

Time freezes. Surely if it was good news Chrissy would be ringing me. I sink heavily onto the stool and rest my elbows on the breakfast bar, bracing myself for what's to come, imagining Chrissy's pale, lifeless body twisted in some ditch.

'You've found her.' It's a statement, not a question and I don't know whether to be relieved or concerned when she tells me they haven't.

'Our intelligence officers have brought a few things to our attention, and some other information has been reported. I wondered if you could pop in, for a chat?'

She makes it sound so informal. One friend to another. 'When?'

'Now.' There's a firmness to her voice I didn't hear yesterday. I tell her I'll be along as soon as I can.

*

Police stations have their own distinctive smell, much the same as primary schools, or hospitals. The second I push open the smeared glass doors and step inside I am clouded by a lingering scent of vomit, disinfectant and memories.

Sitting on hard, grey plastic chairs, Ben beside me, swinging his chubby legs, feet not reaching the grubby floor, as Mum asked the desk sergeant again where Dad was. What he was supposed to have done. When he was being released. His answer was always the same: 'We can't tell you anything at this time. You'd be better off waiting at home for news.'

Outside the sky had fallen into shades of grey and a crescent moon hung over the leisure centre opposite the station. I watched as a family came tumbling out of the revolving door in a mass of love and laughter, hair damp from swimming, a small boy about Ben's age carrying a striped inflatable ball. They were all munching on Mars bars, and my stomach growled in response. From behind his plastic enclosure the desk sergeant scraped back his chair, disappeared from view, reappearing in reception a few minutes later. Disappointment plastered Mum's face as she realised he didn't have Dad with him; instead he carried two plastic cups of hot chocolate which he handed to me and Ben. Powder clumped on the surface and it tasted artificially sweet, not like chocolate at all, but I gulped it down gratefully. That was my birthday tea. That small kindness was soon washed away by the realisation Dad wasn't coming home, then, or ever and it all got muddled in my twelve-year-old mind until I held the police partly responsible for fracturing my family. It was easier than believing it was all Dad.

As I wait for PC Willis to come and collect me for our 'chat' I pace back and forth like a caged lion, unable to settle and, once I am fetched and shown into a small, windowless room, I wish I hadn't come. There's almost a finality in the way the door slams shut behind me.

'Hello, Alison.' I don't recognise PC Hunter from yesterday but his cold, clipped tone is chillingly familiar.

'Have you tested the gloves?' I can't help blurting out. They must have called me in for a specific reason and I can't think what else it would be.

'Yes, we sent them to the lab and the results were pinged back immediately, just like you see on TV. No waiting around for the budget to be approved or for the backlog to be cleared. We wrap up every case in an hour, less the time for ad breaks.' His sarcasm stings me into silence.

'We're going to be recording this interview. Is that all right with you?' He is already fiddling with buttons.

'I'm not under arrest, am I?'

'Not unless there's anything you want to tell us?' His eyes meet mine, and I look away quickly, scared he'll see my panic.

He barks the date and time and introduces himself and PC Willis before asking me to state my name.

'Alison Taylor.'

'And that's your legal name, is it?'

'Yes. It's my married name…' I trail off. That isn't what he meant.

He knows about Dad.

Pressure begins to build in my head but instead of questioning me further he asks me to tell him more about my friendship with Chrissy.

'I met her about six months ago, in the gym.' I'd been nearing the end of my workout, swiping my cardio-damp fringe away from my face. Trying to summon up the energy to drag my weary body around one last circuit. Picturing my thighs in denim shorts. Wrapped around Matt. Overriding those images, though, had been the thought of the home-made fruit cake in the café downstairs, kidding myself it was one of my five a day.

'You look like I feel.' Chrissy had been sipping from a polystyrene cone filled with water from the cooler.

'Knackered?'

'Yes, although some of the sights in here don't exactly inspire me to keep going.' Her eyebrows arched as she raised her eyebrows and nodded in the direction of a huge man, dripping with sweat. He'd grunted as he hefted a dumbbell over his head again, his top had ridden up, displaying a thick carpet of black hair coating his back; in the mirror his stomach hung over the waistband of his shorts.

'Are you single?'

'Divorced,' she had told me. 'And new to the area. Do you fancy getting a coffee? Is that weird? I don't know anyone else here.'

'Throw in a cake and I'm there.'

'We got on really well.' I direct my response to PC Willis, trying to block out the soft whirring of the machine recording my every answer. 'She'd moved for a fresh start after her marriage broke down.'

'Because she had an affair?'

'Yes. I suppose.' It's uncomfortable discussing the morality of someone who isn't here to defend themselves.

'And you found her a job?'

It's frustrating they are asking questions they clearly know the answer to, but I nod all the same.

'If you could speak out loud for the benefit of the tape.'

I lick my dry lips. 'Yes. She was working in a pub but didn't like the late hours, and I knew a vacancy had come up in the shop Jules worked in and I recommended her.'

'And how did she get on with Jules?'

'Okay. Chrissy was always more my friend but the three of us did things together.'

'Did?'

'Do.' My throat tightens and I force down cooling water. 'We *do* things together.'

'There's a post on Chrissy's Facebook page, the last post she made, saying "There comes a time when you have to stop crossing oceans for someone who wouldn't even jump in puddles for you". Have you seen this?'

'Yes.'

'What does it mean?'

'I've no idea.' I'm analysing every word I say, my tone, my body language. I cross and uncross my arms trying to appear casual, but two wet patches have formed under my arms and I keep my elbows tucked into my sides so they can't be seen.

'You and Chrissy aren't Facebook friends.'

'No. Not anymore and I don't know why,' I interject before they can ask.

'She must have posted that after you left Prism? Did you have an argument there?'

'No.' My hands on her shoulders. Pushing. 'Are you going to check the CCTV?' I fight to keep my voice level.

'That would be rather difficult considering Prism burned down last night.'

My head jerks up as though I've been kicked in the spine and I make eye contact for the first time.

'Burned down?'

'Yes. Very coincidental, wouldn't you say? Early reports indicate that it's arson. Where were you last night, Mrs Taylor, between the hours of midnight and 1 a.m.?' Again, he's stopped calling me Alison.

'At home.'

'Alone?'

'With Branwell.'

'And Branwell is?'

'My dog.'

'He can't exactly provide you with an alibi then, can he?'

I swallow the last of the water to wash down my humiliation.

'We just want to find Chrissy, Alison. You must be worried sick. Is there anything you can tell us about that night?'

I grasp gratefully at the sympathy in PC Willis's voice, but release it quickly remembering every crime drama I've watched. No matter how scathing PC Hunter is of TV depictions I'm sure good cop, bad cop is a thing. Stress buzzes in my ears. Mentally I run through how it would sound if I told them about Ewan, even though there is no proof without the CCTV that he exists other than the messages he sent me from a non-existent dating profile. If I told them about the shoes I left by the seafront, the note with the gloves Branwell ate, the flowers I threw away, would it sound as though I was fabricating the whole thing? And yet, if there is anything I can do to help find Chrissy, I know I must. I am drawing in a deep breath, ready to tell them everything, when PC Hunter says, casually, as he's scribbling notes. Too casually.

'What happened to your car?'

'My car?' I can't help repeating.

'You had a new bumper fitted recently? Hit something?'

Someone.

'Look. Am I being accused of something here?' My voice is defensive. Big and brave and everything I am not. 'Do I need a solicitor?' I bite down hard on my lip to stop myself from crying. God knows what they'll find if they come back to the house to do a more thorough search. I flashback to me in my bathroom washing the blood from my hands the morning after the date. There must still be minute traces invisible to the naked eye around the basin. Whose blood is it?

'If you want to seek legal advice that is entirely your prerogative. We're just trying to piece together Chrissy's last known movements. And you're the obvious place to start considering your connection.'

'Just because we live together doesn't mean I know where she is.'

'I wasn't talking about that connection.'

PC Willis and PC Hunter exchange a look I cannot read but there's a heaviness hanging over this cheap plastic table, with its wonky leg and coffee stains, that wasn't here before.

'You must know.' I am asked.

I shake my head, at a loss, no longer caring about recording my responses for the tape.

'Chrissy's maiden name was Marlow.'

I am being watched. I am being studied. I am hooked up to an electric chair with a current running through my body as I squirm and sweat and try to deny what is happening to me.

Chrissy Young is Christine Marlow. The daughter of Sharon Marlow. The woman that was killed in the robbery Dad took part in.

Pressure around my neck.

Shouting. Screaming. Chrissy's furious face.

Me pushing.

Fingers squeezing my throat.

A noose.

The knot pulling tighter and tighter.

Chapter Thirty-Eight

Icy tentacles squeeze my stomach as I stumble out of the police station.

'Stay in the area.' PC Hunter had snapped off the tape recorder before scraping back his chair, draining the last of his coffee, which must have been as cold as his demeanour.

As I drive home I constantly release one hand from the steering wheel, brushing at the opposite arm, my skin itching with the sensation of insects scurrying over me. The crawling sensation of suspicion and deceit. I feel tainted, somehow even more than that night. My mind is scrabbling around for answers and I drive fast, too fast, along the curves that hug the clifftops where Mum, Ben and I would picnic. Where Matt proposed. But the places I don't want to visit are not only physical. They are buried in a box deep inside my mind, and I need to find the key to unlock them.

Christine Marlow.

Did she know who I was when she approached me at the gym? Years ago, the welfare officer who'd been assigned to support me and Ben told Mum she believed in the Carl Jung theory that there are no such things as coincidence, aligning everything to synchronicity instead. Now, I think she was trying her best to alleviate us of our burden of guilt, however ham-fistedly, but Mum had raged, a ball of anger and bitterness and regret.

'So she was meant to die, that poor woman?' Mum had spat. 'Leaving two kiddies without a mother.'

'I didn't mean…'

'Get out! You're not helping, none of you are helping.' And that was when she'd pulled us out of school. Decided that no amount of counselling or educating could allow us to blend into our neighbourhood once more, like the newsagents on the corner of the street, or the red postbox beneath the cherry tree. We'd always stand out like the juice and sushi bar that slid in-between the fish and chip shop and the Indian. Awkward and out of place.

Two kiddies.

A brother and a sister. Chrissy the sister, but where is the brother? Could he be Ewan? Is he the one following me now? Watching me? Sending me things? Was the whole thing an elaborate form of revenge? They must have burned the bar down so the police wouldn't identify them on the CCTV. The only proof vanished, literally, in a puff of smoke.

The indistinct images that pass through my mind are becoming clearer. Louder. Pushing her. The shouting. The crying. Had they revealed who they were? 'Our mind tries to protect us from the things we cannot cope with,' Mr Henderson had said. Is that what I am blanking out? The stark, horrible truth, brutally exposed. Two families torn apart. But we weren't the victims, were we? Not in the eyes of the public who became our judge and jury. Not in the eyes of Sharon Marlow's children.

I race through traffic lights on the cusp of red, recalling why I signed up for the dating app. It was Chrissy who instigated it. I remember.

'It's just a bit of fun,' she had said. 'What's the worst that can happen?' I swallow hard. Her words have left a sour taste that lingers, even as I remember it was Jules who sent the reply and briefly I wonder if she was in on it too, but that's impossible. We've been friends for years, and it was Chrissy who downloaded that particular app.

Coincidence.

Synchronicity.

The victim part of me pulses with an inevitability. Telling me it is no more than I deserve. If I hadn't been desperate for a birthday present, Dad wouldn't have had to steal, and Chrissy wouldn't have lost her mum. Dad wouldn't have lost his freedom. Iris wouldn't have lost her independence. Mum wouldn't have become so stressed, perhaps she'd never have developed MND. My vision blurs with tears and I wipe at them with my sleeve. A chain of events all instigated by my one, small, selfish longing for an iPod and, even now, as an adult, I haven't learned my lesson. I lost Matt his business when I betrayed his confidence about Craig's affair. Julia blamed my honesty on her losing her husband.

I slow as I turn into my road. The adrenaline that had flooded my system at the police station now depleted. Mentally and physically I feel defeated. Almost ready to lie down and take whatever punishment comes my way but, as I trudge up the front path, and unlock my door, there's the happy scrambling of paws, a rough tongue licking my hand. Branwell pirouettes his hello and I know I am not yet ready to give up.

Slinging my bag over the bannisters I take the stairs two at a time, flinging open Chrissy's door.

*

A hundred times before I've walked into Chrissy's room, flopped onto her bed, as she got changed into her pyjamas – the way she would the second she got home from work – swapping stories about our days, discussing what to have for dinner. This time me being here feels different. Intrusive. As though I'm invading her privacy. But we have crossed the line of consideration and trust.

You wouldn't know from looking around that the police have been here. There's still make-up scattered over her dressing table. The box of chocolates on her bedside cabinet. Clothes strewn across the floor. It isn't like the aftermath of a search on TV, with furniture upended and carpets pulled up. 'Of course we make as much mess as we can.' I can almost hear PC Hunter's sarcastic voice but it was what I had been expecting. Instead, it is exactly how she left it. Exactly like a shrine, I think, and the thought makes me shudder. I think she's trying to ruin my life, but still, I will for her to be safe. To tumble through the door in a cloud of Daisy perfume and apologies and 'you'll-never-guess-whats'.

For her to be oblivious to who I really am, the way I was her. We both had different surnames. We never talked about our pasts. Our families. Except Ben, of course. She always was interested in him, and my stomach roils as I wonder whether she has anything planned for him too or if it is enough to take me away from him. But why now? It makes no sense that she'd have tracked me down after all this time without some sort of trigger.

Dad.

His words slide through my mind's eye.

A month before I was released I wrote to Sharon's family, the woman who died. Who we murdered, I suppose. I might not have pulled the trigger, but I've got blood on my hands nevertheless. Everyone involved has and we've all paid the price. We're still paying the price. I wasn't allowed their address but the prison said they'd post it on for me and I had hoped they'd reply before I was released. They didn't. I told her family how sorry I was. How sorry I am. I told them I was getting out and promised I'd spend the rest of my life trying to put right all the wrongs I had caused.

Seven months ago, he'd written his weak apologies and empty promises.

Six months ago, Chrissy had introduced herself to me.

Synchronicity.

Coincidence.

I think not.

Where do I start? I have to do something, I feel so helpless. What could I possibly find that the police haven't? But then again, they only checked the places large enough for a person, leaving drawers unopened, and that seems as good a place to begin as any.

There's a thin layer of dust covering her iPod dock on her chest of drawers and I run my index finger over it, jumping as the Human League's 'Don't You Want Me?' blares. Switching it off I look over my shoulder, as though I'd see her sitting at her dressing table, coating her lashes with mascara, straightening her hair, but I am alone. Not even Branwell is keeping me company, as though he senses the heaviness in the atmosphere, the presence of the police still detectable, like the smell of garlic suspended in the air. I slide open the drawer of her bedside cabinet and start to rifle through the contents. There's receipts, a small packet of tissues, a tube of Polos and, towards the back, under a scarf, I find a hot pink vibrator, and I feel my cheeks turn the same colour as I think what PC Hunter might have uncovered in my room, in the bottom of my wardrobe. I scan the room. If I had a secret and wanted to hide something where would I put it? Dropping to my knees I heft the mattress onto one shoulder and shuffle across the carpet until I have examined every inch of the base of the bed. There's nothing.

There's something here, I'm sure of it. Something's off and I can't quite put my finger on it. A search of her wardrobe reveals nothing. It's tidy. Ordered. The first half of the clothes a size 10, the second a 12. There aren't as many hangers for the latter half; she preferred to be smaller, but when her weight crept up – which it inevitably did – that's when she ended up borrowing my things. I close the doors and turn away from the mirrors.

The chocolates on the bedside cabinet draw my eye. It's unusual for Chrissy to make a box last so long. I lift off the lid. All her favourites have gone; the ones left, the strawberry cream, the orange crunch, are usually ones she'd have passed over to me before recycling the box. Why didn't she do that this time? I lift the plastic insert and draw a sharp breath. Underneath is a piece of paper torn from the notepad we keep in the kitchen. I unfold the note. It's unmistakably Chrissy's handwriting, large and blocky – she never did master joined-up writing at school she had said.

As I read her heartfelt words my knees turn to rubber and
I sit heavily on her bed.

Oh Chrissy.

What have you done?

Chapter Thirty-Nine

A vice tightens around my ribcage until I feel my heart might burst as I scan the words again and again, almost hoping if I read fast enough they will blur together and turn into something else. Something I can cope with. But they remain the same.

> *Last night was incredible. I can't stop thinking about it. Thinking about you. I've never felt like this before with anyone. I know we've talked about this and I know you want to wait, and I understand why, but I think we should tell Ali about us. We're too old to be sneaking around like teenagers with a guilty secret. If we're in it for the long haul she's bound to find out sooner or later and it will be easier coming from us? We've promised to be honest with each other so we should be honest with her too. Whatever you think best anyway. You know I'd do anything for you.*
>
> *Speaking of honesty I've something to tell you…*

Instead of finishing the sentence Chrissy had written 'fuck-fuck-fuck' followed by a series of doodles. Hearts. Flowers. Angels. Lower down the page were small splodges that could have been tears and, in big angry letters,

I CAN'T DO THIS ANYMORE

I turn the paper over in my hands as I turn the words over in my mind. *I can't do this anymore.* What couldn't she do, and with who? My head is shaking 'no', as though I can stop his name popping into my mind.

Matt.

Had he been having an affair despite his promises there was no one else? 'He's often out in the evenings,' Mr Henderson had said. Was that her grand plan, to seduce my husband, break up my marriage? Had her brother got involved and it all escalated into something else?

A murder charge.

I'm adding up two and two and I think I'm making four. Eight. Twelve.

Think.

The day I got out of hospital and went to collect Branwell. Matt wouldn't let me upstairs. He was edgy. Desperate to get rid of me. Bedroom curtains drawn. Was she there? Is she still there? Hiding from me. Laughing at me. Matt offered to repair my car. Would he really have noticed the damage when it was facing forward on the driveway or had he known it was there?

I take another look inside the box in case I have missed something, and I have. Face down is a photo. The white of the back of the print had blended in with the white of the cardboard. Taking a deep breath I scoop it up. It's all piecing together now. The truth is hurtling towards me and I widen my stance and plant my feet, as though I can stop it slamming into me, bowling me over, breaking me entirely. I examine the photo, and frustration bolts through my body like electricity as I study the two people in the image. I'm pretty certain the woman is Chrissy. Long blonde hair. A sprinkling of freckles covering her nose. The fine chain around her neck she often wore, with a gold wishbone dangling in the hollow between her collarbones. The man I'm not so sure. I draw it closer to my eyes, as though that might make a difference. He has short brown hair that could belong to a trillion men. A white T-shirt. Nondescript. Unidentifiable to me. And briefly, I pretend to myself if I can't recognise him, it can't possibly be Matt, it can't possibly be my husband, but the rational side of me knows if it isn't, there would be no need for Chrissy to hide it away like the secret it so clearly is.

I stare at the two of them.

Two birds with one stone.

If I'm in prison Chrissy gets her revenge and Matt gets the house. Knowing all that I am to these people I have loved is a problem to be solved, morphs the fear and the panic and the shame I have felt into something else. Something razor-sharp and ready to wound.

Still holding the photo I stalk out of the room and pound down the stairs.

Tick tock, Chrissy.

Now I'm coming for you.

Chapter Forty

It's nearly time to end this before it breaks us both.

Are you remembering now? Remembering what you lost me, Ali?

Did you really think you could get away with it?

Do you really think I'll let you get away with it? Of course not. You took something from me and now I'll take something from you. Your life or your freedom? Decisions, decisions.

Karma's a bitch.

Chapter Forty-One

At the bottom of the stairs I grab my mobile from my bag and carry it into the kitchen. I message Matt and tell him he needn't walk Branwell tonight, before I smooth the picture of him and Chrissy out onto the worktop and take a photo of it. I text it to Ben and within seconds my phone is vibrating.

'Where did you get that?' Ben asks, and I'm glad he knows me well enough not to bother with opening pleasantries. To sense how upset I am.

'In Chrissy's room, hidden in the bottom of a box of chocolates.'

'Don't do anything rash. I'm coming back. We can talk about it properly.'

'No. Don't miss out on your meeting. Besides there's nothing to talk about. I'm going to fucking kill him.'

'Kill him?'

'He's still my husband.'

Crackling fills the silence that stretches while my heart gallops, waiting, wanting my brother to be as outraged as I am.

Eventually he speaks, slowly, carefully. 'But Matt's not…'

Another beat. I hear him take a deep breath before he can continue.

'But Matt's not yours anymore, is he? He hasn't been for months.'

The truth is as heavy and as blunt as a cricket bat and strikes me with force.

'Sorry.' He almost whispers.

'You're right.'

'I can come home, Ali-cat. If you need to talk.'

'I need to find Chrissy. She must be with Matt. Where else could she be? She's setting me up.'

'Setting you up for what? Why would she do that?' Every word he speaks drips with fatigue, and part of me wishes I'd never rung him. His job is draining enough without the constant worry I am putting him through. I know I have to tell him about Chrissy's connection with Dad, but I don't want to do it over the phone. If he thinks for one second Chrissy and her brother have been targeting me he'll be furious, and I don't want him driving in that state of mind.

'Let's wait until you're home and we can talk it all through properly then.'

I know by this time tomorrow I will have found Chrissy and cleared my name. An idea is taking shape.

Dad's arrest didn't just make the local papers, it hit the nationals too. Somebody had uncovered an old, grainy photograph of Dad wearing a leather jacket and sunglasses, mouth a thin straight line, aiming a gun at the lens, and it didn't seem to matter this had been taken at a fancy dress party, and he'd been dressed up as Arnold Schwarzenegger in *Terminator*. If you looked closely you could see Mum's bare arm before she'd been cut out of the image. She was his Linda Hamilton in a black vest top and jeans. It didn't seem to matter that Dad wasn't the one who actually pulled the trigger. Headlines screamed his guilt, each one worse than the last from 'Young mum gunned down in cold blood' to

'Stamped out in a post office'. On the Monday it was decided that Ben was so young he'd be better off staying at home, but at twelve, it was thought I should go to school, where I'd be safe and nurtured, among friends. Iris had stayed with Ben, while Mum had shouldered her way through the reporters, dragging me by the hand, my eyes a mass of stars from the dozens of flashes. The snap-snap-snap of the cameras almost drowned out by the stupid questions that showered down, and we stamped on them, over them, as we hurried to her car. How did they *think* we felt? Did they *really* believe we knew Dad would break the law? In a desperate situation, are we all capable of monstrous acts? It's incomprehensible we can reach inside the darkest depths of someone else's mind, when we ignore the blackness lurking in our own.

At school, the headmaster had been waiting at the gates, assuring Mum if any reporters tried to access the school grounds he would immediately ring the police. Instead of running over to my friends, as I normally would have, I'd been ushered straight inside, as if I were sick or naughty. I'd sat by the window at the back of the class, my face burning, as the kids outside in the playground stared at me through the glass as though I was an elephant with two trunks. My white school blouse was damp, sticking to my back, my armpits, and that's the first time I ever remember sweating. I had grown up overnight. The bell rang, and Melanie, Izzy and Lauren had been the first through the door, and I'd forced my mouth to smile the first smile it had since I'd run towards the ding-dong of the front door at my party, expecting to find one of my friends on the step. Instead of smiling back, slipping into their usual seats Melanie had fired a look of pure hatred at me, as though I had wronged her, while Izzy and Lauren had avoided looking at me at all. The chairs around me remained empty and when all the desks were filled and a small bunch of kids hovered uncertainly at the front, my teacher had barked at them to sit down.

'But Miss,' one of the children had whined, 'we don't want to sit next to a *murderer*.'

'Yeah,' chimed another. 'My mum says all her family are fucking scum.'

They'd been reprimanded, of course, but it had made no difference. I'd been shunned. No one had wanted to come near me, as though the trauma happening to my family was a contagious disease.

'I can't go back there tomorrow,' I had sobbed, sitting on Mum's lap that night as though I was Ben's age and not a year off being a teenager.

'You can't let them prevent you getting an education,' Mum had soothed. 'Knowledge is power. Don't let them win.'

And that's exactly what I tell myself now as I fetch my laptop.

Knowledge is power.

I won't let them win.

Chapter Forty-Two

I have desperately tried to leave the past behind me. Be a good daughter. A good wife. A good friend. Failing miserably at them all. Longing for the thing I did that took minutes out of the billions of minutes I have lived to fade into nothing. But it's glaringly apparent, as I type Sharon Marlow's name into Google, adding the year and town of the robbery, that nothing in this digital age truly disappears. A sick feeling rises as over a million results load, and my fingers are shaking so hard I find it almost impossible to scroll through the pages. The condemnation. The endless, endless speculation about the case, the verdict. The call for the death penalty. Although every fibre of my being screams at me to start a new search for Sharon's children, I can't help opening one of the more recent reports in an online edition of a red top. A 'Where are the Tanmoor Three?' as though they are faded pop stars or Blue Peter presenters. David Webb, the man who pulled the trigger, had died in prison after another prisoner set fire to him. That must have been the incident Dad wrote about in his letter. Although David was in part responsible for everything my family have been through, are going through, I still shudder at the thought of burning to death and Dad helplessly watching. How on earth could that happen inside a prison with the guards and the cameras and the rigid rules?

It's not like you see on TV, I can imagine PC Hunter saying. *All cell searches and confiscating contraband while guards and prisoners form bonds and everyone gets rehabilitated in the end.* But still, a slow and painful death is not what I'd wish on anyone and, as I think that, I picture Mum growing weaker each day, muscles wasting, speech slurring. Her dignity fading along with our childhood paintings stuck to the fridge and Ben's toddler fingerprints on the walls. Time seemed so cruel back then. Speed-of-light fast and yet impossibly slow. I read on. The second name is more familiar to me – Wayne Lindsell. He visited the house more and more once Dad had lost his job. I vividly remember, one scorching hot summer's day, they drank cheap beer in the garden, while Mum frowned out of the window as she wiped her hands on her apron.

'Tell your dad I want him,' she had said.

I had relayed the message and stood awkwardly on our lawn that was yellowing with thirst, as Dad headed to the kitchen, and I began to follow, but Wayne called me back, asking how school was, in the way that adults do when they can't think of anything to say.

'Fine,' I muttered as Mum's urgent whisper floated out of the open window the way the butterflies were floating around our lavender bush.

'I can't make dinner stretch to feed another mouth. He'll have to go. And it's far too early to be drinking.'

Wayne drained the last of his can before crushing it in one hand, his muscles bulging. I was mesmerised by the tattoo of a lion's head glistening on his tanned arm.

'It's a reminder that I'm stronger and smarter and faster,' Wayne had said. 'King of the jungle. Invincible.'

He was also dead. Ravaged by cancer. There's a photo of him in the prison hospital, all sunken cheeks and jutting collarbones. His hands lying crossed over his chest. His lion tattoo small and shrivelled.

Dad is the only one left. The only one free and, although I know I shouldn't, I can't help opening up the comments at the bottom of the article. The malevolence that spews from my screen snatches my breath. The numerous variations of 'I hope they didn't waste more taxpayers' money giving Wayne pain relief' and the 'someone should set fire to Justin Crawford. Why should he get to live his life free?' And something deep inside of me, a primal, protective instinct, begins to unfurl as I'm back at that funfair, begging Dad to win me a teddy bear on the shooting range. His awkwardness handling a gun, needing to be shown where to put the hard, tarnished pellets, told to close one eye before he squinted through the sight. He still missed the target. He'd hooked a duck instead, tongue poking out the corner of his mouth with concentration, and won me a grubby rabbit whose stuffing spilled out of its seams as he carried me high on his shoulders when my legs became tired.

Branwell licks my hand, as though reminding me to focus, and I start a new search for 'Sharon Marlow + children'.

TRAGEDY STRIKES AGAIN FOR THE MARLOW FAMILY screams at me. I begin to read how Sharon's eldest child, Lewis, was drowned while holidaying in Greece. Christine is the only surviving family member.

No wonder she hates me.

No wonder she wants revenge.

But Lewis can't be Ewan.

*

'I know,' is all I say as I push past Jules and stride into her lounge. 'Why didn't you tell me?'

'I don't know what you're talking about?' she says but, despite her protestations, she can't meet my eye.

'That night. In the bar. On the CCTV. There wasn't any Ewan at all, was there?'

Her eyes flicker to the ceiling, as though she might find the answer painted there against the awful swirls of Artex the previous occupant had left behind.

'I know Chrissy was fucking my husband.' The word is crude and sour on my tongue, but my smouldering anger is burning brighter and brighter. 'I know you recognised the face on the CCTV, so I'll ask you once again, Jules. Who was there that night? Who had so much to hide that they burned the bar down rather than risk the police viewing the footage?'

Jules sinks onto the sofa. 'You really don't remember anything, do you?'

I cross my arms. Waiting.

'I didn't want to hurt you.' Jules drops her head into her hands, fingertips pressing into her scalp.

'Tell me.'

'I'm so sorry, Ali.' Her voice is muffled but I can hear the regret. 'It was Matt.'

It's one of those moments you think you're prepared for. Expecting. Wanting. Longing for it to be over, almost – a dentist extracting a throbbing tooth – but on hearing Jules speak Matt's name aloud my stomach cramps, saliva flooding my mouth. I bolt out of the lounge, my feet pounding the stairs, towards the bathroom. As I round the corner, my left hand pulling on the bannister for traction, I hit something solid and heavy.

'Ali?' James says, steadying me by the shoulders as he comes out of his bedroom. 'Where's the fire?'

Flinching at his choice of words I shrug him off, squeeze past, my fingers stretching towards the bathroom door handle.

'What's wrong?' he asks again and the worry in his voice slows me.

'I know.' I turn to face him. 'I know *exactly* who my date was that night.'

He doesn't ask who it was. He doesn't ask how I found out. He doesn't ask any of the things I thought he might. Instead he says: 'Oh God. I hoped you'd never find out it was me.'

He plants his feet wider, blocking off my exit down the stairs and, although I can't read the expression on his face, I can read the clues that are now visible through his open door: the *Star Wars* poster on his bedroom wall. Ewan McGregor brandishing a lightsaber. The new green jacket he's only worn that once hanging on the front of the wardrobe door. The long black case propped up in the corner of the room that I'm guessing, if I were to check, would contain fishing rods.

Laughing. Dancing. Crying. Screaming. *I don't want to*.

Mouth agape I stare at James who is staring back at me. Waiting for my next move.

Just as I am waiting for his.

Chapter Forty-Three

James was my date that night. My head is spinning. Half-formed scraps of truth fluttering past my mind's eye before I can snatch them, but I know, even if I could catch my splintered memories, lay them out before me, there would still be missing pieces of the puzzle.

'I don't believe you,' I say, but, as I speak, I'm backing away, assessing my option, my escape, knowing it must be true.

'Ali, please.' His hand reaches towards me, and I take another step backwards, my heel hitting the skirting board. The door handle of the bathroom digging into my spine. Slowly I inch my hand behind my back, rooting around for the cool metal.

'I won't hurt you.' James inches closer. 'You don't need to lock yourself in there.'

'But you did hurt me.'

He leans in.

'Don't. Come. Any. Closer.' I spin and push open the door, but before I can step into safety, his hands are on my shoulders and I flash back to that night. The hands on my shoulders, shaking me hard. I scream and scream, and this time it is real and loud and deafening. My vision swimming in and out of focus. All the terror I felt that night comes gushing back, merging with the terror I feel right now. James's fingertips loosen their grip and are replaced with different hands. Soothing hands. The floral scent of Jules's perfume. Arms enveloping me. Stroking my hair.

'Shhh. It's okay,' whispers Jules. But it's not okay. It's not okay at all.

'It was him. James. That night. Not Ewan. James.' I am babbling.

'I know,' Jules says quietly, and I shove her away from me, her betrayal freezing the sweat that had pooled in my armpits, the small of my back. We stand in silence, the three of us who were once friends. My eyes search for something, anything, that will tell me I am not going mad, because – standing in front of James and Jules who not only look like strangers, but now feel like strangers – it's almost impossible to believe anything else in the world is as it should be. I settle on the moon, high and round, outside the landing window. The indigo sky peppered with stars. The glow of the orange lamp post.

'Before you do anything. Say anything. Please hear us out.'

Without looking at her I say 'Fine', and it's not because I want to hear anything they have to say, but because I know they won't let me leave until I do.

*

I am perched on the armchair nearest the front door. Holding a cushion on my lap as though it is a protective shield. My knees jiggle with nervous energy. I can't stop shaking. With fear. With shock. With the horrible realisation that I really can't trust anyone.

James sits furthest away from me, legs pressed together, arms wrapped around his middle, as though he is trying to make himself as small as possible. As though he too wishes he could disappear.

'You've five minutes before I call the police. Talk.' I mean my tone to sound firm and in control, but my voice cracks.

It is Jules who speaks first. 'James has been in love with you for such a long time. And when you split up with Matt and moved next door, he thought… Well he hoped eventually you might come to see him as more than a friend, but you never did.'

'I had no—'

'He wasn't brave enough to tell you directly.' Jules talks quickly. Urgently. Knowing I am judging each and every word. Searching for the lie. 'That night, with Chrissy, when she signed you up to the dating app, I texted James and told him your username and suggested he sign up too.'

'You were the one who took my phone.' I thought back. 'You sent the reply to him knowing who it was.'

'You *liked* him. Remember all those other messages that night? The cock shots? The demands for naked photos. You said James seemed kind, and I thought you might get to know a different side of him. Grow to like him. And you did.'

We shouldn't be out here. I want to go inside. I don't want to do this. Please don't make me.

'No.'

'Ali, you were always messaging each other.'

'I liked someone I thought was called Ewan. What's *kind* about deceiving me? Letting me think you were someone else?' I glare at James.

'He felt terrible. That's why he suggested a proper date that night. So you could see who you were talking to. You both had feelings for each other.'

'You were like a brother to me.'

'That was the problem.' James speaks for himself now. 'We'd fallen into the friendship zone. The games of Monopoly. The family Sunday lunches. I'd asked you along to gigs and you'd always said no.'

I had thought it was because James had a spare ticket but that's not important right now. I take a deep breath and stiffen my spine. Almost detach myself from my body for what I am about to ask.

'Did you drug and rape me, James?'

'No!' He springs to his feet, and I mirror his actions, still holding the cushion, poised to strike out, as though it contains steel and not feathers.

'But we had sex? I can't have been in any state to consent…'

'Ali, I didn't touch you. I swear. Nothing happened.'

Jules yanks his arm and he half falls back on the sofa, and as he raises his hands to rake them through his hair I can see them trembling. I sink back down onto the chair and cover my face with my palms. If I didn't have sex with James, who did I have sex with that night? Closing my eyes I recall the details of the tape. The grainy image. The man staring into the camera. My blonde hair cascading down my back, emerald dress rolled down to the waist.

No.

Agitation drives me to my feet.

'Ali?' Jules tentatively asks but I'm pacing the room, picturing getting ready that night.

'I love this one.' Chrissy had held my green dress up under her chin, smoothing the fabric with one hand. 'If you don't want to wear it tonight, can I borrow it again?'

She'd worn it the week before when I'd had a night shift at work.

'Don't believe everything you see.' Matt had said when we'd had breakfast together.

It was *him* in the tape. Him and Chrissy. What sort of a man would send his wife a video of him having sex with another woman?

The man who knew his wife would never recognise him. My fists furl and unfurl. You fucking. Fucking. Bastard.

Fury is keeping my tears at bay as I spin around to face James. 'Tell me *exactly* what you remember from that night and don't leave *anything* out,' I demand. As he falteringly begins to speak, I close my eyes, letting his words form pictures in my mind. My hazy recollection becoming clearer.

*

Sitting on one of the high stools near the cocktail sign that winked pink and blue, I shift my weight, trying not to slip off the faux leather seat as I scan the crowd. I'd told my date I would be wearing an emerald green dress but now, under lights that strobe green, it looks as though everyone is wearing the same colour. Nervously I fiddle with my straw, pulling it out of my mocktail before pushing it back in, sinking the shiny red half cherry bobbing on the surface. I take a sip of the fruit juice, wishing I wasn't driving: a vodka would calm the butterflies thronging around my belly. I still don't know how I feel about being on a date. Part of me thinks it's too soon. My separation with Matt still so raw.

'You *must* meet Ewan.' Chrissy and Jules had insisted whenever I had expressed my doubts. It was one of the first things they had ever agreed on. 'He makes you smile.'

And he did. The messages we exchanged became more and more frequent, my fingertips were flying over the keyboard, often for a whole evening, as our conversations flowed. Until eventually, tentatively, I had agreed we should meet.

Now, as I sit watching the bodies in the corner that writhe together to the music pulsing like a heartbeat, I wonder whether it is too intimate, almost, to come here. Almost like a proper date.

'Ali.' I pull my eyes away from the dance floor. James leans against the bar, trying to look relaxed but appearing stiff and uncomfortable in a green tweed jacket I've never seen before, more formal than anything the other men here are wearing. His aftershave overpowering – obviously out to impress.

'Hello.' I peer over his shoulder. 'I don't mean to be rude, but I'm waiting for someone.'

'Ewan,' he says.

'Jules told you?' I try to keep the hint of irritation from my voice, hating the thought I've been gossiped about. I really don't want Matt finding out until I am ready to tell him, if there is anything to tell.

'No. It's me. I mean.' He inhales sharply. 'I'm Ewan.' He stretches out his hand for me to shake. Instead I slide off the stool and pick up my clutch bag.

'I suppose you all think this is funny?' Humiliation burns hot behind my eyes.

'Wait.' He places his hand on my arm. 'It wasn't a joke. I… I like you, Ali. I wanted you to get to know me without thinking of me as Jules's younger cousin. Please stay.'

I hesitate. All I have to rush back home to is a lonely Saturday night in front of the TV. But this is *James*. It all feels so weird.

'One drink, Ali. A chance to explain?'

We are being jostled, a hen party coveting our place at the bar. Chrissy is nowhere to be seen.

'Five minutes.' I don't like being lied to. I'm not going to be a pushover.

We have sat side by side before hundreds of times. At his house. At mine. At the pub, where we always come last in the quiz despite Chrissy flirting with the barman for answers. But this time electricity crackles between us as I sit upright and awkward, flinching when our thighs inadvertently touch, our hands brushing together as we lean in to hear each other speak over the throbbing bass, his hand resting transiently on my knee as he listens. As the DJ seamlessly melds one song into another the conversation begins to flow and the tension between us dissipates. One drink leads to two, to three.

'I've a drinking problem,' James admits, and I am shocked until he quickly adds, 'I can't bend my elbow properly in this jacket', and feigns struggling to reach his mouth with his glass.

'It does look very… new.' I laugh.

'I bought it for tonight.'

Confused by the emotions I am feeling I leap to my feet. 'Another round?' He follows me to the bar.

*

'And I wasn't drinking alcohol,' I clarify with James now.

'No. You were driving.'

'And nobody spiked my drink?' What I'm really asking was, did he?

'No. We were having a really nice time.'

'Were? What happened?'

He speaks just one word. 'Chrissy.'

Chapter Forty-Four

After he says Chrissy's name neither James nor Jules can meet my eye.

'And then what?' I strain for some recollection, but I am firmly back in this room with its flat-screen TV, squashy leather sofa and an uncomfortable silence.

'I don't know. She was upset. You were upset. I couldn't hear above the music but you pushed her before you disappeared off together. You told me you'd see me later, but you never came back.' His voice is quiet as he says: 'I'll never forgive myself for not following you, for assuming you weren't interested in me after all and had gone home. I am so, so sorry.'

'But…' My fingertips flutter to the lump on my head, barely discernible anymore but there is still a tenderness when I press down. 'What happened to me?'

'Honestly, I don't know. I finished my drink and when you didn't return I came home. When Ben told us what happened I hated myself for not looking after you properly. Still do.'

'And you knew all of this?' I round on Jules not really needing an answer. I thought about the way they had both been so concerned, always asking if my memories were returning. Self-preservation, that's all it was, and this realisation brings a bitter taste to my mouth.

'Yes.'

'And you sabotaged my hypnotherapy so I didn't remember it was James that night?' I remember the way she insisted on staying in the room although Mr Henderson advised against it. How she shook me out of my trance when my clouded mind began to clear.

'You were distressed.' She catches my scornful gaze. 'And yes. I didn't want you remembering it was James you met that night. He didn't hurt you. He wouldn't. He couldn't. You know that, Ali, if you really think about it. You must believe he wouldn't hurt you.'

'I don't know what I believe. You've lied to me all along. It was James on the CCTV?'

'Yes.' Jules swallows hard.

'And you burned Prism down?' I'm focusing on her. Somehow I can't see James breaking the law, no matter what the circumstances, and as I think this I realise that there's some part of me, a large part, that does believe his story.

'No. That was nothing to do with us.'

'But you told me it was Matt on the CCTV? Another lie?' If we stacked them all together we could build a wall.

'It seemed easier to agree with you when you offered his name.'

'Because you know Chrissy and Matt are having an affair.' My heart is beating a tattoo.

There is gentleness in her voice when she speaks again.

'Yes. I'm so sorry. I know you're far from over him.'

'How long have you known?' Revelation after revelation punches me in the guts. It's like being part of *The Truman Show*. Everything I thought was real pulled away from me.

'I heard her on the phone the day before you went out. All sweet nothings and "we can't tell Ali".'

'Why didn't you tell me? You're *supposed* to be my friend.' I didn't think it was possible to feel any more betrayed by her, but I do. 'You've never really liked Chrissy. I thought you'd jump at the chance to ruin our friendship.'

'I was going to…' She falters. Chews her bottom lip. 'I don't know. My first instinct was to tell you, of course. But then.' She sighs so deeply her shoulders visibly slump. 'It wasn't about Chrissy or the way I feel about her, was it? It was about you, and I care about you, Ali. I know it may not feel that way right now, but I do. I remember what it felt like when you told me about Craig. How much it hurt. And I didn't know if I could… If I should do that to you. Sometimes, you know, I wish you hadn't told me. I wish I didn't know and I was still married.' Tears spill from her eyes and she wipes at them furiously with the back of her hand.

'The problem with knowing things, Ali, is that you can't *unknow* them, and however unfair it is there's a small piece of me, and honestly it's tiny now, but it's there and it blames you for it all, and I'm trying to get over it. I am getting over it. But I didn't know whether it was kinder not to tell you. You and Matt aren't together, and it's only natural he'll move on and the fact that it's with Chrissy… I didn't know if it was my place to tell you, and I was going to sleep on it, but then Saturday happened, and you've been through so much.'

'The police think I had something to do with Chrissy's disappearance. I've been questioned again today.'

'What? God, I'm so sorry.'

'I'll come with you to the station,' James says. 'Tell them everything. I'm sorry, Ali. I really am.'

'I need some time to process all of this.' I stand and to my relief they both remain seated. They are not going to stop me leaving. 'I'll be in touch.'

I am calm and measured as I walk to the front door, and it is only when I step outside and feel the cold biting at my cheeks that I raise my fingers to my skin and realise I am crying.

Although I believe James and Jules I cannot bear to be in such close proximity to them knowing they have deceived me. Flinging open drawers, I throw things into an overnight case, adding toiletries and stuffing the letter from Chrissy along with the photo of her and Matt into the zipped pocket in the lid, before heaping Branwell's bowls, food and his forlorn monkey, now missing an ear, into his basket. I text Iris to let her know I am on my way.

Warm honey light filters from the house onto the driveway, Iris silhouetted in the doorway, speaking on the phone. By the time I have released Branwell from his crate she is by my side.

'That was Ben.' She lifts Branwell's basket out of the boot. 'Sorry. Did you want to speak to him?' she adds as an afterthought.

'I'll call him tomorrow,' I say, although I can't believe I have any words left in me. I'm exhausted. It's an effort to move one foot in front of the other. I settle Branwell in the kitchen, where he sits, wagging his tail so hard as he stares up at the biscuit tin on the worktop, he slowly slides backwards on the tiled floor.

'I'll dump my stuff in my room,' I say to Iris knowing there's no point telling her not to give Branwell human titbits. That by the time I come back down he'll be licking his lips and have crumbs embedded in his furry beard.

I trudge upstairs, squeezing my bag past the stairlift, the constant reminder of Mum that none of us could bear to look at but somehow never got removed. It's almost as though we've stopped seeing it over the years.

If I had to pinpoint a time I knew she wasn't going to get better, it was when two men had arrived in dark blue overalls, carrying in tools and cardboard boxes, as we were leaving to go to school.

'What are they here for?' I asked Iris as I knelt by the front door, scratchy mat grazing my knees, tying Ben's laces in a double knot.

'They're to help your mum,' Iris said but her smile was slow and forced.

'To make Mummy better?' Ben's eyes were wide. 'So her legs work properly again and we can play in the garden.' He mimed kicking a football. 'Goal!' He punched air with his small fist. 'After school?'

'No silly.' Iris ruffled Ben's hair. 'She won't get better that quickly.'

'But soon?' Ben asked.

'Soon,' she said pulling him into her waist so she didn't have to look him in the eye. I was silent as the men unpeeled brown tape from the box labelled 'Stannah'. My heart sank.

I knew, from the internet, that things were getting very bad indeed.

Ben thought it was all incredibly cool when we got home from school that day and I suppose it must have seemed as though the house had been transformed into an indoor playground. He sat on the stairlift as it whirred, painfully slowly, up and down the stairs but he soon grew bored of that, choosing instead to swing from the hoists that hung above Mum's bed.

'Can I have this above my bed when you're better, Mum?'

'You can come and play whenever you want.' Mum spoke slowly. It was an effort for her to form her words, but she could speak, right up until the end, and not once did she ever say what was happening to her was unfair. Not once did I hear her complain, and as I pass her empty room, I think that if what is happening to me right now is the tiniest percentage of what she went through, then I don't really have the right to feel sorry for myself; but I do all the same.

As I settle into my room there's a part of me that wants to tell the police everything I have learned and inform them I believe Chrissy is hiding out at Matt's, but a quick Google search tells me that even if they go to Matt's tonight he doesn't have to grant them entry. Without a warrant they wouldn't be able to search his property, and why would he give them permission if I am right and Chrissy is hiding there? The photo I've got of the two of them and the letter won't count as enough evidence to request a warrant either and then where would I be? Matt and Chrissy would know I've uncovered their sordid secret, Chrissy could disappear again, and I'd be back to trying to clear my name; only this time it would be a million times harder.

I'm longing to confront them myself, but even with the element of surprise it would be two against one. I need her on her own. I need to know what happened to me that night after I left James. 'Softy, softly, catchee money,' I used to whisper as I tiptoed into Ben's room after covering my eyes and counting to one hundred. Even if Ben's giggle hadn't given his hiding place away I knew he'd always be under his bed.

I know where your hiding place is Chrissy and I'm coming for you.

Tomorrow. I can't wait until tomorrow.

I have a plan.

WEDNESDAY

Chapter Forty-Five

The first thing I do when I wake, when the sky has turned from black to grey but is not yet properly light, is to text Matt and ask him to come and walk Branwell at lunchtime. I tell him I am with Iris, and he asks why she can't walk him.

She's not well.

I text, and I don't think this is a lie. Although she insists she is fine – that brave face once more – she seems frailer than she used to. Breathless after walking up the stairs as she poked her head around the door to say 'night, night, sleep tight', and without Ben and Mum here there was only me to join in and say 'don't let the bedbugs bite', and our voices sounded too small.

He tells me he'll be around at twelve.

At eleven thirty I inform Iris that Matt will be here shortly but I've a check-up with Dr Saunders at the hospital, so could she give Branwell to Matt. I loathe to think of him touching Branwell's silky soft fur with hands that have touched Chrissy, but I've little choice if I want to be certain he's out of the way.

I drive the long way around to my old address, not wanting to risk passing him in his car. I park in the next street, so

I don't alert Chrissy to my presence. I want to deprive her of any chance to prepare herself, hide or run away, before I am in the house, standing face to face, asking not why she's tried to ruin my life – I already know why – but needing to know whether any part of our relationship was genuine. The evenings sipping wine and binging on the box set of *Friends*. The nights out, picking at bowls of tortillas, topping up glasses from a pitcher, analysing our past relationships. What was right? What went wrong? At least I know now what went wrong with Matt. *Chrissy* did. With Iris and Ben the only relatives present in my life, my friends were like my family. Looking back is like straining to focus through voile. I'm not quite sure what I'm seeing was real. Jules. James. Chrissy. Matt. It had all felt so genuine at the time, the people I loved who I thought loved me too. Never before have I felt as small and insignificant as I do right now.

Memories crowd as I approach the house that was once my home. The winter-drab borders I dug that will soon be sprinkled with snowdrops and bluebells. Matt hanging the thick bedroom curtains that trail the carpet making the room appear far more opulent than it actually is. Running to the chip shop on the corner as the smell of freshly fried fish drifted through the open window in the summer. Sitting on the swing seat in the garden, eating chips straight out the bag, licking vinegary fingertips. Salt on my tongue. Later, the taste of Matt as we made love under the apple tree at the bottom of the lawn, out of sight of Mr Henderson.

Mr Henderson is by the window in his lounge and he waves as I pass by. He's wearing a tie, so he must be waiting for a client. It's unfortunate he's spotted me, but Matt will know I've been here soon enough. I summon a weak smile and look away quickly. Does he know Matt has moved on with someone new? All the times I asked Matt if he was seeing someone and he denied it, making me feel I was the one with the problem. Once, I thought there was nothing as painful, as corrosive, as suspicion, but now I know that's not true. Cold hard facts are twice as damaging and harder to ignore.

Chrissy.

Her betrayal shouldn't hurt as much as Matt's, but they are tangled together and impossible to separate. The pain is physical; I wrap my arms around my middle as though soothing a stomach ache. My head throbs with the effort of not crying as I fish the door key from my pocket where it had slipped under my mobile phone. No matter what happens inside I'm going to take a photo of Chrissy. Proof of life.

Something is different. At first I can't quite put my finger on it, and I don't think it's the fact the bedroom curtains are still closed. The door is still glossy black. The stainless steel number thirteen screwed to the brickwork. Unlucky for some. Unlucky for me. Something is prickling at me, but I tell myself it's just because I feel uncomfortable – though I shouldn't. The house is still half mine. I've every right to be here. Glancing over my shoulder, as though I am doing something wrong, I poke the key towards the lock.

It won't go in. I try again, thinking it's because my hand is trembling, but then I realise.

The lock is shiny and new, rendering the key in my hand useless.

Keeping me out.
Or keeping someone else in.
Involuntarily, I shiver.
A sense of someone watching me.
Movement.
Footsteps.
A voice whispering my name.

Chapter Forty-Six

'Ali.' Mr Henderson says gently again as I spin around on the step to face him. 'I didn't want to startle you. Is everything okay? You're really pale. Where's your car?'

'It's…' I gesture vaguely with my hand down the street. 'Matt's changed the locks.'

'Yes. He said he bent the key. Did you need something? He's gone out. I'm not sure when he'll be back.'

'I can't wait. I've a hospital appointment. I wanted to pick up my passport. I'm thinking of booking a holiday and I'm not sure how long it's valid for.' I keep my voice low, all the time glancing at the windows for signs of movement.

'Oh, I am pleased. A break will do you the world of good. I've been so worried about you.'

'Thanks.' As we speak I'm inching close to the gate. 'I must go anyway.' I turn, hiding my face before he can see how quickly my smile slips away. I'm just stepping out of the garden when he calls: 'He left a spare key with me. If it's important you get in now?'

'That would be great, thanks.' I don't hesitate for a second. 'It is important. You could say it's life and death,' I say as quietly as I can.

And this time when I flash him a smile, it's genuine.

*

Inside, I leave my shoes on the doormat; only this time it's not fear of traipsing mud through the house, it's fear of being heard. The house smells different somehow. Stale. Unhappy or perhaps it is only me who is unhappy. Still, it is nothing like the freshness of Chrissy's house and I feel slightly relieved she hasn't yet put her stamp on the home I still think of as mine. I had only been living with her for two days when I had arrived home after walking Branwell on the beach, his shaggy fur sea-salt damp. Chrissy had cracked open windows and I had realised just how foul the stench of wet dog must be when you're not used to pets. The next day there were plug-in air fresheners in every socket, hissing out vanilla at regular intervals, but still she'd have to cover her nose with her sleeve as Branwell fired off one of his after dinner farts – 'typical man' – and at the time I thought how intrusive it must be for her sharing her space, oblivious to the fact she was planning on taking mine.

The lounge is to my left. I push open the door, my heart leaping into my mouth when it momentarily sticks, and instantly I think Chrissy is pushing it from the other side, but it is only the thick pile catching. The brown we'd chosen to mask grubby paw prints and hide the stains we hoped our future children would inadvertently leave. The clock above the fireplace fills the silence with its ticking, and it's funny but, while I lived here, I never noticed it making a noise before. The black glossy coffee table we'd chosen from Ikea is covered in a thick layer of neglect, as though this room is unused. No tracks in the dust where Matt rests his feet as he slumps on the sofa after dinner; I'd have been snuggled against him once. I wonder whether they spend all their time in bed.

We've never been big on possessions, Matt caring more about gadgets than cushions and me still having my dad's arrest intertwined with my desire for wanting material things, but a quick scan of the room tells me a few items are missing. The photo of us in a solid silver frame, holding an eight-week-old Branwell up to the camera like a trophy, has gone, and I suppose it's only natural Matt is removing traces of the wife he no longer wants, but it still hurts nonetheless.

Back out into the hallway, I bypass the toilet and head into the kitchen. The hooks which suspended the cast iron pans over the hob are empty. As is the cabinet that housed our honeymoon green glasses. The work surfaces are tidy. Ordered. Not like Matt at all. Usually his idea of clearing up is to stack things on the work surface above the dishwasher hoping someone else – me – will take care of it. That's not entirely fair though. Often we've stood side by side, chopping, stir-frying, chatting about our days.

Focus.

Where is Chrissy?

I open cupboards, as though she might spring out, but it's an avoidance tactic. The bedroom curtains have remained closed for a reason. Hiding someone who doesn't want to be seen.

Common sense tells me to leave the house. The lengths Matt and Chrissy have gone to make them unpredictable. Dangerous. The bruises on my arm. The lump on my head. Who knows how far they will go? But even as I head towards the front door I remember that airless room in the station, the whirring of the tape recording my answers to PC Hunter's barking questions, and I know that I cannot leave. My foot rests on the bottom stair, my fingers grip the bannister. I begin to climb, treading lightly. Every creak of floorboard is magnified in the silence. I wait for the bedroom door to squeak open. For Chrissy to hurl herself towards me, but there's nothing.

To my surprise, our wedding photos still line the landing. We're signing the register. Cutting the cake, the icing version of us balanced precariously on top, meringue dress and wonky top hat. I allow myself a moment of missing him. Once, we had something solid, something good. It was as though we melded into something new when we were together. Something better.

There's a candid shot of Matt whispering in my ear. I'm throwing my head back in laughter. I wish I could remember what he said. Something rude most likely. My hair, shimmering blonde under the bright summer sun, is sprinkled with confetti. Blonde like Chrissy. At least he has a type. The sight of the yellow roses in my bouquet eradicates my sentimentality entirely. *Enjoy the date bitch.* Matt must have purposefully chosen a card adorned with yellow roses to go with the flowers he left on my doorstep. I should have figured it all out sooner.

Angry now, I take the last three strides to the bedroom and press my cheek to the door, imagining Chrissy doing the same on the other side. There's no sound of movement, of breathing. All I can hear is a whooshing noise, the same as I did on our honeymoon when Matt held a conch shell up to my ear, waves roaring, hot sand burning the soles of my feet.

I grip the handle, my palm slick with sweat. Slowly I push the door.

I can't help crying out when I see what is inside.

Chapter Forty-Seven

Our bedroom. It's almost incomprehensible that once this was the place I thought I was safe. This was the place I thought I was loved. It's a mess. The floor littered with moving boxes. I yank open the curtains. Dust motes spin as though happy to see daylight.

What is going on?

'Having a clear out,' Matt had said when he offered me the green glasses, but this is more than a clear out. The boxes are crammed with his clothes. The contents of the loft. Our spindly Christmas tree we vowed to replace each year in the sales as we wrapped tinsel around its threadbare branches, but never did. The string of pumpkin lights we'd hang outside the porch on Halloween.

He's moving. Leaving. My heart cracks that little bit more as I rifle through the rest of the boxes, seeing what he is taking, what he has discarded in the way he discarded me. Is that their plan, to frame me for a murder I didn't commit and run away? Move abroad? The thought of Chrissy causes me to look around the room. Where is she hiding? Every sense is on high alert.

The roar of a motorbike revving in the street outside sounds like it's next to me. I take a step towards our floor-to-ceiling built-in wardrobes, picturing Chrissy hiding behind the door with a knife, a gun. My imagination gallops, until

I convince myself this piece of MDF painted glossy white is all that separates me and imminent death. Despite this I take another step, until I'm touching the handle, filling my air with lungs before flinging open the door. There is nothing but space. Empty wire hangers dangling from the rail.

A quick check of my watch tells me I haven't got much time left before Matt comes home. He never walks Branwell for longer than thirty minutes in the rain and I've already been here for forty-five. I hurry to the spare room we'd once earmarked for a nursery. A single airbed and a sleeping bag are on the floor. A pillow still indented with the shape of a head. Who is sleeping here? Why would Chrissy not be sharing his bed? Where is she? I'd been so certain she'd be here, but I've searched everywhere.

And then I hear a noise from downstairs and remember I haven't. I didn't look in the toilet.

Every shift of the stairs beneath my feet, every creak is deafening, even above the sound of my heart punching against my ribs. Sweat is beading on my brow as I press my ear against the cloakroom door.

Silence.

In my head I count to three before I throw the door wide, jumping back, hands raised to protect myself.

There is nobody there.

Leaning against the wall, body weak with relief, I notice that the postman has dropped the mail through the letterbox and that would account for the noise. Automatically I crouch and scoop up the envelopes, shuffling through the letters. It's mainly junk: a flyer for the new Indian that delivers, a voucher offering twenty per cent off vertical blinds, an A5 sheet advertising guttering clearing and a couple of what looks like marketing mailshots for Matt. In the kitchen I drop them on top of the paperwork that is always heaped next to the toaster.

I can't help noticing that Matt hasn't opened the post for ages, and I start to rifle through the pile to see if there's anything for me he hasn't passed on. Among the thin brown envelopes is a thick cream one stamped 'Markstone Insurance'. It's not a company I'm familiar with and I can't help holding it to the light to see what's inside. Nothing is visible. Curiosity overcomes me and gently I lift the flap of the envelope. Once open I pull out the letter and document inside and begin to read. The words spring at me from the page. I sit heavily on a stool, feeling as though all the air has been knocked out of me. I screw up my eyes, taking three deep breaths before I read again, as though that somehow can have made a difference. As though the letter will now say something entirely different. It doesn't.

Four months ago, despite our separation or perhaps because of it, Matt had taken out a joint life insurance policy on us both. He must have forged my signature. If I die Matt stands to inherit a million pounds. The floor rushes towards me and I put my head between my knees, swallowing the bile that has risen in my throat.

My thoughts rage. Despite the letter I am holding in my hand I find it unfathomable Matt would ever hurt me. My disbelief is fuelled by denial but it's all interwoven with strands of doubt despite him being the one who pushed me away, refused to see a counsellor, packed our marriage in a storage box, tightly nailing on the lid. I scan through the policy in my hand. One million. Enough for a brand new life.

For two.

Was I meant to die that night and when I didn't they thought they'd torment me, send me the antidepressants hoping I'd finish the job myself?

The sound of an engine outside pulls me to my feet. The slamming of a car door. Without waiting to see if it's Matt I slide open the patio doors before running across the rain-damp lawn, my socks sodden. I slip out of the back gate. I can't see him. The man who vowed to honour and protect me. Now a stranger who has put a value on the wife he no longer loves.

I'm still holding the letter in my hands. I won't let him get away with it. I won't.

But he'll know as he pushes open the front door. Stumbles over my shoes on the doormat. He'll know I was there.

Frightened I throw a glance over my shoulder, as my wet feet slap against concrete sending shockwaves of pain shooting through my shins, almost expecting him to be right behind me.

Tick tock.

I'm running out of time.

Chapter Forty-Eight

*Now I have a plan, as I know you will have too. I know you
so well, Ali. You're predictable. You're selfish.*

You're a liar.

I'll almost be sorry to come to the end.

Almost.

Despite everything, I'll miss you.

Chapter Forty-Nine

Visibility is poor as I speed towards the police station, my wipers swish-swish-swishing against the lashing rain. The life insurance policy flutters from the passenger seat to the floor as I tear around a corner, and as I lean to pick it up my car drifts. There's a sharp blast of a horn, and I look up just in time to straighten the wheel, missing the approaching car by millimetres.

Calm.

A speed camera flashes as I pass it in a blur, but I don't care. My mind is racing too, trying to second-guess Matt's next move. Will he come after me? Run? I can't let him disappear along with Chrissy, for if they vanish, I know the cloud of suspicion hanging over me never will. The car park is almost full. I slot in-between a police car and a black Fiesta, its wing scraped white but, as I step out of the car into a freezing puddle, I hesitate. Is the insurance policy enough? Will PC Hunter take me seriously running in without shoes with this one solitary piece of evidence to clear my name. I think of his abruptness. His sarcasm. There's nothing in this envelope linking Matt to Chrissy. 'Circumstantial' I think he'd say, and yes, I did learn that from the TV. My spirits lift as I remember the photo of Chrissy and Matt in my case at Iris's. The letter she had written him. The phone call Jules overheard.

Surely that will be enough.

It has to be.

Yanking my seatbelt across my body, as my foot squeezes the accelerator, I watch the station shrink in my rear-view mirror and promise I'll be back soon.

*

I'm barely aware of where I am until I reach Iris's, where the sight of Matt's car parked in the driveway causes coldness to drip through me like the teeming rain streaming from the guttering.

He's still here. Why?

There's nowhere to park on the road unless I block the driveway and it occurs to me this is exactly what I should do. I can call the police and Matt won't be able to leave. Once I show them the photo, the letter and the insurance policy and have explained exactly what's going on they'll have no choice but to take him in for questioning. This whole nightmare will be over.

But my desire to call the police is overridden by the desire to check Iris and Branwell are okay. I've no idea what Matt is capable of.

Enjoy the date, bitch?

It must have created the perfect opportunity for him when I agreed to meet the man I thought was Ewan.

The house is quiet as I push open the front door. Too quiet. I pull out my mobile phone and as I call 'Hello?' I'm scrolling through the recent calls list. Near the top is an incoming number I don't recognise: it must be the direct line for PC Willis when she phoned to ask me to go into the station.

'Iris?' I shout again. Silence wraps itself around me, suffocating the tiny spark of hope I'd been holding onto that

Matt would be sat at the kitchen table, being plied with tea and custard creams, with no idea I'm aware of what he's done.

Swallowing hard I begin to edge down the hallway. My socks imprinting damp footprints on the oak floor.

There is no bubbling of the kettle, no muted tones of the radio that's always kept on low 'for company', no conversation, no scrambling of paws tearing down the hallway to greet me.

My whole body tingles with an overwhelming urge to run. To get out of this house, where again, a sense of tragedy has settled into the atmosphere, but I can't. I can't run. I can't leave.

The kitchen is empty. Two mugs sit on the table, both half-full. One of the wooden chairs is upended, its spindle back snapped.

A sense of foreboding builds, a pressure in my head as though someone is inflating a balloon.

My thumb presses dial. I lift the mobile to my ear, waiting for PC Willis to answer, as I creep out of the kitchen and towards the lounge, and that's where I see them, poking out from behind the sofa.

Feet.

Iris's beige moccasined feet.

She's lying on the floor, eyes closed, an odd hue to her skin. I think she's dead.

My head starts to spin and as I stumble backwards I notice the message written on the mirror in the orange lipstick she's worn since the 1970s.

You're next

Chapter Fifty

I'm whimpering as I back out of the room, phone clamped to my ear, willing PC Willis to answer. A muffled sound, like somebody trying to hum, draws my attention to the corner of the room.

Ben.

I hadn't seen his car as I'd arrived but then I hadn't been looking for it, lost to my own thoughts.

He's slumped onto the floor, wrists and ankles bound, tie skewed, suit crumpled. The frames of his glasses are bent. There's a strip of what looks like Iris's tea towel tied around his mouth, blood trickling from the corner of his lips.

'Oh God. Oh Ben.'

He makes an urgent, indecipherable noise as I rush towards him, gesturing wildly with his head but I can't tear my eyes away from him, until a shadow shifts in the corner, stopping me in my tracks.

Matt is standing silent. Still. The hate emanating from him is as thick as the fear coming from Ben.

In that split second, I notice everything: the whites of Ben's bulging eyes as he struggles to free his wrists, the stainless steel bread knife clamped in Matt's hand. But it's the scarf looped around his neck that causes my simmering rage to erupt. I bought him that scarf last Christmas thinking the blue would match his eyes that now stare at me with venom.

Until death do us part.

Just as I'm about to spring forward I hear someone say: 'Hello? Hello?'

Thank God. PC Willis's voice drifts from the phone I am still clasping in my hand.

There's a fraction of a second where Matt's eyes flicker from my phone to my face before he leaps forward. I scream.

Instantly, there is a frantic barking from the garden. I think I can reach the back door to let Branwell in. He may be small but he'd never let anyone hurt me. I spin, launching myself towards the door. Matt's fingers grip my shoulder. I turn and kick him as hard as I can in the groin. He crumples to the floor, and I gabble into the handset.

'PC Willis. This is Ali Taylor. My husband. Matt. He's killed my aunt. Hurt my brother. He's trying to kill me. He's going to kill us both.'

'Alison. Where are you?'

Matt is kneeling now, fumbling for the knife that had slipped from his fingers as he fell.

'Iris's: 212 Station Road. Matt's been seeing Chrissy. She's not missing. Oh God.' I edge into the dimness of the hallway as Matt staggers to his feet.

'Ali. Are you safe?'

'No.'

Matt looms towards me.

I'm not safe at all.

'My husband is going to kill me.' I speak slower now. There's an inevitability about it all.

'The police won't be long. Can you get to a room with a lock?'

'It's too late,' I whisper, as Matt prises the phone from my fingertips and smashes the handset against my head.

Blackness.

It's too late.

Chapter Fifty-One

Everything is fragmented. Indiscernible. Vaguely I am aware of being lifted. Cold air. Branches tugging at my hair. Being carried through the back garden. The thrumming of an engine. The creaking of the gate. Lying down somewhere warm and soft. Drifting-drifting-drifting. Blackness once more.

We're moving. My head throbbing. Lulled by the vibrations.

Safe inside the car.

Strapped in next to Dad. Driving to the corner shop. A block of Neapolitan ice cream from the freezer for Sunday tea. Swapping my strawberry for Ben's chocolate.

Sleep.

There's a whooshing sound in my ears as my senses reawaken with a roar. At first I think it's my own flow of blood I hear, my pulse beating rapid and light in my wrist, but then I realise it is the sea. The ground I am lying on is hard and damp, my teeth chattering. Above me I see exposed beams knotted with woodworm. Grey stone walls.

Dark things happen on dark nights.

I realise the photograph on my Instagram page was taken here, the place Matt knew I loved. I'd shared my memories of childhood picnics with Ben and Mum before she got sick. The place where he had proposed.

Rope bites into my wrists as I push myself to sitting. There's a tugging at my ankles, Matt is tying my feet.

'You bastard.' I kick once. Twice. My heel connecting with the soft flesh of his belly.

He slaps me hard. The metallic taste of blood coats my mouth, and I glare at him wondering what road we had taken since we had made our vows that could possibly have led to this. Had I really been such a bad wife?

He pushes his face towards mine, eyes burning into me – and suddenly I know.

I haven't been a bad wife at all. This is not my husband. 'Ben?'

The man so close I can feel his breath is wearing Matt's clothes. Matt's scarf. But the smell is distinctly my brother.

In the corner, the man I thought was Ben is frantically nodding his head. The wire-rimmed glasses that don't fit him properly sliding down his face. As well as feeling scared and angry, I also feel worthless and small. How easy Ben must have thought it would be to fool me with my prosopagnosia, and how right. Ben and Matt have similar hairstyles, short and dark, and when I'd seen Matt tied up wearing Ben's suit and glasses it never for a second crossed my mind to look a little closer.

Don't believe everything you see.

Although I cannot trust what is before my eyes, we all have a unique smell that's almost impossible to replicate. And suddenly I realise exactly what this is about. It has been Ben all along. Taunting me. Scaring me. 'Murderer' painted on my door. Antidepressants in case I couldn't live with what I'd done. Now it all makes perfect, perfect sense.

'Ben.' I'm firmer this time. 'I know it's you.'

He opens his mouth in a gasp and I smell it again, the menthol cigarettes he always smokes when he is stressed, and there is nothing more stressful than killing.

I should know.

Chapter Fifty-Two

I had stayed up late revising for my GCSE mocks, it must have been about eleven thirty before I'd fallen into a troubled sleep. My eyes sprang open at midnight, and I wasn't sure what had woken me at first. I sat up in bed and rubbed the blur from my eyes. Moonlight filtered through the gap in my curtains, the wardrobe shadowed on my ceiling, and that was nothing out of the ordinary, though that night the shadows looked darker. Menacing somehow. Almost reluctantly I swung my legs out of bed, a sixth sense telling me something was very, very wrong. It's the small details I remember now. The fabric of my towelling dressing gown against my goosebumps. The fur of my slippers warming the soles of my feet. The squeaking hinge of my bedroom door as I eased it open, half-hoping it was just Ben that had woken me, but somehow knowing it wasn't. There was still a lingering smell of the sausages we'd eaten for dinner but now these felt heavy and greasy in my stomach.

Ben's door was ajar and in the soft tangerine glow of his nightlight I could see his small body tucked up in his bed. Ollie the Owl had slipped onto the floor; despite having just turned nine, Ben still slept with him. I was about to pick it up, rest it back on his pillow, when I heard it. A noise. A whispering, growing louder and rising in pitch.

I kept my steps long and tiptoe light as I crept towards Mum's room. The door was tightly shut. I pressed my ear against the wood and listened.

There was the sound of muffled sobbing and, at first, I thought it was Mum. My fingertips brushed the handle as I deliberated whether I should go and comfort her, when she spoke and I knew it wasn't her crying. I knew she wasn't alone.

'You have to, Iris.' Mum's voice was thick. Slow.

More and more she'd been having difficulty swallowing, speaking. The muscles of her throat and jaw growing weaker. 'Sometimes the voice can be the first thing to go.' The doctor hadn't looked up as the nib of his fountain pen scratched on Mum's notes. 'You're lucky.' He had said without irony as though Mum should be thankful she could no longer use her left arm, barely use her right. Her legs were too weak to support her. The softness in her tone that used to soothe me back to sleep had long since disappeared.

The crying grew louder.

'I know it's hard. But…'

'Hard?' Iris's voice was scathing. 'You're asking the impossible.'

'But you promised.'

'You can't hold me to that. Remember my first job when I got fired for kissing the assistant manager in the stationery cupboard and you said you wouldn't tell Mum but…'

I pulled a face. I couldn't imagine Iris ever kissing anyone. Mum bit back chasing the image away.

'You can't possibly compare—'

'I know.'

A silence. I held my breath, angled my feet towards my bedroom so I could bolt if Iris came out, but the sound of crying drifted through the door once more.

'I love you,' Iris said. 'And if there's the slightest chance…'

'There isn't,' Mum said. Her tone strengthened by the finality in her words. 'You know there isn't. You've been giving the kids false hope. Clinging on to—'

'False hope is better than no hope.' Iris's words catch in her throat.

'But you know.' Mum's voice is pleading but clearer than I've heard it for months. 'You know.'

There's silence again. I shiver, drawing the belt of my dressing gown tighter.

'I need you. Please. You have to say yes.'

There's a pang in my chest at the sound of Mum begging.

'I'm here, aren't I? I'm looking after the kids. The house. You. I'm doing the best I can.'

'I know you are but it's only going to get harder.'

'You're my *sister*.'

'That's precisely why I'm counting on you. I'd do it for you if the roles were reversed.'

'But Ali. Ben. He's so small.'

'It's *for* the kids. I've already lived longer than they thought I might. I'm going downhill quickly. Do you want them to suffer too? Without Justin, you're all they've got, Iris. Please.'

There's a beat. Two. Mum crying. 'I *can't*,' Iris said. 'I just can't.'

Footsteps thudded towards the door and I darted into the shadows, scooching down by the side of the bookcase. Iris pounded down the stairs. There was the chinking of keys, the slamming of the front door, the firing of a car engine and then nothing but an animalistic whimpering that cut me to the very core.

I was tempted to scurry back to bed, give Mum her privacy, but the sound drew me to her side and, skirting around her wheelchair, I slid into bed beside her, put my arm around her shoulders, and let her sorrow soak my dressing gown. My own cheeks were wet too.

My arm tingled pins and needles by the time Mum lifted her head and her bloodshot eyes met mine.

'Sorry,' she said and there was the familiar slur to her speech as though her conversation with Iris had taken everything from her.

'What's going on, Mum?' Apprehension prickled like the sting from the nettles that grew wild at the bottom of the garden.

'I remember so clearly the day you were born,' she said painfully slowly, a faraway look on her face. 'I was in labour for seventy-two hours and the contractions were unimaginable, almost unbearable but throughout it all your dad kept squeezing my hand, telling me to hang on, reminding me that eventually the pain would end and we'd have something wonderful. You.' Her eyes misted again. 'It was worth it. Every single second. As soon as I saw your face I knew I'd go through it all again in a heartbeat.'

She swallowed hard. I remained silent not wanting my voice to jar her out of the memory she was enveloped in. She so rarely spoke of Dad.

'I love you, Ali. Please know that but...' She shook her head.

'What, Mum?' She was scaring me.

'But this. It's unimaginable, unbearable and there's no one to tell me to hang on.'

'I'll tell you to hang on. So will Ben. Iris.' I rummaged around in my mind for other names to pluck out, friends, neighbours, but it had dawned on me that over the past three years everyone had drifted away and I wasn't sure whether it had been what happened with Dad before, or what was happening with Mum then. Sadness washed over me. Mum was always so social. I thought of the times lately I'd raced upstairs to do my homework, shouting a hello as I passed by her door. Calling 'see you later' whenever I went out as though that was enough. Failure overwhelmed me. I'd let her down.

'I'm sorry, Mum.' Desperately so. 'I'll spend more time with you.'

'I could have a million days with you and Ben, Ali. Live to be a thousand and it would still never be enough, but…' She was hard to understand then. Exhaustion paled her face, deepened the grooves that ran from the corners of her mouth to her chin. 'I'll have to leave you some time. It's the natural order of things.'

'But not yet. The doctor said…'

'I'm not going to get better, Ali,' she said flatly. 'However positive Iris tries to stay, whatever she tells you and Ben, I'm not going to get better. Two to five years the experts said, and it's already been three.'

'I know but…' I trailed off. I wanted to say 'but I want you to get better' as if that could possibly make a difference. Unlike Ben I was old enough to understand. I'd googled. Read the statistics. Mum was going to deteriorate further before she died. It didn't bear thinking about.

'Is it awful?' I'd never asked her before, as though, if she didn't say it out loud she couldn't be suffering. But she was.

'Yes,' she said simply and there was none of the self-pity that would have come if it were me or Ben answering the questions, and I felt a stab of shame at the fuss we both made when we had chickenpox. 'My muscles cramp, there's spasticity in my hands, my joints ache. I've sores where I'm stuck in one position unless someone helps me move. I'm helpless. Reliant on Iris to do everything for me.'

'I'll help more.' I'd always known it must be awful for Mum being so dependent, but I'd only ever considered the lack of mobility. Her frustration with not being able to do things for herself. I'd never really thought about the physical pain she must be in and I felt horrible. 'It must be difficult when you can't move around.'

'It's not just that.' It was an effort for her to force her words out. 'My speech is going. I'm lucky it's lasted so long. Soon I won't be able to communicate with you all.'

'But you will. On the last home visit we were told about the apps, remember? There's options.'

'Like the feeding tube when I can no longer swallow? As it is I can only eat soft things. What kind of life is it to not be able to move, speak, eat? It's been three years since my diagnosis, I'm luckier than most but I'm tired, Ali.'

'Sorry. It's late.' I shifted my weight ready to leave, let her sleep.

'Not that sort of tired,' she said. 'I've been stockpiling sleeping tablets.'

'Do you want one?' That was something practical I could do for her.

'Iris was going to help me take them. *All* of them.'

There was a silence as I turned her words over as though they were written on paper, and it was a gradual unfolding, and even now I don't know whether I didn't understand or whether I didn't want to understand. I covered my mouth with my hands, as though I was the one who had spoken, as I stared at her in shock as though she had betrayed me, and it almost felt as though she had.

'You can't leave us.'

'I will be soon anyway and how long do I wait? Until I can't tell you what I want. I can't bear it anymore, Ali. I want to slip away with what dignity I have left. But Iris. She... she...'

'Shhh.' I held Mum in my arms, her cheek resting against mine, breathing in the rose-scented face cream Iris massaged into her face twice a day. My mind whirred as panic built while I tried desperately to think of ways to help her, but I returned time and time again to the sleeping tablets. I pushed the thought away once more, my skin becoming slick with sweat at the prospect of being without her, as memories gathered and retreated.

Mum outside on a winter-dark morning, hands stinging and raw as she scrubbed at the graffiti sprayed on our garage. Mum shielding me from the baying reporters who pushed and shoved as she took me to school each day during the trial. *Eastenders*, hot chocolate and custard creams. Movie evenings when we could no longer afford cinema trips, curtains drawn, popcorn in bowls, me and Ben lining up at the lounge door as she took the tickets she'd made. So many memories but they all dipped and weaved, carving their own path in my mind, always, always leading to the same conclusion. Mum loved me. And my stomach whirred like the Catherine Wheel Dad had nailed to the fence all those years ago as Mum heaped beans onto jacket potatoes, hot chocolate simmering in the pan while fireworks whizzed and popped.

'You can't just give up.' On us, I wanted to add, but I knew that wasn't fair.

'This isn't something I'm taking lightly, Ali. Leaving you and Ben. I've been mulling it over for the past year. Me and Iris have talked about it tirelessly. I love you and Ben more than anything, you know that, but I want you both to remember me being able to tell you I love you. As the person I was, not the person I'm becoming. Dad's in prison and yet he has more freedom than me.'

She closed her eyes and I had lain back, head sharing her pillow, staring up at the hoist hanging from the ceiling, and I was furious with God, with the universe, with everyone. Furious but certain.

'Are you sure?' I asked. Her eyes met mine and I saw pain and regret but the overriding emotion was a flash of relief. She nodded, her eyes flickering to her bedside cabinet.

'It will be classed as an expected death,' she'd whispered. 'My GP can come and sign the death certificate tomorrow. As I only saw him last week, legally there isn't a need for a post-mortem. No one will ever know.'

Hearing the research Mum had clearly done, the thought she had given to what will happen after, made up my mind. Wordlessly, I pulled open her drawer. My hands were shaking so violently I could barely open the bottles. I tipped the white pills that looked so innocent onto the duvet and snapped each one into four. Mum could no longer swallow them whole. I cradled her head as she forced them down with the warm water that was stale with dust and bubbles – but if I'd gone to fetch her a fresh glass I'd have followed Iris. Run away. Like a coward.

When the tablets were gone we locked eyes.

'Ali,' she said, and I lifted her hand, pressing her palm to my cheek. 'Sarah.' And it had been so long since I had heard my real name I dissolved into tears.

'Don't cry, sweet girl. It's not your fault. None of this is your fault.' I didn't believe her. I thought back to the hours I'd spent hunched over my laptop, pouring over Google, reading page after page of research into MND. The theories stating damaging genetics and environmental factors, including stress, could play a part in the onset. It all circled back to me. Dad stealing to pay for my birthday presents, me letting the police in. However much my heart felt like it was being torn in two this was the least I could do for Mum. I owed her.

'Talk to me,' she murmured and there were so many words I wanted to say but this was the last thing I could do for her, so I said what I had always said in the small, lonely hours as I held Ben and he'd drifted back to sleep. 'The owl and the pussy-cat went to sea…' But my whole body was shaking with shock as the enormity of what I'd done hit me time and time again. I kept losing my thread, starting the verse again, while Mum lay beside me, but like one of Dad's scratched vinyls I kept getting stuck. Then, I don't know when exactly, her muscles were no longer twitching. Her breath no longer rasping.

Dawn finally broke. The sun streaking the sky red – the colour of my shame. Ben would be awake soon and I slid slowly off the bed, noticing the yellowing stain of egg yolk

on Mum's nightie, her slippers half-tucked under the divan,
the grey hair clogging her brush on the bedside table.

*

Everything has stayed with me from that night. The big
details and the small. The whole tortuous mess.

Oh how I long to forget – to forget who I am. What I've
done. But how can I? I cried for me and for her as I kissed
her on lips that would never smile again. Tears blocked my
throat as I wished her good night. I never once thought of
Ben. He's right. I'm a murderer and I deserve to be punished.
I think I always knew I would be. Craved it, almost.

But still, in spite of everything I have to feel guilty about,
it's the fact I didn't finish the poem that endlessly rises again
and again. In my head it's always there, spinning around, as
though saying the words might have made a difference to
her. As though it might have made things easier.

> *And hand in hand, on the edge of the sand,*
> *They danced by the light of the moon,*
> *The moon,*
> *The moon,*
> *They danced by the light of the moon.*

Chapter Fifty-Three

Realising that Ben has been behind everything, and why, is like uncorking a bottle. My memories from that night begin to flow freely. The queue at the bar was thinning as I waved my twenty at the barman before taking a sideward glance at James. James! Who'd have thought we'd be having such a good time? I was still hovering between anger that he'd deliberately tricked me into a date, and gratitude that he had, knowing I'd never have agreed otherwise and underneath the myriad emotions writhing for attention was a sense that, perhaps, this could be the start of something.

'Chrissy's coming over,' he shouted in my ear above the throbbing beat. 'She doesn't look happy.'

'Ali?' I had turned as Chrissy tugged my arm. 'I need to talk to you.'

'Can't it wait?' I yelled over the music, but the look in her eyes told me that it couldn't.

'I've been seeing someone,' she said.

'That's good, isn't it?' I smiled but she didn't smile back.

'It's…' She looked at the floor and for a horrible, sinking moment I had thought she was going to tell me she was seeing Matt, but instead, she said: 'It's Ben. We didn't want to tell you until we were sure it was serious. That it would lead to something.'

'I'm happy for you.' And I was.

Until she said: 'You know that conversation we had the other night, the things you told me—'

I couldn't help myself; I pushed her. Hard. Wanting to stop the words I knew were coming. 'Shut up. Shut up. Shut up.'

Mum. Whether it was the fact it was my birthday that night – always a difficult time – or the wine, or the sharing of confidences, it had all spilled out, and afterwards I had waited for her to judge me, but she'd begun to cry. 'I never imagined you had it so hard.' I had made her promise never to tell anyone and she had crossed her heart, the way I used to at school, and I had believed her. I shouldn't have. I couldn't believe she had told Ben. How betrayed he must feel. How angry.

She stumbled, regained her footing and took my elbow. 'This isn't the time or the place. Come on.'

Dazed, I told James I'd see him later, before collecting my coat and bag from the booth.

The corridor was quieter. The music vibrating through the floor rather than heard. Chrissy stopped by the fire door.

'Ben's outside.'

'I can't go out there.' I was crying.

'You have to talk to him.'

'I. Don't. Want. To.' I was one step away from placing my hands over my ears like a child. I couldn't face him. I just couldn't.

'Ali.' Chrissy grabbed my arms and squeezed, shaking me hard. 'You. Have. To.' She pushed open the fire exit, and I stepped out into the dark. Into the rain. The smell of rotting food from the industrial bins made my stomach roil. The alley was black except a rectangle of light emanating from the door Chrissy was propping open with half a brick and the green glow of the fire exit sign. Ben wasn't there.

'We shouldn't be out here. I want to go inside. I don't want to do this. Please don't make me.' Crying, I had turned and stepped towards the door, but Ben loomed out of the shadows, kicking the brick away from the door so it slammed shut. His fingers dug tightly into my elbow as he dragged me towards him. My heel slipped; my shoulder scraped against the slimy bricks. I could hardly bring myself to look at Ben. His hair was plastered to his head, his cheeks wet, and I chose to believe it was rain and not tears, for I couldn't bear the bewildered expression on his face. I couldn't help myself. I wrapped my arms around him, but he pushed me backwards, hard, against the wall, one hand snaking tightly around my throat.

'Bitch.'

Horrified, my hands covered his as I grappled for breath, until Chrissy yanked him away from me. We stood, chests heaving, eyes burning into each other.

'I know.' His words dripped poison. 'I know what you did.'

'Please…'

'Let's go somewhere dry and private and talk about this properly,' Chrissy said. 'Calmly.'

'Keys,' Ben demanded, holding out his hand as I shivered in my too-short dress. For a second I thought about refusing, my neck still hot from the heat of his hands, but Chrissy was right. We needed to talk about things properly.

I dropped my key ring into his hand before slipping into my coat and pulling on my gloves.

Silently we walked, soaked to the skin by the time we reached my car. There was so much to say but none of us had any words. Ben climbed into the driver's side, while Chrissy settled herself into the passenger seat and I found myself in the back like an outcast.

Three's a crowd.

As we sped through the darkness, towards home, I rummaged around for something I could say, anything, to explain myself. But I couldn't. I was furious with Chrissy for betraying my confidence. I knew I should never have told her. I stared out of the window, the sky and sea merged into one giant pool of blackness.

'Why?' I fired the word at Chrissy.

'I love him,' she said simply, twisting around in her seat. 'I wanted him to know everything about me and that meant telling him everything about you.'

'You don't have anything to do with Mum. With me.'

She fell silent as Ben screeched off the road and hurtled towards the clifftop. For one single, horrifying moment I thought he was going to drive over the edge, but he slammed on the brakes. I clung onto the door handle as we skidded across black ice, stopping perilously close to the edge where the treacherous sea crashed its fury. Nobody came up here in the winter. It was hazardous.

'Go on then,' he yelled at Chrissy. In the moonlight he had a deathly pallor, his fury palpable and I had to keep reminding myself his anger was justified. I'd feel the same if it was the other way around. 'Tell her what you told me.'

Chrissy hung her head and I couldn't think there was anything she could say that could shock me now. *Ben knew the truth.*

'Sharon Marlow was my mum,' she said softly.

'No. No. No!' I screamed so loudly my throat was raw as I thrust open the car door and stalked into the blackness, wanting it to swallow me up. Wanting to walk away from Chrissy and all she represented. How could she be the daughter of the woman who died during Dad's robbery?

'Ali,' Ben yelled and the fire in his voice soldered my feet to the spot.

The rain was slowing, a light sprinkling of snow began to fall, dusting Chrissy's shoulders. She looked like an angel as she stood by Ben's side, wind whipping her hair. She tried to slip her fingers into his, but he wrenched his hand away.

'Ali, my mum was Sharon Marlow.'

'Please, don't. Please, stop.' I didn't want to hear it, but she carried on regardless.

'I got a letter from your dad just before his release and I thought it wasn't fair he gets to live his life with his family. My mum's gone. My brother too. My dad started drinking after Mum died and never recovered. We barely have a relationship at all. I got curious, I suppose, about the life he'd be going back to. The man who had caused it all. He was the only one of the Tanmoor Three left to blame. David Webb and Wayne Lindsell are dead. I wondered what you thought of him. His children. I thought I'd find you on Facebook, just a glimpse into your lives, but I couldn't locate you. There was nothing on Google about you dated after the news reports following his conviction and I thought you must have changed your names. I tried to move on, but I couldn't stop thinking about you all. Wondering if you'd forgiven him. Were waiting for him with open arms. I hired a private detective, and—' She shrugged, her arms wide. 'Here I am.'

'So what did you want? What *do* you want?' I didn't feel I knew her anymore, this woman I'd shared a house with for the past four months.

'I just wanted to see you, just once. Honestly, I thought that would be enough, but then we got talking and I found out about your mum dying and the way your voice went steely and cold whenever I tried to bring your dad up and you told me you had nothing to do with him and I knew. I knew you were hurting as much as me. I knew you had lost both your parents too and I felt a kinship. A connection that nobody but you could ever understand, and I wanted to tell you who I was, but I thought you might reject me. I liked you. Both of you. More than like.' She gazes at Ben.

'Our dad killed your mum,' I shouted.

'He didn't. He was there but he didn't. He tried to stop it, but the papers didn't report that.' She closed her eyes as though remembering. 'Wayne was screaming, threatening to kill everyone. He was out of control. David was waving the gun. Your dad tried to talk him into putting it down. I remember it. All of it. Maybe it came out in court, maybe it didn't. The jury had probably made up their minds anyway. But I wasn't called to testify. I was a mess. Put on antidepressants at such a young age. Pills, pills and more pills when what I really needed was a cuddle. Love. Dad couldn't bear to look at me because I reminded him of Mum.'

'I am so, so, sorry.'

'I know you are, but you can't hold onto the past, Ali. I forgive your dad because holding on to hate for all these years… Well, I've only been hurting myself.'

There was something in her eyes, an empathy. An understanding that was my undoing. I broke down.

'Do you forgive me as well?' I thought I asked the question in my head, but she stepped forward and took me in her arms.

'Ali. There's nothing to forgive you for. It wasn't your fault.'

Those were the words I had waited to hear for most of my life and as soon as they left her mouth the wind snatched them and carried them away along with my shame and my guilt.

I clung to her while she supported my weight, while everything flashed before my eyes, opening the door to the policemen, the scorn on Melanie's face, the cake tumbling to the floor, but this time I didn't push the images away. I allowed them to fully form and then I let them go into the night sky into the blanket of clouds obscuring the stars. Eventually my tears ran dry and I peeled off my gloves and fished in my clutch bag for a packet of tissues, blowing my nose and wiping my eyes before I could face my brother.

'Ben.'

'I don't blame you for what happened to Dad, Ali. I never did. But what you did to Mum? I will *never* forgive you for that. I won't.'

Sobs tore through my body, the freezing air burning my lungs as he turned and ran back towards the car. Chrissy and I trying to keep up with him, our heels skidding in the ice.

'Stop,' Chrissy called as the engine revved. Headlights beamed.

Ben began to spin the car around, turning back towards the road.

'Wait.' I waved my arms. No matter what he thought of me, he couldn't leave us here. We were miles away from town and we'd freeze.

Kicking off my shoes I started to run, the gravel ripping my tights, Chrissy panting hard beside me. Just as Ben began to accelerate back towards the road I broke into a sprint, running into his path. He'd stop. He had to. But he didn't slow. Didn't veer out of the way. I waved my arms.

'Ben!' My cry sucked away by the pounding sea.

Almost in slow motion, he leaned back on his seat, yanked the wheel to avoid me, but the wheels were spinning and fighting against the black ice that kept the car coming at me.

'Ali!' I saw Ben's mouth move. The terror on his face.

'Noooo!' The last thing I remember was Chrissy's hands on me. Pushing. Falling. My head thwacking against something cold and hard.

Nothing.

Chapter Fifty-Four

'You hit her with the car, didn't you?' The blood. The wing mirror. The bumper.

'It was an accident,' Ben says, his voice small, and I am transported back to when he was five, standing forlornly over Mum's favourite vase, smashed on the floor, his bottom lip trembling. 'There was black ice. I thought I'd hit you both. You were so still. So silent. Covered in blood but you had a pulse, and when I checked you over, I realised, apart from your head, there weren't any other wounds. It was Chrissy's blood that had showered you.'

'Where is she?'

'She didn't… she isn't…' He falls silent but he doesn't have to say any more.

'How did I get home?' My mind a blank page after falling.

'You were unconscious. By the time I'd sorted… everything out, you'd come round, taken the car and gone.'

'I drove?' I screw up my face, trying desperately to remember something, anything, about the journey home. There's nothing. I am incredulous I could have picked up my bag, driven home and then gone to bed as though nothing had happened, but then I remember Mr Henderson telling me about shock, how the mind will try to protect us by blocking things out or creating some semblance of normality. For the first time I feel a flicker of understanding for that woman who had murdered her entire family and then cooked them dinner as though nothing had ever happened.

'I thought you'd have driven straight to the police station,' Ben continues. 'I didn't know what to do. I walked across to the cottage and sat for ages, remembering the picnics we had with Mum, do you remember? I'd always bring Ollie the Owl and he'd have his own teacup and saucer. I loved this place. I cried as I watched the sunrise, thinking it would be the last one I'd ever see. Waiting for the police to come and take me away. But they didn't. And I started to think maybe you hadn't told them. Maybe you were protecting me. I had to find out. When I came to yours and realised you couldn't remember anything it seemed like fate. A chance to think. Plan. At the hospital when you asked me to lie to the doctors about falling and you were insistent you didn't want to speak to the police, it gave me… the facial blindness was… an opportunity, I suppose. A chance to make you suffer, like I was suffering. I loved her you know. Chrissy.'

'You took her phone. Posted on Facebook. How did you post on my Instagram page if my phone was in the car?' I can't comprehend what he's telling me. Please don't let it all have been him.

'I logged into your account from my phone. You still use Matt's name as your password for everything. You really shouldn't.'

'Did you send me the flowers?'

'Yes. The fact you couldn't remember anything about your date was perfect. For me. You nearly caught me once, though, when I switched on your radio. I nipped out the back door and Branwell came charging down your driveway.

He knew it was me. I had to drag him onto the street really quickly. You looked me straight in the eye and had no idea. You thought I was in Edinburgh.'

'Even if I hadn't thought you were away, I would never have thought you could do this to me. But wait! It can't all have been you, Ben!' I am desperate for it not to be. 'You chased that man out of my garden. You were beaten up.'

'He was going door to door for the electric, flogging smart metres. I cornered him, demanded his wallet and phone. Let him hit me.'

He grins as though he is proud of what he has done. Look at my spelling test Ali-cat. I got ten out of ten.

'The…' I'm uncomfortable bringing this up in front of my baby brother. 'The sex tape…'

'Me and Chrissy. She liked to experiment. I knew you'd assume it was you and be too embarrassed to show anyone to ask. It's always all about you, isn't it, Ali?'

'You've made it about me. You've put me through hell, Ben. You were the one in the garden banging on my window? I was terrified.' He must have banged on James's window too, to make it seem random at first. Increase my paranoia. 'You can't have hated me that much.'

'Hate,' he says. 'You murdered our mum.'

'It really wasn't like that. Ben you were too small to remember how it was. She couldn't feed herself. Dress herself. Go to the toilet. She had no dignity. She had no life.'

'She still laughed. Made jokes.'

'She put on a brave face for us. That's all.' Kim's Game – the tea towel covering the tray – Ben only remembering what he wanted to be true. 'She couldn't carry on.'

'She had me! She had us.'

'And she loved us. She did. But she wanted to go.'

'I don't believe you. She'd never have chosen to leave me.'

'She was in pain all the time, Ben.'

'She was getting better.'

'She was dying.' We are shouting at each other now. All the while I am working the knots furiously behind my back. Loosening. Twisting my wrists from side to side, the skin chaffing.

'Iris said she'd get better. She promised. She would have known. She was the adult.'

'She was a coward. Look.' I soften my voice. 'We've never talked about it properly and we should have done. You were too young to understand then, but you're not now. Mum had motor neurone disease. You don't recover from that.'

'But Iris promised…'

'Iris was trying to protect you. I was trying to protect you. Ben. Mum wanted to go. She begged me to help her. How could I have said no? She was suffering. It was the kindest thing.'

'It was murder.'

'It wasn't. Not really,' I say weakly.

'If it wasn't. If it was really what she wanted, why didn't you tell me? I had to find out from someone else. Imagine how that fucking felt?'

'It's a shock. I know. I understand. Look. Let Matt go. It's nothing to do with him. Untie me and we can go home. Talk about this properly. I'll answer any questions you like.'

'I can't let Matt go.'

'Why?'

'Because you've already told the police Matt is going to kill us both. "My husband. Matt. He's killed my aunt. Hurt my brother. He's trying to kill me. He's going to kill us both".' He mimics my voice. 'They'll never for a second suspect me. You'll go over the cliff and so will Matt, and I'll say he was trying to kill me too and in the struggle he was the one to fall.'

Ben slices the knife down his arm and crimson trickles over his skin. 'Look what happened when we fought.' I know that even if I could recognise his features he would still be a stranger to me in this very moment.

It takes Ben four attempts to heft Matt over his shoulder. His knees strain under the weight as he carries him out of the door. I scream and scream, my cries mixing with the hungry gulls screeching for food. Ben returns empty-handed and I am broken. Limp, as he picks me up and carries me outside, but when I get to the edge I see Matt is on the ground. He has not thrown him over. Yet. Momentarily I feel an ember of hope that he has changed his mind, until he says: 'I wanted you to see. I want you to know how it feels to have someone you love taken away from you.'

He dumps me on the floor and the wind is knocked out of me. Something hard and sharp digging into my back. 'Ben.' I keep talking, my fingers rooting around for the object I have fallen on. A piece of flint. I begin to saw the knot. Slowly. Methodically.

'Stop!' I cry as he takes a step towards Matt. 'Do you remember I used to read to you when you couldn't sleep? Those nonsense poems you loved.'

'Don't, Ali. It means nothing anymore. My whole child-hood has been a lie. All of it.'

'Not all of it. Not even most of it. I'm so, so sorry about Mum, but if I could go back, Ben, I'd do exactly the same thing. I would.'

He lunges forward with the blade and I duck, but he's so close to my face, I can feel the whoosh of air as the steel slices past my ear.

'Wait.' I'm still working frenziedly at the rope. 'If she hadn't been expected to die, there would have been a post-mortem. They'd have found the tablets and there'd have been an investigation. The doctor knew Mum would have been too weak to undo the lid from the bottle. They'd have known she had help. I'd have been arrested. There wasn't an investigation because it was classed as an expected death, Ben. *Expected.*'

There's a snapping sensation. A release of pressure and my hands are free.

'Ben.' The ground feels shaky as I try to spring to my feet, my knees weak and powerless. He looks uncertain now and I know he is processing what I have just told him. 'Give me the knife.' I put out my hand. 'Please.' We circle each other like sharks, as the ocean below roars hungrily.

'"The Owl and The Pussy-cat went to sea in a beautiful pea-green boat",' I begin, and he begins to cry. Behind him a backdrop of frothy sea and cloudy sky merge into one.

'Benjamin… put down your weapon,' booms a voice. A familiar voice. PC Hunter.

'We traced Ben's phone. Are you okay, Ali?' PC Willis shouts. 'Step backwards.'

But I can't. I am not going anywhere without my brother.

I stretch out my hand. He shakes his head.

'"They took some honey and plenty of money, wrapped up in a five-pound note."' I'm speaking softly now but his lips move with each and every word I say. He's remembering how it felt to be young. How it felt to be loved.

"'The Owl looked up at the stars above and sang to a small guitar—'"

With a guttural cry Ben launches himself towards me, the knife slipping from his fingers. I open my arms to receive him, but I am bowled over, PC Hunter charging forward.

'He's dropped the knife!' I scream. Ben's eyes widen with panic as he backs away. 'Stop. He's dropped the knife!' My throat is raw but it's too late. Ben has stepped backwards again, disappearing over the edge.

Chapter Fifty-Five

There is a moment as Ben disappears over the cliff when time seems incredibly slow and incredibly fast. Incredibly cruel. I'm unable to breathe, making odd half-hiccup noises while a pressure in my chest builds and builds until it is released in one gut-tearing, heart-wrenching scream that rasps like sandpaper in my throat.

The instant I clamber to my feet and start to run towards the edge there are arms around my waist, and I fight against them – 'he didn't have the knife' – but they hold me firm and strong. My knees buckle as PC Willis drives the police car to the edge of the cliff and switches the headlights on to full beam, while PC Hunter barks instructions into his walkie-talkie. Still I don't fall and I know it is Matt who is holding me, and I try to prise his fingers apart, all the while calling Ben's name, but eventually my energy is zapped and I lean back against Matt.

And we wait.

At the theme park all those years ago with Dad I'd felt detached from everything as I had spun around on the waltzer. Present but not. Unable to identify shapes. Sounds. Lights blurring. Seeing everything but absorbing nothing and that's how I feel right now as an ambulance arrives and I am ushered into the back of it, where I sit, wrapped in an itchy grey blanket, dry-eyed.

'Is there any news?' I ask endlessly. Matt hasn't moved from my side and has no idea what's going on any more than I do. The sky is russet now. Dusk staking its claim. But the clifftop is awash with blue flashing lights. 'There are ledges,' I say again, wincing that the thought of Ben's body lying broken and bloodied on rock is preferable to him being swept out into the choppy sea, where the lifeguard's boat bobs orange and small. Overhead, the thrum of a helicopter. With all this they will find him. How could they not? And we'll talk and everything will be okay. That's what I tell myself anyway, but it's a lie even I don't believe.

I'm a murderer.

I rub my wrist, feeling my cold goosebumps, reassuring myself there are no steel cuffs on me.

Yet.

But it's only a matter of time, I know.

Coffee is produced, seemingly from thin air, and I wrap my hands around the styrofoam cup that crumples under my grip, splashing hot liquid onto my fingers.

'We should take you to hospital soon,' the paramedic says once more and, again, I shake my head. 'There's nothing you can do here, and don't you want to see your aunt?'

Iris is alive but unconscious I am told. A heart attack.

'I thought Ben had killed her,' I had said when PC Willis relayed the news in her calming voice.

'She had made me a cup of tea and we were chatting. Ben burst in and before either of us really knew what was happening he hit me over the head,' Matt tells me. His cheek is black and purple, his lip swollen. 'By the time I came to I was tied up. Iris was crying and Ben… I've never quite seen him like that before, agitated, repeating the same thing over and over again.

It was her fault your mum had died. She should never have left the house that night leaving all the medication that had been stockpiled in the drawer. Did your mum?…'

'It's complicated,' I say knowing it's only a matter of time before the whole sordid truth is as open and exposed as I feel right now.

'What did Iris say?'

'She kept saying how sorry she was. She tried to calm him down; she did, but he was ready to break.'

I am not surprised. Ben must have known with the police investigating Chrissy's disappearance it wouldn't take long before his part in it was revealed. Tick tock. Time was running out for us all.

'Iris told him she knew it was all her fault.'

My breath shudders. I'd often wondered whether Iris suspected I'd helped Mum that night. It seemed too coincidental that she passed away naturally after that conversation, but she had never questioned, and I had never told.

Matt continues: 'Iris tried to tell Ben your mum was really sick and would never have recovered. He started crying and asking her why she always told him Mum would get better. "I thought it kinder", Iris had said, "you were so young". "So was Ali, but you know what she did." Ben had spat.'

I thought I was numb, unable to feel, but Matt lifts my hands and rubs warmth into them and when he speaks it's with love.

'Iris collapsed, Ali. Ben didn't touch her.'

She had crumpled under the weight of the truth. I wonder if she had rewritten history over the years to make it bearable the way I had tried to, but it doesn't work, does it, burying secrets? They always become unearthed:

dark and dirty and ready to destroy. My eyes drift to the ruins of the cottage. I can see the ghost of our family picnicking. Mum stating if I ate my crusts my hair would curl; Iris promising Ben that Mum would recover. Those little white lies that bind a family together. The lies told to reassure. The lies we tell because the truth is just too ugly. Too cruel.

There's shouting now. Urgent crackling of walkie-talkies. The helicopter circling and circling. The speedboat slicing a frothy snail trail through the battleship grey waves.

PC Willis glances over, her ponytail swinging jauntily, belying the severity of the situation somehow. Instead of approaching me she turns away.

'No news is good news.' Mum used to say, and I hang on to that, trying not to remember that she stopped saying it after Dad's arrest during the interminable time he spent on remand.

I take a sip of my drink, tasting sea salt on my lips. Above, the moon a sliver in the sky. They'll stop looking soon. It will be too dark.

'I thought it was you,' I say dully to Matt.

'What?'

'All of it. I couldn't understand… I *don't* understand why you didn't want me anymore. Since that night we argued about Craig and Jules you seemed to put your business before our marriage. Everything seemed more important than me. I thought you were having an affair with Chrissy. I found a photo of her and… I suppose it was Ben, but he told me it was you. A note she'd written to him, I thought it was you. Jules overheard Chrissy on the phone to Ben and assumed it was you on the other end.'

'There's never been anyone for me but you.' Matt draws my hand to his lips and kisses my freezing fingertips. I haven't the energy to pull away. 'How could you think that?'

'Matt, someone was trying to hurt me and you took out life insurance after we separated. Packed up the house. I thought you were planning on killing me.' I state this matter-of-factly in the same way you might state 'I thought you were planning on having tea' if someone made a coffee. I'm really past caring about it all. Past caring about everything except Ben.

'Christ.' Is all he says for the longest time as we watch another police car arrive. Another ambulance.

'I fucked up,' he says eventually and it's hard to hear his quiet tones over the crashing waves, the flurry of activity, but I can't tear my eyes away from the place Ben disappeared to look at him. 'I'd put all my eggs in one basket with Craig. Taken a huge risk. The business was struggling anyway, debts had been mounting up for months.'

'Why didn't you tell me?'

For better or for worse.

'Because I'm an idiot. Because I thought it was my job as your husband to protect you. You never asked for anything materially. All you wanted was a family. Love. A roof over your head. I haven't been able to pay the mortgage for months. Your half of the payments are swallowed up by my overdraft the second you transfer it to my account. I've hidden all the letters from you. I thought it was better, you moving out. I tried to source more freelance contracts, even signed up with agencies for a full-time job, but everyone's feeling the pinch and cutting their marketing budgets. I got a second job stacking shelves in Tesco, in the evenings, hoping it would help, but it's a drop in the ocean compared to what I need to clear my debts.'

'So you were leaving? Running away?'

'I was…' He clears his throat. 'Putting my affairs in order, I suppose you'd call it.'

'What's that supposed to mean?'

'It all got too much for me, and I wanted you to be financially protected.'

'*Too much*?' This time, I do look at him. He can't meet my eye.

'I had it all planned. I'd take out the policy and wait a few months before… You know. I was going to make it look like an accident. I was packing everything up so you didn't have to go through my things. I'd even changed the locks so you wouldn't be the one to find me. I knew Mr Henderson would pop in if he hadn't seen me for a few days. It seemed the right thing to do. For you. I love you, Ali. I haven't even been able to bear sleeping in our bed since you left. I've been in the spare room on an airbed.'

I should feel sympathy. I should feel pity. But all I feel is a burning, burning hate as I wrench my hand away from his.

'You selfish fucking bastard. You don't know *anything* about love.'

But what is love? Is it forgiving a father who made a horrible, stupid mistake trying to provide for his family? Is it shielding a brother from the brutal truth when he had every right to expect honesty? Is it holding a glass of water to the lips of a dying mother as she swallows down the tablets you've placed onto her tongue? What is love? I'm damned if I know.

I stand. Something is drawing me forward and, as I walk, I feel Matt's eyes burning into my back and I feel his regret.

His sorrow. His guilt. But I can't be responsible for them. I've enough of my own.

'Ali.' PC Willis steps towards me and we approach each other slowly, warily. 'They've recovered a body. I'm so, so sorry.'

And that's when the tears finally come.

EPILOGUE

It's been six months since we buried Chrissy. It was her body that was recovered that night on the clifftop. Four months since we held a memorial service for Ben and it felt as though my heart was being ripped out as I stood, black heels sinking into the rain-damp grass, the paper in my hand shaking so hard the words hopped into each other. It didn't feel right saying the things I had written, that would echo empty and meaningless around an almost deserted churchyard. Instead, I had screwed up my notes and recited the Edward Lear poem he loved so much. It seemed apt. It had proved impossible to correlate the Ben who tormented me with the brother I've always been so close to, and eventually I stopped trying, fearing I was driving myself mad. In the end, a lifetime of memories warmed the ice-cold betrayal that was running through my veins; Ben curled up on my lap, rubbing sleep from his eyes, begging for 'just one more page'; Ben driving, both of us singing along to 'Don't Look Back in Anger', and the lyrics have never seemed more poignant than they do now, because despite everything I don't blame him. He had dropped the knife in the last few seconds of his life and I know he wasn't going to hurt me. I think if I had had the chance to explain everything properly he might even have understood, but Ben's sensitivity had always fuelled my burning desire to protect him. It's little wonder his fragile mind couldn't cope with years of deceit. It must have felt as though everyone was keeping secrets from him, and I know, as I look at the bare skin my wedding band once circled, just how heartbreaking that can be.

We never did recover Ben's body, but I'm told that's not unusual, the tides being as wild and unpredictable as the human mind. He'll likely turn up somewhere, some time, the marine police say. I hate to think of him out there, alone, in the dark and freezing sea, but I think of the Owl and the Pussy-cat and picture him snug in their little wooden boat, with their honey and plenty of money, and although it sounds silly, it's a comfort somehow. I said my final goodbyes. Choking back ceaseless sobs as I carefully set his battered Ollie the Owl, with its frayed green ribbon, and threadbare fur, in the place where Ben's body should lie. Dropping a handful of earth into the open grave I raised my eyes to the forget-me-not sky and imagined Ben reunited with Mum; and now, when I picture her, it's always the way she was before MND ravaged her body: smiling, at peace.

Sometimes, as I slipped into the warm waters of sleep that I knew would become dark and choppy, as they always did once the nightmares took hold, I imagined it was easier for them than it was for me. The one who was left behind. But time rolled on, as it always does.

It seemed impossible that the snow dusting the rooftops would melt, daffodils would poke their yellow heads from their darkened slumber. But they did. The world is still turning even if mine has shattered. Life has continued.

Matt and I talk regularly now. There's an understanding between us that wasn't there before. Compassion. We're not together but we dance in symbiosis. Every now and then after he's visited I find a Terry's Chocolate Orange and it always makes me smile. He's having counselling for his depression and I'm still coming to terms with the fact my facial recognition will never come back. Two fragile minds don't equal one strong one. Neither of us has filed for divorce and, despite everything, I don't want to. One day perhaps we'll be more than just friends but, for now, I'm content with my own company, my Sunday lunches with Mr Henderson, meeting PC Willis for the odd coffee: Steph as I now call her. She's been a fabulous support. The truth about Mum's death came tumbling out, as the truth often does, and as I confessed I felt a weight being lifted from my shoulders, and I knew that if I went to prison I would still be freer than I have been for years. The wait was interminable but after long deliberations and discussions I wasn't a party to, it was declared that due to my tender age at the time and the number of years that had passed, no charges would be brought. A 'victim of circumstances' I was called, and I shook my head when Steph relayed this. I still hate the word victim, even after everything I've been through. Especially because of everything I've been through.

I no longer work at the care home. Unable to tell the residents apart, I was in danger of handing out the wrong medication and letting me go was absolutely the right thing to do. It didn't make it hurt any less. I still visit regularly though, taking Branwell in, letting the residents fuss him, including Iris who lives there now. She's often quiet. Reflective. She always sits silently by the window, watching, as the visitors traipse up the winding path, and I wonder if she's waiting for her sister. For Ben. She'll be reunited with them sooner than I will, and in a way I envy that.

I despaired of finding a new job. My condition clouding everything I tried, but then I was offered a role working for the charity that had been my lifeline, supporting others with prosopagnosia – there's more of us than you think. I work long hours, often manning the phone lines during evenings and weekends too and, in the time in-between, I take Branwell for long walks along the seafront, through the parks, but not along the clifftops. Never along the clifftops.

The home Matt and I owned was repossessed. It had been so long since he'd paid the mortgage and I didn't want to stay in the house I shared with Chrissy. I moved to the outskirts of town, desperate to move away but equally desperate to stay in this place that ties me to Ben.

James and Jules email often and I'm replying more and more. It turns out neither of them burned Prism down in a bid to keep James out of the whole sorry mess. Carl did. The bar wasn't making the money it used to; no wonder he was so eager for cash to pay his suppliers with. He thought an insurance claim was the easy way out. Until he was arrested. But who am I to judge? I think we've all been guilty of carrying out acts we think are a good idea, until we're caught. Haven't we?

I've told James and Jules if they pass me in the street not to tell me who they are. I'm not ready to talk to them face to face yet, but I am working towards it. Sometimes I still think of the jolt of electricity I felt as James's hand brushed mine in the bar, the way he made me laugh. Forgiveness sets you free, Chrissy had told me, but I'm taking that one step at a time, starting with Dad. We've been writing, proper letters that you pop into postboxes, and today we're meeting for the first time since his release.

'How will I recognise you?' he had written, and I had almost laughed, I'm probably the last person you should ask that question of, but then I remembered my coping techniques. The little markers I use to make my life easier, and they do.

'I'll be the one with the black and white dog with the over enthusiastic tail.'

Facial blindness is both a blessing and a curse. I'd never have chosen it, of course, who would, but the truth is it keeps me present. Engaged with my surroundings. I observe the little things others don't. Automatically assessing body language, mood. Noticing colours more vibrantly so I can identify them later. Show me a blue top and I'll tell you if I've seen it before, and if you think that sounds simple, there are seventy-three shades of blue and hundreds of variations in-between. It's the small things I remember, always.

Dad will be here any minute. I bend to stroke Branwell. His ears are pricked, muscles tense. Not straining against the lead, longing to race around the park as he usually does. He knows we're waiting for something. For someone.

Dad. I turn the word over in my mind. It's been so long. Fleetingly I wonder whether this is a bad idea. Whether I should go home now before he comes but a sixth sense whispers it's too late. He's here.

Looking up, my heart skips with a knowing hidden deep inside my consciousness. *Dad.* He's still familiar as he hovers by the duck pond, studying me intently, uncertain and afraid. I smile. A throng of picnickers tramp in front of my eyeline, old-fashioned wicker baskets crammed with food, kids carrying cricket bats, footballs. A family. The one thing I don't have, except now perhaps I do.

He's still there. Unmoving. And even from here I can sense his trepidation and I wonder what he's expecting. Anger? Frustration? Tears? But love? Is he expecting love?

To my left is jeering. The men playing football catcalling a teammate, but I don't turn and look. Everyone's a stranger. Everyone except him.

There are only a few metres between us but there are miles and miles and years and years, and I know he is picturing being back in that house too. I wonder whether he is tucking me into bed, twirling Mum around the kitchen as 'Sweet Talking Woman' plays, the smell of gingerbread men floating from the oven, or if he's thrashing against the handcuffs snapping onto his wrists as the horrified faces of his children are scorched into his mind.

I stand, swotting away a bee that buzzes lazily past my ear. It's the perfect, perfect day. White tufts of clouds suspended in a cornflower sky. He nods. Just once and so do I, taking a step forward, and then another. My throat hot and swollen with emotion. Reminding myself I am too old to be swung into his arms. I'm almost as tall as him now.

He moves towards me, biting his lower lip as though the moment is too much for him. I scan his features. Until now I'd been cradling a small kernel of hope that I'd recognise him still, the way I recognise Mum, but I don't. He fills my heart, though, and a rush of love courses through my veins. How could I ever have thought I hated him? This man who gave me life.

Despite the warmth in the air, the hairs on the back of my neck prick up as though someone has trailed a finger over my skin.

'Sarah?' A familiar voice behind me. A voice that has comforted me a thousand times. Read me a hundred bedtime stories.

'Dad?' I whirl around to face him.

'Sorry, I should call you, Ali,' says the man who is unmistakably Dad. But then who was watching me?

Confused, I glance back over my shoulder at the duck pond. The man who had nodded at me is retreating now, his eyes still fixed on mine. He raises his hand in a single goodbye and, as he turns his head away from me, I see him wipe something from his cheek.

I think it's a tear.

Ben?

And they sailed away for a year and a day in a beautiful pea-green boat.

A LETTER FROM LOUISE

Dear Reader

Thank you so much for choosing to read *The Date*. Firstly, a huge thank you for reading, reviewing, sharing and supporting my first three books.

I can't quite believe this is my fourth! The idea of *The Date* sprung from the unlikeliest of sources – *My Life*, a long-running CBBC documentary series featuring children with unique stories. Five years ago, my family and I watched an episode featuring Hannah Read, a girl who acquired prosopagnosia at the age of eight after an infection caused inflammation of her brain. Hannah's story was equally heartbreaking and inspiring. In one scene she was led into a room containing her family and friends but also some strangers. She walked around the room and studied each face intently and you could feel her panic as she was unable to identify anyone she knew. Hannah was also shown a selection of photographs and became extremely upset that she couldn't recognise her own picture. Hannah said she felt 'cut off from the world around her' and her anxiety whenever she left her house was palpable. The documentary makers introduced her to other teenagers with the condition, and a university carrying out a research project subsequently taught her coping strategies. By the end of the programme Hannah felt less isolated and more positive, but her distress and her story stayed with me long after I switched off my TV. It is still with me. Imagine waking up one day in a world where everyone looked like a stranger? How utterly terrifying.

A year after watching, Hannah often crept into my thoughts. I knew I had to write a story about Face Blindness. After I finished *The Sister* I started playing around with an opening, but I didn't know what to do with it – there was almost too much scope – and so I put it to one side and wrote *The Gift* instead. The time came to write my third book and, instantly, I thought of Hannah again. I pulled out my notes and this time wrote the first 10,000 words and sent it to my editor. 'How are you going to progress it?' she asked. I was at a loss to know how to sensitively approach a story surrounding a subject that had really touched me. Again, I put it to one side and, instead, wrote *The Surrogate*. By the time I'd finished my third book, my main character, Ali, had been brewing in the back of my mind for four years. I was determined to have another attempt. This time I felt more confident I could write a pacy, unnerving thriller, but also stay true to the emotions and challenges faced by those who have prosopagnosia. I wanted Ali to show the same courage and determination that Hannah did.

I do hope you have enjoyed this story, and if you did I'd be very grateful if you could leave a review for *The Date*. I'd love to hear what you think, and it really does make a difference helping readers discover my books for the very first time.

I adore hearing from readers. You can find me over at Facebook or Twitter or via my website, where I regularly blog flash fiction and writing tips.

Take care, Louise x

www.louisejensen.co.uk

@Fab_fiction

fabricatingfiction

BOOK CLUB QUESTIONS

1) Before reading *The Date*, had you ever heard of Prosopagnosia (Face Blindness?) How hard do you think it would be to adjust to a loss of facial recognition?

2) How did your perception of the characters change throughout the book?

3) 'I can see the ghost of our family picnicking. Mum stating if I ate my crusts my hair would curl; Iris promising everything would be ok. Those little white lies that bind a family together. The lies told to reassure. The lies we tell because the truth is just too ugly. Too cruel.' If a lie is told with the best of intentions, is it forgivable?

4) Who did you think was tormenting Ali?

5) 'I won't find the sense of safety I was seeking here, among the secrets and lies and the tangled, torturous past. Stupid to ever think that I could.' Did you feel Ali had managed to move on from her past until she went on her date?

6) 'You don't want to go to the police, Ali. You've got blood on your hands.' Could you empathise with Ali's

reluctance to talk to the police? What would you have done in her situation?

7) Did any of the theories you formed throughout reading the story turn out to be correct?

8) 'In a desperate situation, are we all capable of monstrous acts? It's incomprehensible we can reach inside the darkest depths of someone else's mind, when we ignore the blackness lurking in our own.' Can we ever really know someone properly? How well do we know ourselves?

9) When Ali's secret is revealed, how did you feel about her?

10) What do you think the future will hold for Ali after the Epilogue?

ACKNOWLEDGEMENTS

I'm stunned to be writing the acknowledgments for my fourth book and once again it has taken a fabulous team to bring it to life. As always a big thank you to Lydia Vassar-Smith, without whom I might have been forever languishing in a slush pile. Thanks to all at Bookouture, in particular to my editor Jenny Geras for her insight, along with Jennifer Hunt, and to Kim Nash and Noelle Holten for their publicity wizardry. Janette Currie for her copyediting skills. Another huge thank you to Cath Burke and the team at Sphere, Little, Brown for publishing my paperbacks. I've got cover lucky again with another fabulous design by Henry Steadman. A big thank you to Rory Scarfe for your calming presence and all the agency things you do behind the scenes.

I'm so thankful for all the amazing readers and writers I've had the pleasure of meeting, both on and offline. You all brighten my day.

I've been incredibly moved and incredibly inspired by all the YouTubers vlogging their journey with MND. A heartfelt thank you for sharing your vastly different experiences. I shall continue to tune in and cheer you on.

Thanks to Professor Daniel Lasserson for his neurology expertise and to Lisa Hardy for her input on police procedures. Any mistakes are entirely my own.

Mick Wynn, your input has been insightful as always. Symon Adamson for your continued support. Lucille Grant thanks for always being on hand. Emma Mitchell – I bloody love you (and no I didn't cut and paste that…).

To my friends who have supported me (and seen very little of me these past couple of years) in particular Sarah Wade, Hilary Tiney and Natalie Brewin – I treasure your friendship.

My family – I'm still here! Especially Mum, Karen, Bekkii Bridges and Pete Simmons.

Callum, Kai and Finley – you guys are growing far too quickly and I am so ridiculously proud of you. (Finley, no animals were harmed in this book – a promise is a promise!).

This book has been an emotional write for me, thank you Tim for your love and support.

And Ian Hawley, are you watching?

Read on for the beginning of
Louise Jensen's bestselling novel,
The Surrogate

LATER

There is a rising sense of panic; horror hanging in the air like smoke.

'They're such a lovely couple. Do you think they're okay?' says the woman, but the flurry of emergency service vehicles crammed into the quiet cul-de-sac, the blue and white crime scene tape stretched around the perimeter of the property, indicate things are anything but okay. She wraps her arms around herself as though she is cold, despite this being the warmest May on record for years. Cherry blossom twirls around her ankles like confetti, but there will be no happily ever after for the occupants of this house, the sense of tragedy already seeping into its red bricks.

Her voice shakes as she speaks into the microphone. It is difficult to hear her over the thrum of an engine, the slamming of van doors as a rival news crew clatters a camera into its tripod.

He thrusts the microphone closer to her mouth.

She hooks her red hair behind her ears; raises her head. Her eyes are bright with tears.

TV gold.

'You don't expect anything bad… Not here. This is a *nice* area.'

Disdain slides across the reporter's face before he rear-ranges his features into the perfect blend of sympathy and shock. He hadn't spent three years having drama lessons for nothing.

He tugs the knot in his tie to loosen it a little as he waits for the woman to finish noisily blowing her nose. The heat is insufferable; shadows long under the blazing sun. Body odour exudes from his armpits, fighting against the sweet scent of the freshly cut grass. The smell is cloying, sticking in the back of his throat. He can't wait to get home and have an ice-cold lager. Put on his shorts like the postman sitting on the edge of the kerb, his head between his knees. He wonders if he is the one who found them. There will be plenty of angry people waiting for their post today. 'Late Letter Shock!' is the sort of inane local story he usually gets to cover, but this… this could go national. His big break. He couldn't get here fast enough when his boss called to say what he thought he'd heard on the police scanner.

He shields his eyes against the sun with one hand as he scouts the area. Across the road, a woman rests against her doorframe, toddler in her arms. He can't quite read her expression and wonders why she doesn't come closer like the rest of them. At the edge of the garden, as close as the police will allow, a small crowd is huddled together: friends and neighbours, he expects. The sight of their shocked faces is such a contrast to the neat borders nursing orange marigolds and lilac pansies. He thinks this juxtaposition would make a great shot. The joy of spring tempered by tragedy. New life highlighting the rawness of loss of life. God, he's good; he really should be an anchor.

There is movement behind him, and he signals to the cameraman to turn around. The camera pans down the path towards the open front door. It's flanked by an officer standing to attention in front of a silver pot containing a miniature tree. On the step are specks of what looks like blood. His heart lifts at the sight of it. Whatever has happened here is big. Career defining.

Coming out of the house are two sombre paramedics pushing empty trolleys, wheels crunching in the gravel.

The woman beside him clutches his arm, her fingertips pressed hard against his suit jacket. Silly cow will wrinkle the fabric. He fights the urge to shake her free; instead, swallowing down his agitation. He might need to interview her again later.

'Does this mean they're okay?' asks the woman, confusion lining her face.

The trolleys are clattered into the back of the waiting ambulance. The doors slam shut, the blue lights stop flashing and slowly it pulls away.

From behind the immaculately trimmed hedge, hidden from view, he hears the crackle of a walkie-talkie. A low voice. Words drift lazily towards him, along with the buzz of bumblebees and the stifled sound of sobbing.

'Two bodies. It's a murder enquiry.'

CHAPTER ONE

Now

Don't turn around.

Behind me, the laughter rings out again. I tell myself it can't be her, but I know, even after all this time, it is. The world falls away from me and I grip the counter so hard my knuckles bleach white.

Don't turn around.

In front of me, Clare's mouth forms the question: 'whipped cream?', but I can't hear anything above the thrumming in my ears. I shake my head as though I can dislodge the buzzing that's growing louder and louder. Clare lowers her arm; the nozzle to the cream had been poised over my mug. I always have the same drink every time I come here, but today the sound of laughter has thrust me back into the past. The smell of the hot chocolate I usually find so tantalising is causing my stomach to roll.

'Are you okay, Kat?'

I'm hot, tugging at my scarf as though it is choking me. White frost still patterns the pavement outside, but in here it is stifling; the coffee machine hisses and spits and steam rises towards the oak beam ceiling.

An impatient cough from the man shuffling his feet behind reminds me I have not yet answered Clare.

'I'm fine,' I say but my mouth is dry. My voice a strange croak. Pushing coins over the counter with one hand, I pick up my drink with the other. Hot liquid slithers down the side of the mug, trickling over my fingers, scalding my skin. Reluctantly I turn around. There it is again.

Laughter.

Her laughter.

My eyes dart around the café, and when I see her, everything else fades into the distance. She has her back towards me but I'd recognise that glossy black bob anywhere. She runs her fingers through her hair as she speaks animatedly to the elderly lady sat opposite her; tilting her head to the side she listens to the response. It seems like I saw her only yesterday, but of course I didn't.

Lisa.

My palms feel hot as they start to tingle. I haven't had a panic attack for such a long time, but underneath the mounting anxiety is an inevitability about it all, a resignation almost.

I'm unsure what to do at first; my feet roasting in my UGG boots. My scalp prickling. The room around me tilts and sways. I move to lean against the wall and it bears my weight while the lunchtime crowd stream in for their bowls of home-made soup and paninis dripping with melted cheese. There's no way I can leave without her seeing me and I can't face the confrontation. Already, I am emotionally drained and longing to check my mobile once again for news. Focusing all my attention on placing one foot in front of the other, I inch my way towards the round table in the corner, all the time feeling as though I might faint. Sinking into a tub chair, I plonk my shopping bags on the floor as I try to make myself as small as possible. My drink remains untouched in front of me, a thick skin forming on the top. My throat is tight and I cannot swallow. *What is she doing here?* We are sixty miles from home, and as I think this, it jars me I still automatically refer to *that* place as home, and not here, where I have made a new life. Fingering the gold cross hanging around my neck, memories crash and tumble around my mind: our first day at school; Lisa crouching to tie up my shoelaces as I hadn't yet learned; cross-legged in my garden in the hot summer sun, threading daisies into chains, and later, stuffing toilet tissue in our bras, and practising kissing on the backs of our hands. I have missed her so much but I don't know what to say to make amends. What I can possibly do to make it right. I can pretend I don't need her, but that doesn't stop the aching inside my chest when I think of the friendship we once had.

A loud clearing of the throat draws my gaze sideward. A couple glower at me as they wait for an empty table, their tray laden with steaming coffee and slabs of cake with cream cheese icing. Apologies spill from my lips as I pull on my coat, gather my bags. Taking a deep breath I stand and march towards the exit, head down, eyes fixed firmly on the floor. I have almost reached the door, my fingers brushing the cool metal handle, when a voice calls, 'Kat.' I can't help turning around.

'Lisa.' I study the face of my ex best friend, expecting to see anger, hurt, at the very least, but a smile creeps across

354

her face. Her eyes crinkling at the edges. You would think
the blazing row we had the last time we were together never
happened. Or what came after. Especially what came after.

'I thought it was you!' She looks genuinely pleased to
see me.

'What are you doing here?' My tone comes out more
accusatory than I mean it to, and I soften my words with
a tentative smile.

'I'm on a week's placement at St Thomas's Hospital. I'm
a nurse now.'

'Like your mum?' I blurt out. I never usually allow myself
to think of her family. Or of my own.

The here and now.

'What about you?' she asks.

'I've lived here for a few years.'

'What a coincidence.'

Is it? I hate the sense of mistrust creeping its way into
my being. After all, Lisa is not the one who did anything
wrong, is she? Before I can respond she has enveloped me in
a huge hug. 'I've missed you so much,' she says, and despite
my misgivings, I find myself hugging her back.

'You're not leaving already, are you?' she asks.

I glance out into the street. At the grey skies laden with
swollen clouds. At the people rushing by, heads down,
pushing against the biting wind. I know I have hesitated
for a moment too long when she asks me if I have eaten
lunch and my stomach growls in response.

'Aren't you with?…' I gesture towards the old lady at
the table.

'No. I was just passing the time.'

Lisa always did have the ability to chat to anyone, to fit in anywhere, and I feel the dull weight of the loneliness I always carry.

A quick bite to eat. It can't do any harm, can it?

'I think we've lost your table.' Two teenage girls are slipping into the empty seats.

'I vote we find a pub.' Lisa grins, and the years fall away. Tears inexplicably spring to my eyes as I find myself pleased she is here. Not a chance to recreate the past; I shudder when I think of the past, but there is comfort in the familiarity: the way she links her arm through mine; the floral perfume she still wears. Icy air gusts into the coffee shop as she shoulders open the door.

'We can walk to the pub over there.' I nod towards the building opposite: warm honey lamps glowing in the window, sign creaking in the wind. Nick and I often eat there.

A light snow has begun to fall, and as we pick our way across the icy road to The Fox and Hounds, I taste frost and hope on my tongue. Almost ten years. And just when we are approaching the anniversary, fate has brought us back together. That has to be a good thing, doesn't it?

*

'Here's the local celebrity.' Mitch puts down the glass he is polishing and slings the gingham tea towel over his shoulder. 'The usual?' He pours a shot and fizzes open a bottle of tonic.

I take a sip. The vodka heats me from the inside out, thawing my chilled bones. Leading the way across the pub,

I ignore the seats by the open fire that crackles and spits. Instead, we slide into my favourite booth in the corner.

'This is nice.' Lisa looks around. 'Not exactly The Three Fishes, is it?'

'Thank God!' We spent too much time there as teenagers, perching on bar stools with long chrome legs and faux leather pads. Sipping overpriced wine tasting of vinegar. 'Do you remember how often we used to slide off those stools?'

'Yes! I permanently had one foot ready to break my fall.'

'So, how are you?' I ask. There's a drawn-out pause.

Lisa tucks her hair behind her ears. 'Fine,' she says, eventually, with a smile that disappears before it is fully formed, and I get a sense there was something else she wanted to say, but instead, she asks: 'What was that about? "Local celebrity"?'

'It's nothing.' I pick at the beer mat on the table, peeling back the cardboard on the corner.

'It's hardly nothing.' Mitch rests a chalkboard on the corner of our table with the specials scrawled in his spidery handwriting.

Today's soup is carrot and coriander. I wrinkle my nose. I don't eat carrots unless they're in a cake.

'Kat and her husband were in one of those glossy Sunday supplements, at a posh charity dinner, mingling with the rich and famous. Wasn't as good as the food you get here though, was it, Kat?'

'Nothing quite beats your sticky toffee pudding.' I sense Lisa's eyes on me as I study the menu, my long hair falling forward, shielding my cheeks. I know they must be flaming.

'Roast turkey.' Lisa rubs her hands together.

It's only the 1st of December but Mitch has had a ridiculously tall tree in the corner for weeks now. Red and silver tinsel twisted around its plastic branches. Cheesy Christmas songs drift out of discreetly positioned speakers. The Pogues sing 'Fairytale of New York'.

'Pasta for me.'

Mitch bustles towards the kitchen. A heavy silence descends, pushing me back into my seat. I could stretch out my fingers and touch Lisa but the gulf between us seems impossible to breach. And for once, she seems nervous, fiddling with her cutlery.

'Lisa…' I trail off, sifting through my mind for the words I know I should say. Trying to put them in some sort of order before they spill from my lips, self-pitying and damaging.

'Shh. It's ok.'

'I hit you.' Even now my palm still stings when I think about it.

'We both made mistakes. Did things we regret, didn't we?'

'Yes, but your mistakes didn't kill anybody,' I whisper.

There is a pained expression on Lisa's face, and I feel compelled to carry on.

'About that night…' A hard lump lodges in my throat and I drain the dregs in my glass trying to wash it down.

'Kat.'

Lisa covers my hand with hers. Her skin soft and familiar. Tears rise and I bite them back, remembering the way we used to link fingers as we'd dash out into the playground, eager to get to the hopscotch before anybody else.

'You must hate me?' The hate I have for myself is ever present, smouldering away in the pit of my stomach. It would be a relief, almost, if she slapped me, screamed, at the very least.

'I did hate you,' she admits, and although not unexpected, her words still spear me, 'for a long time, but not so much for what happened – that wasn't your fault – but because you ran away, I suppose. We could have got through it together, and I have got through it.' Her voice is strong and determined.

'I had to leave. It wasn't my choice…' My voice cracks.

'We don't have to talk about it. Not right now anyway. Let me get some more drinks. Same again?'

'Please,' I say, even though I'm such a lightweight I should have a lemonade. But although the hot flush of panic has cooled, my heart is still racing a little faster. My breath is still coming a little quicker. The warm bloom of alcohol will calm me, I know.

Lisa slides out of her seat, and I take the opportunity to check my mobile again. Instead of a text alert, a picture of me and Nick kissing on our wedding day fills the screen. My mood dips when I see there is still no news. While Lisa is ordering our drinks, I slip into the toilets and splash cold water onto my face. Patting my skin dry with a rough paper towel I catch sight of my reflection in the mirror, my pale face framed by dark poker straight hair, the deep purple bags that shadow my eyes.

Back at the table I tip tonic into my glass, watching as tiny bubbles shimmy amongst the ice cubes.

'I don't know how you can still drink vodka,' Lisa says. 'Do you remember Perry Evans's party? We must have drunk nearly a whole bottle between us.' She pulls a face as though it was yesterday.

I haven't partied like that in over ten years. Nick keeps trying to persuade me to have a big celebration for my birthday next year, but I keep putting off thinking about turning thirty.

'I remember holding your hair back while you were sick all over the washing-up in the sink.'

I laugh at the memory and the sound momentarily startles me.

'I've never touched the stuff since.' Lisa shudders theatrically. 'Jake was there that night too, wasn't he?' Her question is casual, as if she can't quite remember, but I know she can. I see my own hurt reflected in her eyes.

Before I can answer, Mitch sets down a bowl of steaming carbonara and buttery garlic bread in front of me. As I lean forward to reach the salt, the gold cross around my neck hangs down, and Lisa lightly touches it with two fingers.

'You still wear this?'

I don't answer. I don't need to. I know we are both remembering, and I wonder whether, even after all this time, Lisa thinks she should be the one wearing this cross, but as usual, I'm connecting dots that aren't there. She's been nothing but friendly.

We fall silent for a few minutes as I twirl pasta around my fork. Lisa tackles one of Mitch's legendary roast potatoes which Nick and I always joke should come with a chainsaw.

'Tell me about this husband of yours then. Nick, isn't it? He's the patron of a charity?'

I've a mouthful of food so I nod my response, and at first, I am grateful for the change of subject but, just as I begin to swallow, I realise Mitch never referred to Nick by his name and neither did he say Nick was the patron of a charity. The bread sticks in my throat. Is it really a coincidence she is here or has she purposefully tracked me down? And if so, why?

Revenge whispers the voice inside my head.

I drain my drink to silence it.